SILENT RUNNING

An Art Marvik Mystery

Pauline Rowson

This first world edition published 2015
in Great Britain and the USA by
SEVERN HOUSE PUBLISHERS LTD of
19 Cedar Road, Sutton, Surrey, England, SM2 5DA.
Trade paperback edition first published
in Great Britain and the USA 2015 by
SEVERN HOUSE PUBLISHERS LTD.

British Library Cataloguing in Publication Data

Rowson, Pauline author.
    Silent running. – (An Art Marvik thriller)
    1. Missing persons–Investigation–Fiction. 2. Murder–
    Investigation–Fiction. 3. Veterans–Fiction. 4. Suspense
    fiction.
    I. Title II. Series
    823.9'2-dc23

ISBN-13: 978-0-7278-8500-5 (cased)
ISBN-13: 978-1-84751-599-5 (trade paper)
ISBN-13: 978-1-78010-650-2 (e-book)

Typeset by Palimpsest Book Production Ltd.,
Falkirk, Stirlingshire, Scotland.
Printed digitally in the USA.

Dedicated to all those who serve and have served their country to protect and keep us safe.

ONE

Marvik knew they were cops.

In the gathering gloom of the late February day, from behind the sparse cover of winter foliage, he watched the two men peer through the grimy windows of the semi-derelict coastguard's cottage on the cliff top of the Isle of Wight. The larger and older of them stood back and eyed up the crumbling, ivy-clad house, then with a wave of his hand he indicated for his colleague – a thinner, younger, balding man – to check out the rear. They were going to affect an entry. It was Marvik's cue to leave.

Keeping low, swiftly and stealthily he ran southwards through the shrubs and into the dense cover of nearby woods. After a few yards he swung east and darted through the jagged undergrowth of countless landslides over the years until he was just above a sharp cliff edge before the rock and grass-strewn land sloped more gently to the narrow isolated sandy bay. Beyond, in the English Channel, he caught the pinpricks of lights on a ship sailing to France before turning and climbing expertly down the cliff. It was probably where Ashley Palmer was heading, or Spain, his escape route already planned, long before he and the cops had shown up here.

The daylight was fading fast but Marvik didn't need it as he sprinted across the shale and sand to the powerful motor cruiser anchored in the shallow water. The wind had sprung up, bringing with it the taste of salt and a chill dampness. Leaping on board, he glanced up at the cliff edge. There was no one there.

Quickly, letting up the anchor, he pressed the starter. The engine gave a satisfying deep throb and sprang to life, sounding exceptionally loud. He thought it would be heard twenty-three miles across the other side of the island, which was where he was heading, never mind just beyond that cliff top. But still no one appeared. He throttled back and chugged slowly away, hoping that if either of the two cops heard the sound of a boat they'd think it was a night fisherman. He looked back. All was quiet.

Slowly he headed north, keeping the rugged coast on his left. It was a sea he knew well so he wasn't concerned about running aground, and the ships and ferries didn't come this close. When he reached the Solent there would be more vessels crossing to and from the mainland and heading out to the English Channel, but even then there wouldn't be many on a late winter's day. His thoughts returned to what he'd discovered in the derelict cottage – nothing. It was as he had expected and probably what Shaun Strathen had anticipated. Marvik recalled their telephone conversation earlier that afternoon. The call had taken him by surprise because it had been so soon after they had renewed their acquaintance after a gap of a year. Twelve days ago they'd met accidentally in East Cowes Marina and had exchanged phone numbers but not reminiscences; their days in the marines together were over and probably seemed as distant a memory to Strathen as they did to Marvik, even though it had been just over a year for both of them.

'I need you to do something for me,' Strathen had said urgently and without preamble. Marvik thought he'd caught an edge of desperation in the words but perhaps that had been his imagination: Strathen had never sounded desperate in his life, even when he'd lost his left leg in combat in Afghanistan. If Strathen considered something to be urgent then it was.

'A computer research scientist at Chiron, one of my clients – all right my only bloody client – has gone missing. He didn't show up for work on Monday and Professor Shelley, the managing director, has tried his mobile number without success. So have I. Sod all. And Palmer's not at home. I went there this morning. No sign of any disturbance or of him.'

'You had a key?' Marvik had foolishly asked, anticipating the answer which Strathen gave.

'Of course I didn't. The house couldn't have been easier to enter if he'd left the ruddy door on the latch.'

Strathen was an expert at getting into difficult places, much like Marvik had been, once.

'But I found the indentation of an Isle of Wight address on a Post-it notepad in his office with today's date on it and a time: five p.m. I think he's meeting someone and that he's heading for trouble.'

'Why should he be?'

'It's complicated. I haven't got time to go into detail but the projects Palmer works on are potentially very valuable to Chiron's competitors. He could be selling highly sensitive information and to the wrong sort of people. This is not the kind of stuff you give to a man in a mac up a dark alley or hand over in a brown envelope under a table in a café or pub. What Ashley Palmer knows is in his head and that means he could be in danger. He's very clever but also very naive and has no idea of the nasty things that nasty people get up to in this world, like you and I do, Art. Call it a hunch, intuition, whatever you like, but I need someone at that address in case he shows up, and don't say call the police because I want to be sure first. If he's not there then I'll get Professor Shelley to call in the cops. If he's there, ask him what the hell he's playing at and persuade him to return with you.'

'And if I can't?'

'You can't. But at least I'll have tried. Or rather you will have tried. I can't get over there in time; you're on the spot so to speak.'

Marvik had agreed to go. Now as he peered into the darkness he wondered why Strathen couldn't have come himself. His boat was just as powerful. Admittedly it was moored on the mainland but it wouldn't have taken him long to reach here. Perhaps he had trouble with the boat's engine and didn't want to chance breaking down in the Solent. Perhaps it would have taken him too long to fuel up and cross, or perhaps it was that hint of desperation that Marvik had caught in Strathen's voice that had made him accept without further questioning. He recognized that his reasons for accepting were coloured by pity and guilt. Both were wasted emotions: Strathen had made that clear when they'd met up again. Strathen didn't want his or anyone else's sympathy. 'A prosthetic leg doesn't stop you from having a life,' he'd said twelve days ago. And it didn't seem to have done. While Strathen had adjusted to civilian life, without his left leg from just above the knee, Marvik was still struggling to come to terms with it. Maybe that was why he had promised to go. He needed to prove he was still up to the job. But was he? Maybe Strathen had reconsidered and thought he wasn't, judging by the presence of the police. And Marvik's more recent record bore that out.

As the lights of Portsmouth on the mainland came into view Marvik thought that by now Ashley Palmer might be experiencing some of those nasty ways of those nasty people, if Strathen was right. But perhaps Palmer had just taken off for a few days and had forgotten to tell anyone.

He reached for his phone, preparing to break the bad news to Strathen, but got his voicemail. He rang off with a frown of annoyance and without leaving a message. Why wasn't Strathen answering after insisting this was so urgent? Maybe the police had already reported back to him and Strathen didn't think it necessary now to wait for his call. Well if he couldn't be bothered to answer his phone then Marvik saw no urgency to try him again. He'd done as Strathen had asked. Now let the police look for Palmer. That was what they were paid to do. Palmer wasn't his problem. Nothing was his problem. He was content to let life pass him by from now on. The peace and solitary existence that awaited him in a quiet spot of the island was all he wanted. And yet as he eased the boat into the blackness of Newtown River on the north-west of the island, he knew it wasn't. He was fooling no one, least of all himself. He'd enjoyed the surge of adrenalin that Strathen's call had summoned up. Perhaps he was ready to return to work. But for Nick Drayle as a private maritime security operative? How could he when a man had died on his watch?

'It wasn't your mistake,' Drayle had said in July and a few times since then.

But Marvik disagreed.

'Lee lost it, not you,' Drayle had added.

'But I should have seen it coming,' Marvik had insisted. He had far more experience than Lee Addington, his colleague on board Harry Salcombe's yacht. Addington was ex-army but with only six years' experience behind him as opposed to Marvik's fifteen, and six of those spent in the elite of the marines, the Special Boat Services. Addington didn't know that treacherous stretch of water in the Indian Ocean like he did. Addington, at the helm, had seen the pirate boat approaching. Marvik had ordered him to change course and speed. He'd done so but the pirates had pursued them. Marvik had fired off a flare. Everything was done according to standard practice and training until Addington had left the helm to the boat's owner, Salcombe, and before Marvik knew it he'd engaged the pirates. They'd returned fire. Harry Salcombe had got a bullet in the chest, Marvik in the shoulder and had struck his head as he fell. The next thing he could remember was waking up in hospital several days later. His shoulder wound was nothing that a bit of physio wouldn't cure, but the blow to his head had worried the medics because of his record of traumatic brain injury incurred in combat while in the marines. But he was fine.

Subconsciously he rubbed at the scars on the right side of his face, the legacy of being too close to an improvised explosive device while on a mission in Afghanistan. He tasted the bitter bile of failure that Salcombe's death had left him with as he eased the boat alongside the pontoon, not noticing the thin drizzle that had started to fall, and hated it. His commando training had declared there was only one outcome: winning. But he hadn't won. He'd failed – first time out. The humiliation gnawed at him. He'd tried to shut it out. He'd come here to recuperate, reflect, regain his strength, his resolve and his confidence. And decide what he was going to do with the rest of his life. Five months on and he still didn't know.

Shutting off the engine, he stood in the dark, listening to the silence, hoping that it would erase his irritation but tonight it couldn't. Tonight there was something wrong and suddenly he realized that it wasn't solely within him. He caught a sound. He stiffened, his senses on full alert, straining his ears for it. Yes, there it was, footsteps, but here in the middle of nowhere and nothing surrounding him but sea and countryside? Perhaps he'd imagined it. But no, it came again, and as he drew closer to the cottage a shadow came into view. He froze. Nobody came to visit him because nobody knew he was here.

The figure disappeared around the rear of the building. Marvik picked his way noiselessly and carefully forwards. He knew every stick and stone, every pothole, rut and bush on and alongside this path. He knew how many paces he could take to reach the front door and how many paces to the rear. He knew exactly what lay ahead and around him. He could do it blindfolded if necessary.

So who the hell was it? An intruder? After what? He had nothing of value to steal except a laptop computer and that wasn't worth much. But when did thieves and druggies need an excuse to break in? They'd steal pennies if that was all there was to take to help them buy their next fix. But this wasn't a town or city, it wasn't even suburbia; no one came to this part of the reserve except the Brent geese in winter and the sailors in summer. And there was no car in the gravel lane except his old Land Rover Defender. No tyre tracks either, he thought, swiftly studying the ground. Nor had there been any boats in the river, except his. And burglars didn't walk miles to rob a house. The figure emerged from the rear of the house. It was a woman and Marvik recognized her with a shock.

'Charlotte!' he cried, stepping forward.

She spun round.

'Art, is that you?'

She ran towards him and before he knew it she was in his arms, trembling. He held her close and tight. It had been four years since their relationship had ended and two since they'd last communicated, and then only briefly by text and email. What had brought her here now and in such an emotionally charged state? And how the devil had she found him? Only his bank, the Ministry of Defence and the National Trust, who he was renting the property from, knew his address. He had cut off all ties with his small number of distant relatives and his former Marine colleagues. Not even Strathen knew his address. He'd bought his battered Land Rover Defender by cash and although his address was on the licensing authority database, Charlotte wouldn't have been able to access that.

Gently he eased her away and studied her. She looked terrified. He needed to get her inside the cottage and to calm her down. 'Drink?' He could do with one himself. The day had been full of surprises.

She let him lead her to the rear of the cottage. The state she was in he thought she'd have gone with him if he'd told her they were to take a moonlight swim – not that there was any moonlight, and the sea was far too cold at this time of year to enter it voluntarily.

Unlocking the rear door he swiftly disabled the alarm, noting the fearful glance she tossed over her shoulder before entering. He tried not to show his concern. But in the light her changed physical appearance struck him more forcibly. Her ashen face was gaunt, her blue eyes wide like a frightened child's. They were still the colour of cornflowers but they were bloodshot from crying. Her fair skin had lost its sheen and her face was harrowed and etched with worry lines across her forehead and around her eyes. She'd aged in the last four years, but then who hadn't. He could smell her fear which was so unlike her that he felt livid at whatever or whoever had caused it. The Charlotte he recalled, who had nursed him after a successful but dangerous amphibious attack in Sierra Leone, when he'd been injured the first time, had been almost as fearless as his team. She'd seen and absorbed so much horror and death. Too much perhaps. Had it finally tipped her over the edge? But that didn't answer what had triggered it, or why and how she had tracked him down.

'Wine? Whisky?'

'Tea.'

He placed the kettle on the large range. 'Sit down. Take off your jacket.'

She placed the rucksack on the floor and shrugged out of her waterproof jacket. He noted that the bottom of her jeans were filthy and her boots were caked with mud. She shivered as though cold and wrapped her arms around her chest, hunching her shoulders.

'Have you eaten?' he asked.

'I'm not hungry.'

'You'll eat and then you can tell me what's troubling you,' he said firmly.

She was too worried and weary to argue.

He cut off some large chunks of bread, then heated up some soup he'd made yesterday, realizing that it was hours since he'd last eaten and then only a snatched sandwich before Strathen's call and his trip to the eastern coast of the island in search of Ashley Palmer. He switched off his phone. Strathen could wait. Charlotte was far more important.

He watched her tuck in to the soup, realizing she was hungry after all. Occasionally she'd start at a sound outside and look nervously towards the window. There were no blinds because there was no one within three miles of him except the birds and wildlife. He caught the sounds that seemed to scare her but he was used to them. It was just the wind catching the reeds and shrubs. They ate in silence and when they had finished he opened a bottle of red wine and poured them both a glass. The colour was back in her cheeks and she had relaxed considerably, although there was still an edginess about her.

She pushed her fair hair off her face and smiled at him, and in that smile Marvik saw something of the old Charlotte emerge. He recalled the days and nights they'd spent together after he'd been declared fit for duty. Their romance hadn't lasted longer than a couple of weeks but it had been pleasant. The decision to end it had been mutual.

'I'm sorry for being so weak,' she said with an attempt at lightness. 'What a baby you must think I am.'

'Hardly,' he answered quietly and seriously, remembering she'd been part of the Commando Forward Surgical Team working in danger zones with them and seeing to the men's injuries without a murmur. Christ, she was as brave as the Marines he'd known. She'd been deployed in Afghanistan and on the primary casualty reception ship RFA *Argus*, as part of a rapid reaction surgical team, and she'd been on board other RFA vessels. He wondered if she'd seen too much action, too much pain and suffering, and it had finally got to her.

'I had to speak to him. I didn't know if he'd agree to see me at first but he did,' she said, nursing her glass of wine in both hands.

Marvik couldn't make any sense of what she was saying but he said nothing as she took a breath and clearly made an effort to mentally gather and rearrange her thoughts into some kind of order. She took a long swallow of her wine before continuing.

'I'm stationed at the Queen Elizabeth Hospital, Birmingham, the Royal Centre for Defence Medicine, critical care unit.'

Marvik knew it well, having spent some time there after receiving his head wound. Strathen had been there for four months before being transferred to the military rehabilitation centre at Headley Court in Surrey.

'Just before Christmas a Marine with 40 Commando, Paul Williamson, got badly wounded in Afghanistan. An IED detonated while he was on patrol. It killed two men with him. He was treated at Camp Bastion before being flown back to Birmingham. He died three weeks ago.'

And clearly she'd been close to him, just as she had been to Marvik, only he'd survived.

'He was twenty-three. He'd saved the lives of two men on previous occasions. His colleagues said he was fearless and he was, but it wasn't just training and instinct that made him that way; he had something to prove to himself. There was a great anger inside him.' She took a swallow of wine and a deep breath before continuing.

'Just before he died he told me something that he said he'd never told anyone. I learned that his father had murdered a woman in 1997 and had been imprisoned for life. Paul barely remembers his father. He was only six at the time. His mother and he left the UK to live in Spain before returning and settling in Wales. She never spoke about his father except to say that he had left them and was probably dead. Paul soon stopped asking about him. It was only when he came to enlist in 2010 and his background was thoroughly vetted that he discovered the truth. He couldn't ask his mother about it because she had died shortly before he decided to join the Marines.

It was a great shock to him. He felt ashamed of what his father had done and he needed to prove to himself that he wasn't like him.'

She took another sip of wine. 'Paul said he'd been told his father was still alive and serving his prison sentence. But Paul didn't want to know anything about him and he didn't name him as his next of kin. That was a distant cousin of his mother's. I spoke to the cousin, a Colin Bell, at the funeral, but he said he didn't know anything about Paul's father and that he didn't even know Paul. He'd been amazed to be named as next of kin. He also said he didn't know that Maggie, Paul's mother, had died. Apart from Colin Bell there was no family at the funeral, only the nursing staff and his colleagues.'

She poured herself another glass of wine and Marvik did the same. The wind was rising outside and rattling around the ancient cottage and the drizzle had turned to an impatient and restless rain that sporadically hurled itself against the small windows. As the wine and confession did their work, Charlotte began to relax.

'I couldn't get it out of my mind. I was angry at Paul's death and that he'd died ashamed of his father when he should have died at peace and proud of what he'd achieved. I thought his father should know how brave his son had been and how he had died. Paul had told me his father's name so I looked up the newspaper reports on the Internet and found details of the murder and the trial. It attracted a lot of media interest at the time, mainly because Paul's father, Terence Blackerman, had been a navy chaplain.'

Marvik eyed her, surprised.

'I know. Paul never said, but he must have known. How could a chaplain have done such a terrible thing? I wondered if he'd suffered from post-traumatic stress, but there was no mention of it in the articles I read. He'd strangled Esther Shannon after making love to her in her room at the forces club in London, the Union Services Club at Waterloo, on Saturday November the eighth 1997.'

'The day before Remembrance Sunday.'

'Yes. Terence Blackerman and Esther Shannon were there for the Remembrance Service at the Albert Hall on Saturday. Esther's father had been killed in the Falklands War in 1982. I contacted HM Prisons via their website and emailed the Prisoner Location Service to find out where Terence Blackerman was serving his sentence. If he was still in custody my details would be passed to him and he would need to agree to disclose his whereabouts.'

'And he did,' Marvik said, quickly catching on. 'Which is why you're here.' Blackerman had to be in one of the Isle of Wight prisons, either Albany or Parkhurst, both of which were in the same location, just outside Newport, the small capital town of the island.

'Yes. He's in Parkhurst prison.'

'And you've been to see him.'

She nodded and took a gulp of her wine. 'He's not how I imagined.'

Marvik considered her words. 'In what way?' he asked, curious and deeply interested not only to hear what she had learned but also burrowing away at the back of his mind was still the question of her fear. Blackerman was in prison, so why should she feel afraid of him? Because she had been afraid, and still was. He didn't believe she'd been spooked by the dark. But again he wondered if nursing Paul had pushed her over the edge. That didn't account for how she'd tracked him down though.

'He was a quiet, gentle man. I could see immediately that he'd suffered a great deal and that he hadn't been told about his son's death. When I told him, he didn't look shocked or angry, there was just this tremendous sorrow. It was as though . . .' She hesitated in an attempt to find the correct words. 'As though I was seeing someone who had been physically and brutally abused; the scars were in his eyes and on every line and in every pore of his face. It tore at my heart. I cried. *He* comforted *me*. My God, Art, I'd gone there all geared up to be righteous and angry and all I could do was blubber like a baby.'

Had she cried at Paul's death or at his funeral? Marvik doubted it. Maybe her grief had caught her unexpectedly. He knew it often happened like that and could be triggered by anything, even the smallest, seemingly insignificant thing.

'I'd thought telling him about the sacrifice his son had made would make him ashamed. I wanted to hurt him because he'd hurt Paul and so many others through his actions, and I succeeded, but I wish to God I hadn't. I wish I had never gone there. It was a mistake. When I was leaving he said, "I didn't kill Esther Shannon but I don't expect you to believe me any more than anyone else has ever done."'

Don't they all say that? thought Marvik.

As if reading his mind she declared with fervour, 'I swear to you, Art, he's no killer.'

Maybe he was just very convincing, but again Marvik didn't express his opinion.

'I told him where Paul was buried and said that the prison authorities might give him permission to visit his son's grave on compassionate grounds, but he said, "It's over." I asked him what he meant but he just smiled with a sadness that I couldn't understand. It was as though he didn't want to leave prison, that he'd given up.'

Marvik wondered if perhaps Blackerman had become institutionalized. For some prisoners staying inside was less terrifying than being let loose in a world where you had to fend for yourself. The Marines wasn't prison, far from it, but they'd taken care of him for fifteen years and he hadn't fared well since coming out, he thought with bitterness.

'He thanked me for coming. Said "God bless you", and that was it. I felt as though I had let both him and Paul down.'

He reassured her she hadn't.

She shifted uneasily. 'There's something else,' she added, 'and before you say I'm emotionally overwrought I know I am. But that doesn't change the fact that I'm being followed.'

He studied her with concern, puzzled by her declaration. It would account for her terrified appearance and anxious state when he'd first seen her. 'Go on,' he encouraged.

'I asked the taxi to stop by the woods at Corf Copse. I walked from there.'

That was just over a mile from the Newtown Old Town Hall and the handful of houses close by it. She'd had another two-mile trek to locate his cottage.

'And was there anyone?' Marvik asked, gravely.

'I couldn't see who it was but I'm certain there was someone.'

And Marvik wouldn't dismiss that claim. He knew all too well that when in danger you had to trust your instinct, if you had it. And those that did lived longer than the ones who didn't. His instinct had deserted him with Lee Addington and Harry Salcombe on that private yacht. He rose. 'I'll take a look around outside.'

'Thanks.'

He pulled on his jacket and took his torch. She insisted on clearing away. He instructed her to lock the kitchen door after him and to only let him in when he called her name and knocked four times. 'Two long and two short. Just a safety precaution. And when you've finished, switch off the light and wait at the table for me.' He could see that his precautions worried but also reassured her. He wasn't taking any chances.

Outside, he heard her shoot across the bolt. He stood in front of the lit kitchen window. He didn't think anyone was in the undergrowth with a high-powered rifle aimed at the window or at him, and maybe he was tempting fate by being so visible, but if there was someone then they weren't after him. But why would they be after Charlotte?

He was relieved when the light was extinguished. In the darkness he walked slowly around the cottage, his ears straining for any unusual sounds, his eyes, which had long grown accustomed to the dark, searching for signs of movement in the shrubs. His senses were again firing on all cylinders, which made twice in one day, and it felt good. Fleetingly he wondered if Strathen was trying to get hold of him.

He surveyed the countryside in the rain, assuming a casual stance so that if anyone was watching they'd simply think it was his usual night-time routine. He could hear the sea washing against his boat. He saw the boat's outline on the end of the wooden pontoon. There was no sound nor sign of anyone. Yet, as he did his full circuit of the house, he felt that pricking sensation between his shoulder blades that told him someone was out here somewhere. It wasn't just Charlotte's imagination or his heightened senses.

Charlotte let him back in as arranged. He smiled reassuringly, hiding his concern. 'All quiet.' He showed her where the bathroom and the spare bedroom were and then returned to the kitchen and fired up his laptop. He hadn't asked her how she knew where to find him, but he would, later.

He could hear her moving about upstairs as he entered the name 'Terence Blackerman' into the Internet search engine. Soon he was absorbed in what he was reading from the various newspaper reports of the time, no longer conscious of the sound of creaking floorboards overhead or when they stopped. It was as Charlotte had relayed to him: Esther Shannon had been staying in the Union Services Club, close to Waterloo Station, where Terence Blackerman had also booked a room for the night. The fact that he was a chaplain made the story even more salacious, a man of God who, Marvik read, had slept with Esther Shannon having only just met her and had then brutally strangled her.

The trial had taken place at the Central Criminal Court in London, or the Old Bailey as it was more generally known. Blackerman's prints and DNA had been found in Esther Shannon's room, but then Blackerman hadn't denied having sex with her. Marvik wondered why he had. Mutual attraction? A moment of madness? It was a rather impulsive and uncharacteristic act for a man of the cloth, but then he was human like the rest of them. Perhaps he was simply lonely and feeling down after the Remembrance Service. Perhaps they both were and conversation had turned to comfort, which in turn had led to sex. Not the desperate, frantic, hungry kind of sex but the sharing of tormented emotions, the need to reinforce the belief in life. Or perhaps that was just how it had been with him on certain occasions. Maybe even Charlotte had been one of those occasions.

Marvik recalled the chaplains who had gone into battle with them. They'd trained as commandos, and they were tough, but they didn't carry arms. There was one in particular, David Treagust, who he'd admired, respected and to whom he owed a great deal. He wondered where he was now. Had Blackerman been like Treagust? Had his officers respected him? What had they thought of this man who had killed a woman after making love to her? And why would he kill her? There was no suggestion of forced sexual activity in the reports that he was reading. And no mention of a marital rift in Blackerman's life, but he was only reading journalists' versions of the trial. There was obviously a lot more to the story.

According to the reports the post-mortem had confirmed sexual intercourse before Esther Shannon's death by strangulation. Blackerman had pleaded not guilty and had strenuously denied the murder charge, claiming he had returned to his own room in the early hours of the morning and had left the club at six o'clock the following morning to catch the train home to his married quarters at HMS Excellent, Gosport, near Portsmouth, without any knowledge of Esther Shannon lying dead in her room. A jury had returned a majority verdict. Marvik didn't know a lot about the law – and obviously there was more to the trial than he was reading here – but the evidence seemed pretty flimsy to him. Perhaps Blackerman had had a crap lawyer and the prosecution had an ace one. Charlotte was convinced that Blackerman had been genuine when he claimed he hadn't killed Esther Shannon and she'd probably heard as many confessions as any priest to know when they rang true. The dying don't lie.

Footsteps sounded on the stairs and he pushed down the lid of the computer and rose as Charlotte entered. Enveloped in a large sweatshirt of his she looked both tired and beautiful. She also looked strained and vulnerable. He put his arms around her to comfort her but soon he was kissing her. He hadn't meant to but she didn't push him away. Instead she responded hungrily and clung to him.

After a moment she pulled back. Eyeing him pleadingly she said, 'I don't want to be alone.'

'You don't have to be.' And Marvik couldn't help wondering if those were the very words that Esther Shannon had uttered to Terence Blackerman on the last day of her life seventeen years ago.

TWO

Thursday

He eased himself out of bed, trying not to disturb her. It was just before six and he'd been awake for an hour. Thoughts of Blackerman had plagued him during his fitful night's sleep and, as he'd lain listening to the birdsong, he'd wondered if Blackerman had appealed against his sentence. Marvik had seen no mention of it in the reports he'd read on the Internet but perhaps the media hadn't covered that, it being old news. And Marvik knew there was no chance of Blackerman getting parole if he was sticking to his 'I didn't do it' story.

Charlotte stirred and opened her eyes.

'It's early, go back to sleep,' he said but she shifted and propped herself up on one arm.

'Sorry about last night.' She squinted up at him bleary-eyed. 'All that stuff about being followed. I made an idiot of myself. I was tired. That visit to the prison was awful. It smelled of fear and I kept thinking of how Paul had suffered and—'

'Breakfast,' he interjected brightly.

Her expression cleared. 'Good idea. I'm famished.'

He showered and by the time he'd made breakfast, she'd also showered and dressed. 'How are you getting back to Birmingham?' he asked, while dishing up her fried egg and bacon.

'Ferry from East Cowes to Southampton, then train.'

'I'll take you over if you like.'

'You have a boat?' she asked with delight.

'Of course.' Having spent most of his childhood on board his parents' boat accompanying them on their marine archaeological expeditions, and then years in the Special Boat Services, he couldn't live without one. He had to go over anyway. He wanted to see Drayle. He also needed to contact Strathen. He'd found three voice messages on his mobile phone from Strathen, each growing tetchier. 'What are you going to do about Terence Blackerman?' he asked her.

'Try and forget him, I guess, although that's going to be hard.'

'I don't see what else you can do.' And he'd do the same. 'You've kept the promise you made to yourself for Paul. Blackerman has to come to his own decisions about his son. Put it behind you, Charlotte, and move on.'

'Like you have.' She eyed him closely.

'Yes,' he said with a stab of unease.

'This doesn't look like it.'

She was right but he wasn't going to tell her that. 'I'll make the boat ready.' He shrugged into his sailing jacket and picked up his binoculars. He told himself there was no one following Charlotte but no harm in checking. He stopped and examined a couple of plants as he made his way around the cottage but his studies had nothing to do with the flora and fauna. He was checking for signs of unusual activity, human, not animal. He found none.

He jumped on board and rolled back the canvas cover so that the cockpit was fully exposed. Instead of turning to the helm though he faced back on to the harbour and, raising the binoculars, panned them across the wide expanse of the flat countryside, taking in his cottage and the grounds beyond, the shore close to it, the river, the reeds and then the land opposite before swinging the glasses back in the direction of his cottage. He caught a glimpse of movement in the reeds. It was only a heron. There was a tiny flash of light just for a second, then it was gone. Had he imagined it? No, but it was probably the weak early morning sun striking something in the grass, a piece of glass perhaps.

Returning to the cottage he found Charlotte ready to leave. He set the alarm and locked up. She admired the boat, asked how long he'd had it – since October, when he had taken on the cottage, he answered – and an easy silence fell between them as they headed out to the Solent. With each mile across it she grew more relaxed. The anxious frown and haunted look in her eyes evaporated. The sea was weaving its magic on her, but not on him. Strathen's request yesterday to help find Ashley Palmer had stirred up Marvik's latent feelings of restlessness and Charlotte's arrival and her question about moving on had fuelled them. He felt out of sorts with the world. The Marines had been his life for so long. He missed the comradeship, the danger, the adrenalin-fuelled operations, the routine, the discipline, the sense of purpose. He missed being valued. Drayle's job hadn't and could never replicate any of that and it was the answer he decided he'd give Drayle shortly, albeit couched in a different language. He wondered if anything could ever replace what he'd had and knew it couldn't.

Irritated by his maudlin thoughts he turned his mind to the other matter that disturbed him: how Charlotte had managed to track him down. He'd thought she might say but she made no mention of it and, as Marvik moored up at the Town Quay, he thought it was about time he asked her. He walked with her up to the busy boardwalk, which was packed with commuters arriving off the Red Jet ferry from the Isle of Wight and those making for the small Hythe ferry coming into dock. She said she'd take a taxi to the station. Marvik could see them lined up along the side of the boardwalk. Making sure to keep his voice light he said, 'How did you know where to find me, Charlotte?'

She looked confused for a moment then smiled. 'You told me.'

'I did? When?' he asked, disguising his surprise.

'You sent me a text.'

Now he was really puzzled. 'What did it say, remind me?'

'That you were living on the Isle of Wight and if I was over, to drop in and see you.'

'When was this?'

'You must be getting senile,' she laughed. 'It was two weeks ago. I replied to say that I was hoping to be over soon. Then yesterday I sent you another text to confirm I was coming to the island and you said to make sure I came to see you. You gave me your address.'

'You don't still have the text, do you?'

'Yes.' She reached for her mobile phone and within seconds was showing it to him.

'Sorry, I didn't receive it,' he said with a smile, handing the phone back to her. 'Must have got lost in the ether.'

But a shadow crossed her face. 'Will I see you again?' she asked.

'You know where I am.'

'Yes but do you *want* to see me?'

'Of course.'

But she eyed him dubiously before adding with a resigned and sorrowful expression, 'It's OK, Art, I know the drill. It's a pity. I'll miss you.'

He hugged her tightly as though to compensate for his lack of enthusiasm and watched her walk away with a pang of regret. He was genuinely fond of Charlotte, and they were good together, but he didn't want any ties. So what the hell *did* he want?

He turned back towards his boat, withdrew his mobile phone from his jacket and punched in the number he'd memorized from her text. There was no answer. In fact there was no line.

Replacing his phone he climbed on board and headed into the Solent. So who had sent those texts? Why would someone pretend to be him? What if Charlotte had decided to reply by phone instead of text? Would the impostor have faked his voice? Would Charlotte have been fooled? Possibly if it was a bad line or the impostor had claimed to have a cold. If the purpose had been to confront them then why not do so at the cottage, especially if Charlotte's claim that she was being followed had been true. There had been ample time and opportunity. It didn't make any sense. The trilling of his phone broke through his thoughts and he answered it to find it was Strathen.

'Where the hell have you been, outer bloody Mongolia? Don't you ever answer your phone?' Strathen said with exasperation.

'I called *you* twice last night and *you* didn't answer,' Marvik replied irritably. 'Besides, you know that Ashley Palmer didn't show because the police were there so I didn't think you needed my report. Did you call them in?'

'No. Professor Shelley did. I had no idea Shelley had contacted the police until he told me this morning. Apparently Palmer sent him a text late yesterday afternoon to say where he was going and that he wasn't coming back to work. He'd had a better job offer. Shelley suspected him of selling out to a competitor; he called the police. I said it would have been nice to have been kept informed as I'm your security expert. You can imagine what he said about that. Some security expert who loses a key employee a month after being engaged.'

'Neither of us seem to have a good track record in civvy street. Is the text genuine?'

'It came from Palmer's mobile phone, which is now disabled, but I don't think he sent it. Did the police see you?'

'No.'

'I had to tell Shelley about finding the indentation of that address on the note pad on Palmer's desk and asking you to check it out for me. I gave Shelley some brief background about you, said you were completely trustworthy, and that you lived on the island.'

'But you don't know where I live, do you, Shaun?' Marvik wondered if Strathen had sent Charlotte to him. Strathen knew Charlotte from his time spent in the critical care unit at Birmingham. But why should he, and why do it in such a covert way? Marvik couldn't see Strathen acting as matchmaker.

'The island is hardly Australia. Wherever you lived it wouldn't take you long to reach that coastguard cottage, especially by boat.'

Strathen had a point. The island was roughly 150 square miles. And it sounded as though he was telling the truth. But for Strathen, who had been a Special Forces Communicator in the Marines, a highly intelligent and resourceful man, tracing him would have been child's play.

'Shelley's informed the police about you, they're here now going through Palmer's office and they want access to his work PC and everyone else's in the company, which I've already checked with nil result. Not that they'd trust me, of course. I'm just a security guy with no brains,' he added scathingly. 'They'll probably come knocking on your door.'

'Why? I can't tell them anything.'

'I'm walking around the car park taking this call so the buggers can't hear me. Did you find anything in that cottage?'

'Only dirt and dust. There was no evidence that he had been there. Did he catch the ferry to the island?'

'The police say he was on the three forty-five Red Jet from Southampton to West Cowes yesterday afternoon. He bought the ticket by cash; one of the terminal staff recognized him from a photograph the police got from his house.'

Marvik thought they had been very busy in such a short space of time.

Strathen said, 'The police have searched his house and say there's no evidence in it of who he was meeting. I could have told them that but thought it best not to. I asked Feeney, the fat DI in charge, if they'd found a computer but he said they hadn't. I already knew they wouldn't but if everyone thinks I'm dumb then I might as well play along. You never know where it will get you. I think the poor bugger might be dead.'

'Maybe he went willingly and is of greater value alive to whoever has persuaded him to go with them.'

Strathen grunted doubtfully before adding, 'Professor Shelley and his sister Beatrice are in conference with Rodney Dearman, Chief Executive of DRTI, the Defence Research and Technology Institute, the body that is funding Ashley's project. I expect Shelley's wetting his pants that the money will stop and that Ashley's research will show up at one of his competitors.'

'Would it be that disastrous?'

'It's a highly competitive field. Ashley's involved in the development of intelligent software, more commonly known as artificial intelligence. His remit is in relation to the medical field, Chiron's specialist area. Artificial intelligence has the ability to revolutionize medicine; it can more accurately diagnose, carry out intricate invasive surgery and screen patients for faulty medical implants without ever having to insert intrusive instruments down the throat or in any other orifice. Robotic applications never get tired or need copious amounts of caffeine like doctors do. Ashley's been working on developing artificial intelligence systems that can advance the development and use of prosthetic limbs, predicting movement, sensation, and muscle-locking which could also have implications for those suffering from neurological illnesses. It's big business, Art, and growing rapidly. But his work can and does cross over into other applications, especially those associated with defence.'

'Hence the police's rapid response to Shelley's summons.'

'Yes. It could be used for object detection and manipulation, navigation, mapping, path planning, and systems that make for faster collection and analysis of critical information for improving reaction time and decision-making in military actions.'

'So if the wrong people got hold of it—'

'Or him. Then he won't be around long enough to spend the money he's being paid, if he went willingly,' Strathen said, worried.

'Where was he between Monday when he didn't show for work and catching the Red Jet ferry yesterday?'

'Good question. That's what I'd like to know. He wasn't answering his mobile phone and he doesn't have a landline. And he certainly wasn't hiding in that house yesterday. He could have been with a mate or a girlfriend but my bet is he was holed up somewhere having been told that it was essential he lay low until the pick-up time. He must have written down that address on Friday before leaving work although there's no trace of him taking a telephone call on the office phone but he might have done so on his mobile. I didn't check his desk until yesterday afternoon when it became clear there was a problem and that's when I found the address.'

And just as that text message Charlotte had received bothered Marvik, so too did that note, or rather the indentation of it. 'Would a clever man betray himself so easily?'

'Perhaps he scribbled it down in a moment of distraction and hadn't realized he'd pressed too hard on the pad. But he did go to the island.'

'It would have been a hell of a long and awkward journey though, from Cowes to just beyond Rocken End beach and that cottage. There are no trains to that part of the island and only a limited number of buses involving at least one change.'

'He could have taken a taxi.'

'Perhaps he was met at Cowes.'

'Well the police are dealing with it now. It's out of my hands and Shelley will probably dispense with my services and hire someone he thinks more capable. Especially if I have overlooked something, but I've been monitoring everyone's emails, calls and browsing history and I swear nothing has been going on of a dubious nature. Look, I'd better go back in otherwise they'll think I'm phoning the Kremlin.'

'Let me know what happens.' Marvik rang off without mentioning Charlotte. Strathen had enough worries of his own. And so did he without puzzling over the disappearance of a computer research scientist.

As he headed towards Thorn Beach and Drayle's extensive grounds on the coast bordering the New Forest, Marvik reconsidered the text messages that had been sent to Charlotte. The first had been two weeks ago. The timing corresponded with Paul Williamson's funeral. The second had been sent yesterday, as she was on her way to visit Paul's father in prison. Someone had known that was where she was going and had drawn her to him after it. So, if whoever had sent the messages knew her movements, why follow her – *if* they had? And why had they wanted her to visit him?

The deep throb of a helicopter caught his attention and he squinted up at it, knowing before he saw it that it was a Chinook. He and Strathen had flown in them countless times on exercises and missions. But that was another life.

The sky was darkening with heavy clouds rolling up from the west and he felt the first spits of rain. He turned his thoughts to his meeting with Drayle. Ahead, just beyond the Beaulieu River, he could see the pontoon that stretched out from Drayle's estate. It was a good location for his business, isolated from any neighbouring properties but with easy access to the Solent. Drayle's extensive staff and consultants included Marvik's former colleagues from the UK's Special Forces Unit and other veterans. Drayle was ex-service himself. Maybe they'd all adjusted to civilian life better than he had.

As he eased his boat on to the pontoon he looked up to see Drayle emerge from the brick and flint building across the landscaped grounds. Drayle was accompanied by a dark-haired stocky man, in an expensive, well-cut suit, about early fifties. Spotting Marvik, Drayle raised his right hand in acknowledgement. The man beside him glanced over but the sound of a boat approaching caught Marvik's attention and he turned to see a modern motor cruiser heading towards the pontoon. He recognized both the boat – it was Drayle's – and the man on board it, Lee Addington. Despite his tension at seeing Addington and the memories that he conjured up, Marvik smiled and stretched out his hand to the broad-shouldered, dark-haired man in his late twenties as he jumped off the boat. It wasn't Addington that he had anything against, it was his own failure to control the situation that infuriated him. But more than that it was the uncharacteristic lack of confidence that the incident had resulted in him feeling and he acknowledged that part of him resented Addington for making him feel that way.

'How's the shoulder?' Addington asked.

'Healed thanks.'

'And the head injury?'

'Fine.' Marvik saw that Drayle was finishing his conversation with his guest, a new client perhaps. The man climbed into a top-of-the-range BMW and Drayle headed purposefully towards them. Addington nodded a greeting at the smart but casually dressed sixty-two year old before leaping back on to the boat and Drayle drew Marvik further away from the pontoon.

'Well, Art, have you come to a decision?' he asked in the quiet calm voice that Marvik knew well.

'I'm sorry, Nick, but I don't think being a private maritime security operative is for me.'

'Lee's said the same. He's off to pastures new at the end of March. Crewing for a millionaire in Monaco.'

Marvik raised his eyebrows. He hadn't said, but then Marvik hadn't given him the opportunity to.

Drayle continued. 'So how about returning as a consultant? I need someone with your expertise. The client list keeps growing. There'd be opportunities for travel, variety, challenges.'

'Consultancy on what?'

'Maritime security, of course. Your service in the marines, your background, and your experience first-hand with pirates and, tragically, Salcombe's death. Yes, Art,' Drayle quickly added, obviously seeing his dubious look, 'what you went through means you're ideally placed to advise our clients. You might even get to spend time in your native Finland, advising the coastal authorities there.'

Marvik didn't correct him. It was his mother's native Finland not his. He hadn't been back for years and then only on a joint exercise with the Finnish Coastal Jaegers. Maybe he should return. But that might be construed as running away, again.

'So when can you start? I've got shipping clients, ports and offshore exploration companies lining up for the valuable advice you can give them.'

Clearly Drayle expected an instant decision and Marvik was sick of prevaricating. Charlotte had asked him if he'd moved on – well he had. Taking refuge in the sanctuary of Newtown Harbour was at an end. It was time. 'Give me a fortnight.'

Drayle smiled. 'Perfect. Great to have you back, Art.'

Marvik took the firm grasp and returned to his boat. He nodded a farewell to Addington and cast off. But as he crossed the Solent he felt no eager anticipation at the prospect of his new role with Drayles. Perhaps that would come later, once he knew more about it and once his thoughts were clear of Charlotte and that phoney text message. Perhaps it was some nutter who knew about their past relationship and was jealously stalking her. He didn't like that thought. He should have told her he hadn't sent them but that would only have added to her worries. Maybe he'd call her later. But the more he considered it the more uneasy he became. It was the timing of those two messages that bothered him.

By the time he reached Newtown Harbour the wind had risen but the rain had come to little more than a few threatening and erratic flurries. He secured the boat and made for the cottage feeling troubled. A blackbird flew squawking into the air. On the surface everything looked the same. The cottage door was shut, the windows too; it was exactly as he had left it that morning. But there *was* something.

He scrutinized the garden and surrounding area. There was a branch of a shrub broken but nothing else. The rear door was locked and the alarm still set. He disengaged it and stood motionless for a moment, listening. Only the sound of the wind and the birdsong came to him. He studied the kitchen. Nothing had been disturbed or defiled. The kettle was exactly where he had left it on the dark blue range, the kitchen cupboards closed and his laptop computer was on the table in the centre of the room. He stiffened. No, that was wrong. It wasn't exactly how he had left it. It had been moved just perceptibly. Or was that just him getting compulsive, obsessive and paranoid?

He crossed to it and studied the computer and the table around it. The lid was down. It was the same distance from the edge of the table, the chair was in the exact position and yet as he studied both he knew it was fractionally different. Was it just his imagination? His eyes swung to the door which led into the hall and his pulse quickened. It was ajar as he had left it but he remembered looking back as he had set the alarm before leaving and like a snapshot the image reframed itself in his mind. Having a photographic memory was a gift and he'd developed that to become a skill over the years in combat. The door was open slightly wider than when he had left and Charlotte couldn't have done that because she had been beside him when he had set the alarm.

Swiftly he went through the rest of the house looking for more signs of the intruder. He found them in his bedroom and in the living room. They were minuscule and would not have been noticed by anyone else but he knew exactly where and how everything had been left. There was a drawer not quite closed, a book slightly at an angle, a tube of toothpaste moved ever so slightly in the bathroom. Whoever had been here had been no common burglar because nothing had been stolen or wrecked. He had no television, no valuables, no money lying around, only his laptop and that was practically an antique. Whoever had entered the house had been expert, but not expert enough. His blood was pumping fast, the adrenalin was coursing through his body – not caused by fear or anger, he swiftly acknowledged, but by exhilaration.

He recalled the flash of light he'd seen earlier through his binoculars and knew that Charlotte had been correct. Someone *had* followed her here and *had* been watching the cottage. Seeing them both leave he had seized his chance. But how the hell had he known the alarm code?

Marvik returned to the kitchen. His brain was racing. There could be several ways. By training powerful binoculars on the rear door the intruder could have seen him punch in the number. And if he'd used surveillance equipment which could also record then all he needed to do was replay the recorded images slowly, have some knowledge of where the numbers were located on the keypad – not difficult when most were in the same place – and then imitate it. The other scenario was more worrying.

Marvik crossed to the table and from there he studied the alarm. Charlotte could have planted a skimming device above it. He'd seen nothing on the alarm system that morning when they'd left but that didn't mean it wasn't there, just that he hadn't been looking for it. Then all the intruder had to do was remove it when he entered, after keying in the code. But why the hell should she have done so?

And how had the intruder entered?

The last question was easier to answer than the first. The lock wasn't that difficult to pick, not for an expert, and he never secured the bolts. The front door was much more difficult to unlock. He gazed down at his laptop, his mind teeming with questions. Had the intruder come by car? If so then someone in the hamlet might have seen it, but that would have been too risky. So his intruder must have parked some distance away and walked to the cottage. Had he stayed outside all night? He'd have got bloody cold and wet, but maybe he didn't mind that. Was he watching him now? Had the intruder believed his search would go undetected? What had he hoped to find? And had he discovered it? What did the intruder expect him to do next? Maybe nothing. But that wasn't an option.

Marvik hurried out, not even bothering to set the alarm. He climbed into the Land Rover Defender and headed for Parkhurst prison.

THREE

'Only visitors named on a visiting order are allowed to visit prisoners,' the prison officer relayed to Marvik forty-five minutes later in the bleak reception area of Parkhurst. He'd hoped he might be able to persuade the prison authorities to allow him to see Terence Blackerman, but that seemed out of the question. He didn't know the system, which was obviously more complex than he'd expected. But action was better than sitting around contemplating why someone was interested in what he'd viewed on the Internet or why Charlotte had thought she was being followed, which clearly she had been.

'And how do I get one of those?'

'You don't. The prisoner must issue one to the visitor for him or her to be allowed a visit.'

So Blackerman had issued one in order for Charlotte to be able to visit him after he'd agreed to disclose his whereabouts to her. He had no reason to do the same for Marvik.

'And visits have to be arranged twenty-four hours in advance,' the prison officer continued. 'The usual procedure is to book by phone or email. And there are only certain days you can visit. This is not one of them.'

'If I leave you my details could they be passed on to Terence Blackerman so he could put in a visiting order?' Marvik asked, wondering what Blackerman would make of that. He quickly added, 'It's about his son's death. I'm a former Royal Marine. Commandos.'

That seemed to open the door. The prison officer's until then implacable features broke into a grin. 'Ex RAF Regiment,' he said.

They exchanged some reminiscences about their service life and Marvik left ten minutes later with the officer's promise that he'd pass his details on but there was no guarantee that Blackerman would want to see him. It wasn't quite a wasted journey though because Marvik had also pumped the prison officer for more information on Blackerman, and he'd got it.

'He's never seen anyone in the eight years I've worked here,' the officer, who had introduced himself as Ron Hubbard, said in answer to Marvik's question. 'Except for a woman who came yesterday. Nice looking but nervous. Her first visit inside a prison I guess.'

Marvik didn't enlighten Hubbard about Charlotte's service background. There was no need for him to know it.

'But perhaps he's keen to see more of this woman – and on the outside – because he applied to see the prison governor yesterday, maybe to own up to what he did.'

'What's he like?' Marvik had asked. 'Paul never spoke of him,' he added for authenticity.

'Quiet, does as he's told when he's told.'

'But?'

Hubbard raised his eyebrows. 'Is there a but?'

'Sounded like it to me.'

Hubbard gave a wry smile. Then his expression clouded over. 'There's something about him but I can't put my finger on it. It's as if . . .'

'Go on,' Marvik encouraged, hoping he hadn't overplayed his hand.

'As if he has some inner strength or knowledge that helps him to deal with prison, but then he is a former chaplain and he's maintained his religion inside so maybe he thinks God is helping him. Not that he spouts about religion or tries to convert the other prisoners – on the contrary he says nothing. But he's probably confessed his sins and knows he'll be forgiven in heaven and all that crap.'

Obviously Hubbard was a non-believer or was just trying to sound tough. But their conversation had given Marvik an idea. Was it worth his while talking to the prison chaplain? Maybe he would if Blackerman refused to see him but he doubted the prison chaplain would confide confidential advice about one of the inmates to an outsider any more than the navy chaplain Marvik had confided in would to others.

Charlotte had claimed that Blackerman maintained he was innocent and his refusal to budge on that and be granted parole bore that out, so perhaps, Marvik thought as he headed back to his Land Rover, God was giving him inner strength. Did he believe that? He'd certainly prayed when facing what he thought was death, and sometimes in the quiet and beauty of the harbour he'd felt close to something, but whether that was God or just Mother Nature doing what she did best he didn't know and he didn't stop to consider.

He called Charlotte but got her voicemail. Glancing at his watch he saw it was almost three o'clock. She would have been in Birmingham long before now but perhaps she had gone straight on duty. She hadn't said she was going to, but then he hadn't asked. He didn't leave a message. He certainly wasn't going to tell her that his cottage had been entered and searched. Neither did he want to worry her about Blackerman, so he'd keep his visit to the prison from her, but he was curious to probe her for more on her impressions of Blackerman and what they'd discussed. He was annoyed he hadn't asked her more last night or this morning but he'd had no need to then. He'd had misgivings about her health. Now he knew there was nothing wrong with her nerves. He'd try again later.

He grabbed a bite to eat in the quayside café in Newport. His thoughts returned to those two text messages ostensibly sent from him. Why would someone be keen to draw him into this? He'd never heard of Terence Blackerman before yesterday. And neither had he heard of Esther Shannon, the woman Blackerman had murdered in 1997, the year before he'd joined the Marines and the year of his parents' death in a diving accident on a marine archaeological expedition. Was there some connection between Terence Blackerman, Esther Shannon and himself, of which he was unaware? He didn't think so, but he couldn't be certain because he didn't have all the facts. Perhaps Blackerman's son, Paul Williamson, was the link. Paul had been in the Marines at the same time as Marvik, albeit in different units. Had their paths crossed? It was possible. They might even have spoken but Marvik hadn't recognized the name when Charlotte first mentioned it and he didn't recall it now. Could the person who had sent Charlotte that text message, who had followed her to his cottage and entered it, be Paul's former buddy and somehow he blamed Marvik for Paul's injuries and death, or wanted something from him? What, however, he couldn't fathom.

He polished off his sandwich and made for the Land Rover and home. There had been no further intrusions in the cottage. Whoever had come had got what he wanted the first time. Marvik again rang Charlotte and again got her voicemail. She must be on duty.

He switched on his laptop and checked his browsing history, not that he really needed to because he knew which websites he'd viewed last night and so too would his intruder if that's what he had been looking for. But why should anyone be interested?

The sound of a car pulling up outside caught his attention. He rose and made for the front door to see the same two men he'd seen

last night at the derelict coastguard cottage climb out of a dark blue
Ford. The bigger man, according to Strathen, was DI Feeny. Strathen
had warned him of a possible visit; Marvik just hadn't thought it
would be so soon. He invited them in and showed them through to
the kitchen where he offered them refreshment. They both declined.
And both refused to sit. Marvik therefore also chose to stand.

Feeny began the questioning while the leaner, younger man whose
ID claimed he was Detective Sergeant Howe took his notebook from
the inside of his jacket pocket. 'Mr Strathen told us you went to the
rendezvous point yesterday late afternoon to meet Ashley Palmer.'

'I went there, yes, on Shaun Strathen's request, but it was with
the intention of hoping to find Ashley Palmer there and to persuade
him to return to the mainland.'

'Why would he want to return with you?'

'He probably wouldn't have done, *if* he'd been there. He wasn't.'

Howe looked up. 'You know Mr Palmer then, sir?'

'No. I've never met him or heard of him until yesterday just
before four p.m. when Shaun phoned me.'

Howe looked blankly at him while Feeny's lips twitched in the
ghost of cynical smile. They obviously didn't believe him. That was
their problem. But even to Marvik it sounded feeble. Howe's eyes
dropped to Marvik's computer. He'd see nothing but a blank screen.

'Why did Shaun Strathen ask you to help?' Howe asked, looking
back up.

'Because I live on the island and we've worked together in the
past.'

Howe continued. 'But tracing people wasn't what you did in the
Commandos.' So Shaun had told him that.

Marvik said, 'Our missions often involved searching for people
others didn't want found and hopefully extracting them before they
were killed. We didn't always succeed,' he added.

'And you think Ashley Palmer is dead?' Howe asked.

'I don't know enough about him or why he's gone missing to
think that.'

'What's your occupation, sir?'

'I work for Drayles, the maritime security company.' They'd
probably already run a check on him and knew that. They might
even know he was involved in Harry Salcombe's death.

Feeny said, 'Is this your cottage?'

'No. I rent it.' And they probably knew that too.

'For how long?'

'I'm on a six-month renewable lease.'

'When did you arrive?'

'October.'

'Why here?'

'Why not?' Marvik suppressed his irritation. They were only doing their job but he wished they would do it with a little less scepticism. They obviously thought he was involved in Palmer's vanishing act and maybe they also suspected Strathen. Well they were wasting their time.

'What do you know about Ashley Palmer?'

'Hardly anything. Only what Shaun told me. That he's a computer research scientist working on developing artificial intelligence systems for the medical industry and that's it.'

Feeny nodded at Howe who produced a photograph. 'Have you ever seen this man before?'

Marvik took it and studied it. He was looking at a man in his late twenties of stocky build, but not fat, wearing faded jeans and a baggy white T-shirt emblazoned with a logo and the words 'Caring for the Marine Environment' printed underneath it. He was standing with his back to the sea, at the entrance to Portsmouth Harbour, so the picture must have been taken at Old Portsmouth outside the Spice Island or the Still and West pub. He was holding a bottle of beer and smiling into the camera with apprehension in the studious blue eyes. His hair was short and very fair. 'Is it Ashley Palmer?'

Feeny nodded.

Marvik had imagined him older and more shambolic. 'No, I've never seen him.' He handed the photograph back to Howe.

'Did you enter the cottage?' Howe asked.

'Yes, but I wasn't in there long. I searched the rooms and saw no evidence that he'd been there but I didn't search the grounds.'

'Why not?'

'I saw no need to.'

'How did you get there?'

'By boat. It's moored on the pontoon here.'

Would they ask to search it? Did they think he had met Palmer and done something with him?

'And you returned when?'

'I got back just after six thirty.'

'Can anyone vouch for that?'

'Do they have to?'

'Just routine.' Feeny smiled like a poisoner inviting him to eat something he'd contaminated.

Should he tell them about Charlotte? But that meant involving her and he didn't want that. And how did he explain why she had been here? They would question her to confirm his story. No, it was too complicated.

'I was alone,' he said, holding Feeny's gaze.

'And you live alone?'

Why did Feeny make the question sound like a sneer? If it was to goad him then the detective was going to be disappointed. 'Yes. I'm sorry but I can't help you find Ashley Palmer.' He held Feeny's cool gaze.

After a moment Feeny said, 'Well, thanks anyway.' He nodded at Howe to follow him. Marvik showed them to the door. He watched them climb into the Ford and drive off with an uncomfortable feeling in the pit of his stomach. He was certain they didn't believe him but they would have to. There was nothing linking him to Palmer, except his visit to that cottage and Shaun Strathen. He reached for his phone and rang him.

'The police have been here,' he said as soon as Strathen answered, and quickly he relayed the gist of the interview. 'They seem to suspect me of something, probably abducting Palmer.'

'They're fishing.'

'And they probably think we've conspired to do it together. Any further news?'

'Palmer's former girlfriend, Louise Tournbury, has been contacted but she says she hasn't seen or heard from Ashley since just before Christmas when she was with him at the Portsmouth Diving Club social function. They used to go diving together in the Solent and on holidays but she said that Ashley's been so heavily involved with his work at Chiron this last year that he's not been diving and he didn't renew his membership last April. She's a teacher at Woodlands Primary School, Bordon, Hampshire.'

Marvik knew the area. So too did Strathen. Bordon was an army town and home to the School of Electrical and Mechanical Engineers at Prince Philip Barracks. It had once also been the married quarters for Royal Air Force Oakhanger, home of No. 1001 Signal Unit, responsible for supporting satellite communication services for the British Armed Forces worldwide. The station had been decommissioned in 2003 when support to British military satellite communications had been outsourced.

Strathen said, 'Palmer's parents are both dead. The police are probably tracking down any relatives and friends.'

'Are they going to give his photograph to the media?'

'Not yet, because of what he was working on. They've called in their own hi-tech experts but I'll be astounded if they get anything from Palmer's PC or anyone else's at Chiron, but the police can access international databases that I can't get into, so they might turn up something. I'm searching the Internet for any references to the applications he was working on and I'm trawling the social media networks for any sign that Palmer was active on them, but so far I've drawn a blank. Don't worry about the police, Art. I shouldn't think they'll be back.'

Marvik rang off. He tried Charlotte's number several times with no answer. She was obviously avoiding him. He didn't blame her; after all he'd made it clear he didn't want to renew their relationship and maybe she felt the only way to prevent herself from being hurt was not to answer. But he had to speak to her. And he would in the morning.

The smell of her in his bed made it impossible for him to sleep. At one a.m. he stripped off the sheets and went downstairs where he tossed them into the washing machine and made a coffee. The cottage felt cold despite the heat from the Aga. He checked his phone and his emails. There were no messages. He toyed with searching the Internet again for more items on Blackerman but didn't. He returned to bed but found no refuge in sleep. His mind was too active, and his senses attuned to a possible intrusion.

At six thirty he rose and drove to Brading Down where he went for a punishing run, pushing himself, testing his fitness levels, pleased to find that while not at his peak, he wasn't too far off it. It was an hour after sunrise by the time he returned to the cottage and thirty minutes later he was calling the critical care unit asking to speak to Charlotte Churley.

'She's not here.'

Marvik's eyes flicked to the clock on the kitchen wall. It was eight thirty.

'Can you tell me when she's next on duty? I'm a friend. She came to see me yesterday. Art Marvik. I can't get through on her mobile number.'

There was a portentous pause and Marvik felt a cold chill run through him. 'What is it? What's happened? Is Charlotte OK?' he asked anxiously while his mind rapidly ran the gauntlet of possibilities. She'd been taken ill on the train; she'd been knocked down by a vehicle on her way to the station; she was wandering about suffering memory loss.

After a moment the woman answered with concern in her voice, 'She was meant to be on duty last night but she didn't show up. No one's seen or heard from her. She's been reported missing.'

Marvik's heart lurched. His head was whirling. Did she get on that train to Birmingham? He should have made sure she did. He should have made certain she was safe. It was his fault if anything had happened to her.

He quickly rang off and headed for his boat wondering if the police would come to interview him. Two missing persons laid at his door was enough to make them highly suspicious but he didn't give a damn about that. He had to find Charlotte. And Southampton, where he had left her, had to be the starting point.

FOUR

T hirty minutes later Marvik was mooring up on a visitors' berth at Ocean Village Marina, and running the short distance to the Town Quay where he began a methodical and thorough process of interviewing every taxi driver who had been on duty the previous morning, wishing he had a photograph of Charlotte to show them. None of them had taken her to the station or anywhere else.

He repeated the process inside the shopping centre with the same result. No one remembered seeing her. Feeling increasingly worried and desperate he headed for the railway station where his enquiries drew looks of astonishment and disbelief. He was told countless times that it was a busy station, that she could have slipped through unnoticed. Only those who caused a fuss or were particularly friendly and pleasant, which he gathered was about as rare as an honest politician, were noticed.

Both the Town Quay and the railway station had CCTV but as

a civilian he had no chance of being shown it. He needed the police
to authorize that and he'd make damn sure they would. Maybe they
were already on to it. Would DI Feeny and DS Howe be on the
investigation? Her disappearance would also involve the Royal Navy
Police. They investigated crime both on ship and shore establish-
ments. Charlotte's disappearance had been at neither, however, and
it probably wasn't considered a criminal matter. She was absent
without leave, yes, but they'd probably put that down to a health
problem.

He called her unit but this time he was met with a guarded
response that Charlotte Churley was unavailable. He rang off.
Perhaps the police would treat it as low priority but he wouldn't.
He *couldn't*. His gut told him time was critical. Charlotte was in
danger and he had to do something to help locate her.

Deeply disturbed, he returned to his boat, considering what to
do next. The obvious answer was to go to the police and tell them
that Charlotte had visited Terence Blackerman in prison and that
afterwards she'd spent the night with him. It would expose the fact
that he'd lied to the police and that would draw deeper suspicion
from Feeny over his possible involvement with Ashley Palmer's
disappearance, but to hell with that.

'Art Marvik?'

He spun round to find he was being addressed by a dark-haired
man in his early fifties with deep brown eyes in a round weather-
worn face. He was wearing a sailing jacket of a well-known and
expensive brand over casual trousers and deck shoes. He was also
carrying a small sailing holdall. Marvik had never seen him before.
And neither had he heard him come up behind him. My God, had
he become that sloppy? At one time he'd have heard a fly land on
the pontoon behind him. Where the devil had he sprung from? How
did he know him?

'Yes?' Marvik answered warily and tetchily.

'We have a mutual acquaintance'

'I'm sorry, I'm in a hurry.' He didn't have time for casual chit
chat.

'Yes, I know, to find Charlotte Churley.'

Marvik started in surprise. Christ, was he looking at the bastard
who had taken her? Was this man here to demand some kind of
ransom?

'Can I come on board? It will be easier to explain.'

Yeah, and easier to be attacked, thought Marvik, but two could play that game, and he was younger, fitter and trained to kill. He nodded him on to the boat. He'd have to turn his back on him to open up but he didn't think he'd be in danger of an attack then. This man wanted something first. But Marvik waved him into the cabin ahead of him.

He reached into his pocket. Marvik made to spring forward.

'My ID,' the man said quickly and handed a wallet across to Marvik.

He found he was addressing Detective Superintendent Philip Crowder. 'Are you from the Birmingham police?'

'No. Shall we sit.' It wasn't a question.

Crowder slid on to the bench seat and put his sailing holdall on the table. After a moment Marvik took up position opposite. He was beginning to wonder if this was the man who had entered his house and browsed his laptop. If so then he was bloody good, but not good enough that it had escaped his trained eye. Yet Marvik knew he'd made mistakes. He needed to sharpen up.

Crowder withdrew a laptop computer and a Manila folder.

'Terence Blackerman,' he said.

'What?' Marvik exclaimed.

'At least you didn't say who and pretend you hadn't heard of him.'

'Why should I?'

'Because Charlotte visited him yesterday in prison before coming to see you.'

'How do you know that?'

Crowder fired up the computer. 'We know you've been asking at the taxi rank and at the railway station if anyone saw Charlotte Churley after you dropped her off there yesterday at nine fifty-seven.'

'You had someone following me?' Marvik hadn't spotted anyone. Had he really lost it so completely? It seemed so. The thought depressed him.

'We don't need to. It's obvious you'd do so after discovering she hadn't returned to duty.'

Marvik was puzzled. He didn't understand any of this.

'Have you been called in to investigate her disappearance?'

'No.'

He rapidly thought. 'Then you've got a tap on my phone.'

'Not on yours but we have been able to keep tabs on Charlotte and her calls until yesterday morning when, at ten fifteen, we lost track of her, or rather we found her phone in a dustbin on the Town Quay.'

Marvik went cold inside. 'Then you know I've been calling that number.'

'Yes. But Charlotte didn't have your number logged in her address book. We found the text you'd sent to her from another mobile number and her reply to you.'

'Who's "we"?' Marvik didn't bother to say he hadn't sent that text. Not yet. He needed to know what this was all about.

'The police, of course,' Crowder answered solemnly.

But which branch? wondered Marvik, though he could tell by Crowder's set expression that he wasn't going to expand on that if he asked, so he didn't bother. 'If you knew Charlotte's movements why didn't you prevent her from going missing?'

'Because we didn't have anyone following her; we were only tracking her via her mobile phone.'

'But you knew she was being followed.'

'No.'

'You didn't follow her on Wednesday?'

'We had no need to; we knew where she was going, to the prison and then to you.'

Marvik wasn't sure he believed him about not following Charlotte.

'We have CCTV images of her after you dropped her off at Town Quay.'

Crowder swivelled the computer around. Marvik thought that Crowder had to be a genuine police officer otherwise he'd never have been given permission to have this stuff. With keen interest he studied the screen as Crowder continued.

'You can see Charlotte on the quayside walking towards the taxi rank. Her bright red jacket is distinctive. Then the catering supplies delivery van shows up and she disappears behind it. That's the last sighting we have of her.'

Marvik speedily recalled the layout of the Town Quay. 'There's a door into the centre just behind that van. She might have gone inside and walked to the street exit from there.'

'She didn't. Here are the pictures over the street exit for the period following her disappearance into the centre.'

Marvik peered at the people coming in and out: none of them was Charlotte, even if she'd changed her jacket.

Crowder said, 'We've also studied the CCTV images inside the centre. There is no sign of her in any of the shops or entering by any of the doors on the outside to the first-floor offices and neither does she show up in the corridors. She didn't double back and leave by the south exit and neither did she board a private boat or catch the ferry to West Cowes or Hythe.'

'Could she have been bundled into that catering van?'

'We're checking out the driver and the company. The catering van was there for fourteen minutes. The driver unloaded some drinks and supplies on to a trolley and wheeled it into the centre. No other car drove up behind the van and neither is there a motorbike or motor scooter arriving or leaving shortly after Charlotte's disappearance. It's possible that Charlotte changed her clothes in the ladies' toilet inside the centre, stuffed her jacket and trousers into a bag and left. She could have been told how to dodge the cameras.'

'But why should she?' Marvik said, puzzled.

'Maybe she *planned* to disappear. Perhaps she'd got fed up with being a nurse or being in the navy.'

But Marvik could see that Crowder didn't believe that any more than he could. It was what some might say though. 'She could simply have applied to come out of the navy.'

'Perhaps she couldn't wait that long. Perhaps she's met a man and has run off with him, or is suffering from post-traumatic stress and just wants to be alone.' The latter was a view that Marvik had considered himself, so it would be easy for others to believe it.

He said, 'But why go to the bother of changing her clothes?'

'To delay the navy's investigation into her disappearance and give her time to get away.'

'She might have been forced to change her clothes.'

'There is that possibility. But there's another: she's been forcibly abducted because of her visit to Terence Blackerman.'

And that had been, and still was, Marvik's belief. 'But why, for Christ's sake!'

'That's what we need to find out and why we need your help.'

'I'd never even heard of him until yesterday.'

'But someone intended you to because someone sent Charlotte Churley that text message purporting to be from you. It was sent from a pay-as-you-go phone which no longer exists. Of course it could belong to you. You could have bought it for the purpose of luring Charlotte to your cottage and then killing her.'

'What!' Marvik cried.

'You took her out on your boat either late last night or early this morning and you killed her and ditched her body in the sea.'

'But she's there on your CCTV images!'

'Where? That's just a blonde woman in a red jacket like Charlotte's.'

'You can't honestly believe that!'

'You and Charlotte were in a relationship four years ago. You've grown bitter since it ended, and jealous. You were determined to make her see that you were the only man for her. When she declined you got angry. Maybe you didn't mean to kill her; things just got out of hand.'

Marvik made to retort then snapped his mouth shut as he studied Crowder's implacable expression. Did he really believe that? No. But others might. In the silence that followed Marvik was conscious of the sound of the wind slapping the halyards against the masts outside and the gentle rocking of the boat. His mind flew back to what Charlotte and the prison officer, Ron Hubbard, had told him and what he'd read about Terence Blackerman in the early hours of yesterday morning.

After a moment he said, 'You think Blackerman was framed.'

'Possibly.'

Marvik's mind raced. 'And if he was framed then it's possible he told Charlotte something that the real killer of Esther Shannon doesn't want to be made public. But why wait this long to tell? And why reveal it to Charlotte?' But Marvik already knew the answers. 'That first text message was sent to Charlotte just before Blackerman's son's funeral, after Charlotte had applied to find out where Blackerman was serving his sentence, and the next when she was due to come over to visit the prison. The killer believes Paul told Charlotte something and she visited the prison to check it out with Blackerman. But she never mentioned anything to me, except to say that Blackerman told her he was innocent and she believed him.'

'Perhaps that was enough to stir things up. To make it uncomfortable for the killer.'

'But why me?'

Crowder said nothing, just waited for Marvik to get there on his own. His fists clenched. 'The bastard's elected me to be framed for Charlotte's abduction.'

'And possible murder.'

'Because he knows about our previous relationship.'

'You've also suffered a brain injury and you've had psychiatric help.'

'That means I'm fair game, does it?' Marvik declared hotly.

'It means others might think you unstable. You have also been treated at the hospital where Charlotte works, you're single, and you live on the Isle of Wight.'

'It's someone I know?' Marvik said, narrowing his eyes.

'Anyone can find out these things,' Crowder dismissed. 'But now that you *are* involved – and I don't think you have abducted and killed Charlotte – I'd like your help in trying to find her and I believe we can only do that by discovering what really happened to Esther Shannon in November 1997. If you ask enough questions and stir things up—'

'The killer will come after me. You want me to act as bait.'

'Yes.'

'While still being under suspicion of being involved?'

'*If* the Birmingham and Navy Police come to the same conclusion as I have previously illustrated.'

'And you trust me?'

'I've seen your service record.' Crowder left a second or two's pause before continuing. 'This will involve danger. If Blackerman is innocent, as he claims, then the real killer of Esther Shannon has killed at least once, probably more, and he will kill again. I think you can handle it.'

Marvik took a breath. He wasn't afraid of danger. He was afraid of botching it. Crowder must know about Harry Salcombe's death. But what if he did? All that mattered was finding Charlotte and hopefully still alive, although if what Crowder said was true it might already be too late.

'OK.'

Crowder nodded and briskly continued. 'We know from our prison intelligence officers that Charlotte visited Blackerman in prison and that you also visited Parkhurst prison yesterday and requested that your name be given to Blackerman with a request that he see you. That has not yet been passed on. It could be later, depending on what you discover. We know Blackerman claims that he didn't kill Esther Shannon but he offers up no further information on who he suspects or who he knows for certain did it.'

'Perhaps because he doesn't have that knowledge.'

'We think he does and that he's protecting someone who is now getting very nervous that he might be exposed.'

'But why go to prison for this person? And keep silent all these years?'

'That's what you need to find out.'

'It must be a very powerful secret for him to have kept his mouth shut for seventeen years.'

'He might not have had much choice. Either that or death.'

Marvik recalled what Charlotte had told him. 'Blackerman was a chaplain. Surely a man of God wouldn't fear death.' The chaplains he'd met hadn't. They were tough, brave buggers – David Treagust included or rather especially.

'Then perhaps he fears something more than death.'

Marvik understood that. He'd faced death many times. That didn't scare him; what did was being disabled and ill. Strathen's disability didn't seem to hamper him, but the thought of being incapacitated frightened the living daylights out of Marvik. And yet he still chose high-risk occupations, and he was choosing a high-risk assignment now. He didn't stop to analyse why. Maybe he knew why. The psychiatrist, Langton, had said it was because he was running away. On the contrary, he'd never run away from danger in his life. It wasn't that kind of running Langton had been referring to, though, but rather a running deep inside him that had started with his parents' death. He pushed such thoughts away and concentrated on Crowder.

'There is no doubt that Blackerman slept with Esther Shannon. He never denied that. But committing adultery is not murder. There is the possibility that he sees imprisonment as a punishment for that sin, but if that were the case,' Crowder quickly continued, anticipating Marvik's interruption, 'then he's been punished enough. Your job is to start asking questions of those who were involved in the Esther Shannon murder.'

'How will I find them?'

'There is some brief information in this file.' Crowder tapped the Manila folder beside him. 'But I can't let you have the case files or trial notes because I don't have them and I'm not going to request access to them.'

Marvik swiftly considered this and put it together with the fact that Crowder was here alone and undercover. 'You believe someone within the police is involved in Esther Shannon's murder.'

'Or is withholding evidence connected with it. Accessing the file would alert him and he'd make sure the trail that leads to him is wiped clean, including silencing Charlotte.' Crowder delved into the holdall and withdrew a mobile phone. 'It's a pay-as-you-go phone and it doesn't have GPS tracking. Don't use the email on it. Call me if and when you need anything further or need a meeting, although I suggest we keep the latter to a minimum.'

Marvik took it and saw that a number was already entered on it.

Crowder packed away the laptop. 'Don't use your computer or your own mobile phone or landline for anything connected with this case. If you have to use a computer go to a cyber café or a library. Meanwhile the navy and the police will officially continue with their search for Charlotte. I don't think it will take them as far as the Blackerman case, but it might bring them to you.' Crowder slid out of the seat. 'If there is any news of Charlotte I will call you. But the sooner you find the truth behind Esther Shannon's death the sooner you find Charlotte Churley.'

Marvik nodded and rose.

In the cockpit Crowder said, 'Start stirring things up, Marvik. I'll leave you to decide where to begin but when you've read the details in that file, burn it.'

'And if the people I question ask me how I found them?'

'You'll think of something to say.'

Marvik nodded. He knew that he would.

He watched Crowder leave, taking his farewell as though they were sailing buddies. He climbed on board a small but powerful motor cruiser further down the pontoon. Was it his or had it been hired for the purpose of affecting a meeting with him? Marvik scanned the horizon looking for other boats that were occupied, or people on the pontoon, but couldn't see any evidence of anyone being connected with Crowder. He could possibly have colleagues on the boat he'd boarded who had been in the cabin below, perhaps even monitoring their conversation. Crowder could have been wired up. Or was he working completely alone? No, not completely; someone would have had to sanction the operation. Marvik waited to see if anyone followed Crowder's boat out of the marina. They didn't. He was keen to read what was in that folder and eager to get started. Every minute counted.

He returned below and opened the folder and was surprised and slightly irritated to find that all it contained were two names and addresses and very little else. The first was Helen Shannon, Esther's sister, who lived at Locks Heath, a large conurbation just off the M27 motorway between Southampton and Portsmouth. The other was DCI Duncan Ross of the Sussex police. There were some brief notes on him. He'd been a detective sergeant with the Metropolitan Police when working on the Esther Shannon murder investigation under DI Bryan Grainger. Ross had transferred to the Sussex police in 2000 when he'd been promoted to DI and then to DCI. He was due to retire in April. He spent most of his weekends restoring his boat in Littlehampton Marina. That was about forty-five miles by road and approximately thirty-four nautical miles to the east.

Interesting that Crowder was pointing him in Ross's direction. Why? There must have been many officers on the investigation who would be able to tell him about it, including Grainger. And what of the DCI or Detective Superintendent who had been on the case? Perhaps they were dead or living abroad. Or perhaps Ross and Grainger were the only officers in full possession of all the facts, or rather the officers Crowder suspected of knowing more about it than they had let on. There was only one way to find out. Committing the information to memory, he struck a match to the paper over the sink and watched it burn. Then he went on deck and set a course for Littlehampton Marina.

FIVE

He made good time. As he motored past the bleak stony shores of the West Beach to the entrance of the River Arun he radioed up Littlehampton Marina to say he was approaching and asked if they could accommodate him for one night, possibly two. They could. Marvik had assumed there'd be no trouble with that. At this time of the year the marina wouldn't be full.

Several times on the way he had wondered if he was wasting his time. This might be the one weekend Ross wasn't working on his boat. He might be on an investigation or on holiday. But if Marvik read between the lines he was certain that Crowder had meant him to come here now. Ross wouldn't show until tomorrow but that gave Marvik a night to reconnoitre the area. He'd had no need to return to the cottage. He had everything he required on board, and what he didn't he could buy in Littlehampton.

There was no sign of Ross, or anyone else, on the pontoons of the small marina. But Marvik located an old classic wooden boat that was most probably Ross's.

He reported to the marina office, where he paid a fee for one night, and then struck out along the road away from the marina, past a handful of small light industrial units on his right and a mobile home park on his left on the river side. After half a mile he turned left at the crossroads and walked briskly over the narrow footbridge that spanned the River Arun. There was a pub on each side but Marvik ignored both and made for the town centre wishing he could see Ross today rather than hanging about until tomorrow or possibly Sunday. It was time he could ill afford. Every minute counted in the search for Charlotte and he was frustrated at having to kick his heels waiting around. Despite what Crowder had said about the police looking for Charlotte he thought he couldn't rely on them.

He stopped at the Lifeboat Centre and stared across the river at the masts of the yachts moored opposite across the grey ebbing river. Two missing people in two days and in the same area, with him as the common factor. But he had no connection with Ashley Palmer. He'd never even met him – but could Charlotte and Palmer be connected? Was the common thread between them Terence Blackerman? He didn't see how it could be but he reached for his phone and called Strathen. He asked first if there was any news of Palmer.

'Nothing. None of the taxi drivers at the Cowes terminal on the Isle of Wight claim to have picked him up. The police have circulated his photograph to the bus drivers but as we said before I can't see him boarding a bus to Rocken End, if there is one, or a bus to anywhere else come to it. They've also circulated photos to the marinas at both East and West Cowes.'

'Did he take any clothes with him?'

'The police don't know, because neither they nor any of us know what was in his wardrobe. I gave them a description of the bag he usually carries and that's not been found in his house, and neither is there a passport. I'm going through my contacts at the Border Agency to see if he's shown up abroad.'

'Aren't the police doing that?'

'Probably, but I can't leave everything to them,' Strathen answered sarcastically, mirroring Marvik's thoughts. 'They've also searched that coastguard cottage and the area around it and drawn a blank.'

As Marvik knew they would. He said, 'Do you remember Charlotte Churley?'

'Of course I do, she nursed me when I first got flown to the hospital from Camp Bastion. Didn't you go out with her?'

'Yes. She's missing.'

There was a moment's silence. 'As in AWOL?'

'Yes. She came to see me Wednesday night after I'd returned from looking for Palmer. I dropped her off at the Town Quay yesterday morning. She didn't show up for duty at the hospital. She never arrived in Birmingham. The police are involved but like you said, Shaun, we can't leave everything to them. I need you to check her Internet profile, see if she's posted anything about coming to see me. And I need you to see if there is a connection between her and Ashley Palmer. I can't explain now, it's too complicated, but I'll give you all the details tomorrow.' Marvik suddenly realized he'd spoken on his own phone and not the pay-as-you-go Crowder had given him. Had someone really tapped his mobile phone? If so he'd given little away except that he'd drawn Strathen into this.

'Don't call me. I'll call you tomorrow.'

There was a second's pause before Strathen replied. 'OK.'

He found a supermarket and stocked up on provisions. He had intended eating on the boat but as he reached the footbridge he turned into The Arun View and ordered a beer and a meal and took a seat in the window overlooking the river. The pub was relatively quiet, it being early evening, but later he suspected it would be crowded with the first of the weekend revellers. From where he was sitting he had a good view up the river towards the marina and of the caravans and mobile homes that bordered the waterfront. He turned his attention to the pub. There were two families with young children on tables to his right and a few couples in the bar. There was also a man in his fifties reading a newspaper and another in his early thirties doing something with his phone. Towards the entrance there were another two men, both in their thirties and both well built. Cops? Marvik wasn't sure this time. Were they on duty? And if so were they watching him? But why should they be – unless Crowder didn't trust him, or wanted to keep tabs on him.

His meal arrived. He ordered another beer and ate slowly without tasting the food, making sure to appear relaxed and at ease while acutely aware of the two men near the entrance who seemed to be making a pint of beer last a very long time. The man reading the newspaper left and the one on his phone was still playing with it while looking out of sorts. The children were growing noisier and the pub was filling up. The river was now in darkness and lights were on in the mobile homes opposite. It was time for Marvik to leave.

He returned to the boat, walking slowly up the long wide road that led to the marina. The only turning was to his right into the caravan and mobile home park and the road terminated at the marina. He'd hear any vehicle approaching. But nobody passed him by car and nobody followed him on foot.

He was keen for action but there was a waiting game to be played and, although impatient, he'd learned that preparation and waiting were part of the success of an operation. Well he could wait but his preparation for this operation was sadly lacking because the information he had was so meagre.

As he lay on his bunk he listened to the sounds of the night, acutely aware of anything that sounded suspicious, fully prepared in case he needed to act. He slept the kind of half-waking sleep that could be shaken off in an instant and replaced by action if required. But none was. The cawing seagulls announced the dawn and he rose to find a grey light slowly filling the sky to the east. He changed and went for a run. His head was clear, his muscles screaming for more exercise, his eyes alert to his surroundings, his ears attuned for any danger. He took a circuitous route. He would have liked to run along the river's edge into the flat marshy countryside but he chose the road, his eyes scanning the parked cars. Surely the police wouldn't be stupid enough to be sitting in their car, and they weren't. If those guys in the pub had been cops then they would have known he'd come by boat and could up anchor and leave at any time. He noted the cameras over the marina and along the road. The police wouldn't have to physically watch him, they could be sitting behind a console in a nice warm operations room.

By the time he returned to the boat the morning was bright and breezy with a wind from the north-east that brought an edge of sharpness with it. He watched two swans head further up the river towards the small historic town of Arundel before he made for the marina showers. After breakfast he took a stroll around the pontoons. It was a little after nine thirty but he'd already seen a slender, balding man about early-fifties arrive with a Border Collie. The cover was off the old classic yacht and the dog was lying on the pontoon in front of it. Good. It was easy to strike up a conversation with a person who had a dog but even if Ross hadn't had a pet the yacht would have been a good enough topic. Marvik halted in front of the boat and bent down to ruffle the dog's fur. It hauled itself up like an old man and sniffed around Marvik's leg, thumping its tail.

'You've made a friend,' a voice hailed him and Marvik looked up to see a man's head poking out of the cabin. The rest of him followed. He climbed up into the cockpit wiping his hands on an oily rag. 'But then he's everyone's friend.'

'What's his name?'

'Rune. It's a letter from an ancient Germanic alphabet. I looked it up. It's related to the Roman alphabet. It's a mark or letter of mysterious or magical significance, a secret.'

Very apt, thought Marvik, wondering what secret Blackerman harboured that had kept him in prison for so many years.

'But there's nothing mystical about that old boy,' the man continued, nodding at his dog who once again flopped down beside Marvik's feet.

Marvik smiled. He didn't know for certain this was Duncan Ross but he'd bet on it.

'You staying in the marina?' the man asked.

'Came in yesterday.'

'From?'

'The Isle of Wight,' Marvik lied.

'Lovely place. Sailed there many times. Not on this. On the boat I had before. This was meant to be my retirement project but I've had more time on my hands lately than I anticipated.'

'You've been made redundant.' Perhaps he'd got it wrong, or Crowder had, and this wasn't Ross.

'No. My wife left me.'

'I'm sorry to hear that.'

'Why should you be? I'm not. Hazard of the job.' Marvik looked blankly at him, hoping he'd elaborate. He did. 'I'm a police officer.'

So it was Duncan Ross.

'I'm amazed we stayed together for so long,' Ross continued.

'But with retirement looming in April we both came to the conclusion six months ago that we didn't want to spend the rest of our days looking at one another and not knowing what the hell to talk about.'

Marvik smiled. 'Will you miss the job?'

'No. Everything's changed. It's all paperwork, public relations, targets and human rights. We think more of the villains now than of the victims.'

'Will you take up another job?'

'I've been offered a couple – security, private investigation. I could even go back into the force in a civilian role, there are a lot of posts that are now being done by civilians. They're even recruiting civilian investigators and superintendents. But I've done my bit.'

'I'm thinking of joining the police,' Marvik said, taking the opening presented to him. 'The Met. I'm a former Royal Marine, Commandos.'

'Tough job.'

'So's the police.'

Ross shrugged and looked thoughtful for a moment. 'I was in the Met. But the wife wanted to move out of London. Said it was getting too crowded, dirty and noisy. So we came to the seaside in 2000 and I transferred to the Sussex Police.'

'A bit quieter on the crime front, I should imagine.'

'A bit.'

'You must have had some interesting cases in London.'

'A few,' he answered, smiling wistfully. But Marvik thought he caught an edge of bitterness in those two words. Perhaps Ross had regretted leaving London and the Met. And now that his wife had upped sticks and deserted him, he resented it, and her, even more. Marvik thought he'd plunge in and see where it took him, especially as Ross seemed the friendly, talkative type.

'I heard about a murder that happened at the services club in London, the Union Services Club, in 1997, when I was staying there some time ago now. One of the bar stewards told me a young woman had been killed, were you on that?' He kept his tone light but eager. He hoped that Ross would be flattered into talking to a possible new recruit, demonstrating the range and depth of his career. In Marvik's experience, showing a keen interest in someone's job never failed to elicit information and confidences. And he wasn't wrong now.

'I was. DI Bryan Grainger was the guv'nor. He became Detective Chief Inspector Grainger after it. I was only a detective sergeant then.'

Marvik's interested deepened. There had been something in the way Ross had spoken that alerted him.

'You mean he got promoted because of the success of the case.'

'Probably.'

'But you're not sure it was deserved.'

Ross studied Marvik critically. He wondered if he'd pushed too fast and too hard. Perhaps he had sounded too eager.

But Ross said, smiling, 'You'll make a good police officer.'

Marvik returned the smile. 'Because I'm nosy.'

'You need to be.'

'The case also caught my attention because I was told the man who was convicted was a navy chaplain and I've known a few chaplains and I can't imagine any of them killing.'

'That's what they all say,' Ross answered cynically, then seemed to acquiesce. 'But you're right. It was one of those cases where everything fitted and yet your gut told you it was wrong. It was too neat and I remember when I saw Terence Blackerman being sentenced, it didn't seem right. He didn't seem right.'

'You think he was innocent?'

'No. Everything pointed to him being the killer but I was convinced there was something he was holding back, something that might have made a difference to the life sentence he got. He didn't look shocked at the sentence, just sorrowful and I don't know . . .' Ross rubbed a hand over his chin. The dog looked up and gave a small whine as though sensing something in his master's demeanour. Marvik could see Ross was recalling the incident and thinking back down the years.

'It was as though he was steeling himself to shoulder the punishment, not because he was guilty, which is what Grainger said when I voiced my views to him, but because there was something he knew only he wasn't telling.'

His words echoed what Crowder had told him. 'You think he was protecting someone who could have been involved in this woman's death.' Marvik almost said her name then.

'There was no one else involved. There was only his DNA and fingerprints in the room, aside that was from the cleaner who was at home with her family at the time Esther Shannon was killed, and the previous occupant's DNA and she was sixty miles away at the time of the murder. Anyway it was a long time ago. Terence Blackerman's probably out by now.'

Again Marvik bit his tongue, though something inside him was telling him to come clean with Ross. Maybe he would, later. He hadn't expected him to be quite so open but perhaps now Ross was nearing retirement he'd already slipped into the habit of reliving his past glories, and was ready to regale them to anyone prepared to listen and even those who weren't.

'Perhaps you should write your memoirs when you retire, about your most interesting cases,' Marvik encouraged.

'It would bore the pants off everyone. Don't they say never look back.'

They do, Marvik thought with conviction. 'Perhaps Grainger will write his memoirs.'

'If he does they'll be worth a few bob because they'll come from the other side. He was killed in a hit and run nine months after retiring in 2004. Car came out of nowhere as he was crossing the road in Brighton.'

So that was why his name wasn't in the meagre file Crowder had left him. 'That's tough for his family.'

'He was divorced years ago, no kids.'

Marvik left a moment's pause before saying, 'Why did Terence Blackerman kill this woman, Esther Shannon?'

Ross shrugged. 'Perhaps she wouldn't let him have sex the way he wanted it. Maybe he went in for bondage and she wasn't playing. Or maybe he could only get aroused if he was violent.'

'Did he admit that?'

'No, and there was no evidence she was beaten up. He denied any kind of sexual pressure or quirks. As you said, he was a naval chaplain, with an exemplary record, well liked, married with a kid. No hint of any marital tension or stories that he liked the women or that he'd ever been violent before.'

'But he would have seen violence,' Marvik insisted thoughtfully. 'He'd have gone into battle with his men. He'd have served in the Gulf War, perhaps even the Falklands War in 1982.'

'Not the Falklands, but Esther Shannon's father was killed in the Falklands War.'

'Blackerman would still have seen conflict. Perhaps he was suffering from post-traumatic stress.'

'Not according to the medical reports.'

So he had been medically examined. Marvik wondered what they'd found. 'Whoever examined him might have been incompetent.'

'Possibly.'

'Was Esther Shannon in the services? Perhaps they'd met some time before and had an affair?'

But Ross was shaking his head. 'We found no evidence of that or that he knew Esther's father. She was in London for the Remembrance Service and so was Blackerman.'

'So they met at the Albert Hall.'

'No, at the Union Services Club, in the lift.'

Marvik's ears pricked up at this new information.

'It got stuck. They were trapped in it and struck up a friendship.'

'How long for?' Marvik prayed silently that Ross would continue to be talkative. He half expected him to ask, 'Why all the questions?' But he didn't.

'Eighteen minutes. He went back to her room and into her bed. That's pretty quick work for anyone.'

And especially a chaplain, thought Marvik, and yet he remembered Charlotte's words on Wednesday night. *I don't want to be alone.* Had Esther Shannon said the same to Blackerman? Had she been frightened? Had she told Blackerman why she was afraid? Was that why she was killed?

Ross was saying, 'Blackerman returned to Portsmouth early the next morning before her body was discovered by the chambermaid. When Esther Shannon didn't hand in her key, the maid went in to investigate and found the poor woman dead. Blackerman claimed he left her room at one thirty a.m.'

So not so scared that she didn't ask him to stay the night. Why not? The case had obviously stuck in Ross's mind, probably because, as he'd revealed, he'd had doubts about the conviction. 'Did she attend the Remembrance Service every year?'

'No, that was the first time according to her sister, Helen, and obviously her last.'

But her father had been dead for fifteen years so why not go before? Enquiring about that might be one question too far. Ross had already been surprisingly forthcoming. And perhaps tomorrow he could ask him a few more. 'You must have had lots of interesting cases.'

'I have, and disturbing ones. But not for much longer,' he finished brightly. 'How long are you staying?'

'Just for tonight.'

'Well, good luck with your application.'

That was Ross's way of getting shot of him and it sounded as though he didn't intend being here tomorrow. Marvik patted the dog and headed up the pontoon towards the Boathouse Café where he bought a coffee and sat close to the window but not directly in it.

Sipping his coffee he kept his eyes on the pontoons. From here he could see Ross's boat. He watched him emerge from the cabin with a mobile phone pressed to his ear. Nothing wrong or unusual in that. Perhaps he'd got a call from work or a family member. Marvik wished he could lip read because there was something about the man's posture and his serious expression that told him it wasn't a social call. He frowned, puzzled. There was also something different about Ross's demeanour. His body language was more assertive. He looked more like a man in charge, in fact a Detective Chief Inspector, rather than a man with an oily rag tinkering with an engine inclined to talk about the old days. Or rather the one old case Marvik had pumped him about.

Ross rang off and disappeared into the cabin. Marvik swallowed his coffee and ordered another. He took it back to the same seat. There were three people in the café but nobody he recognized or interested in him. Eight minutes later he saw Ross stride up the pontoon with the dog following more slowly at his heels. For a moment Marvik wondered if they were heading towards him. But Ross made for a saloon car in the car park. The dog jumped in the back, Ross climbed in and pulled away. Marvik waited a couple more minutes, then left the café and headed into town.

He found the library in Maltravers Street just off the B2140. Soon he was seated at a computer terminal and searching the Internet for information on the hit-and-run incident that Ross had told him had killed former DCI Bryan Grainger. He was certain the local newspaper must have covered it. They had and in some depth, he was pleased to see.

He read that Grainger, a former Detective Chief Superintendent with the Metropolitan Police, had been killed in Broad Street, the opposite of its name it appeared, because it was described as a narrow one-way street that ran north from St James's Street to

Marine Parade, in the south, the latter being the main A259 running along the seafront not far from the junction with the Sea Life Centre and the pier. It had been dark, raining heavily and very windy. The streets had been deserted. It was shortly after eight thirty p.m. on the twenty-ninth of October. There had been only one witness, a woman called Linda Hannam, who had been visiting her sister who ran a guest house in Broad Street. And she hadn't seen exactly what had happened. She'd heard a car rev up and shoot off and had turned to see a man's body on the ground. She thought it had been a large black car but couldn't say what make or give the registration number. She was in shock. She didn't even know in which direction it had turned when it reached the junction with Marine Parade. She rushed to see if she could help and had phoned the emergency services but Grainger had been pronounced dead on arrival at the hospital. Enquiries by the police, Marvik read, hadn't discovered why Grainger was in that street. He lived alone in Chichester, a cathedral city just over thirty miles to the west of Brighton and about fifteen from Littlehampton. He hadn't been registered at any of the guest houses and no one could remember seeing him or serving him in any of the bars and pubs in Broad Street or nearby. A house-to-house had unearthed no further witnesses and the CCTV cameras along the seafront had failed to pick out the vehicle. No one had come forward to admit to the crime and as far as Marvik could see no one had been arrested for it.

There was a small piece about Grainger's career in the Met, but no mention of his cases or the Esther Shannon investigation. According to what Marvik was reading, Grainger had worked for the Serious Organized Crime Agency, and had had an exemplary record. So what had he been doing in Brighton? Taking the night air? Hardly on such a wild night. Visiting or meeting someone? Possibly. But that person had never come forward and that meant he or she didn't want to be involved. But whether the hit and run was deliberate or the action of a drunk or drugged driver, Marvik didn't know. And if it was deliberate then it might have nothing to do with Esther Shannon. It could have been connected with another crime Grainger had investigated in the past while working in the Serious Organized Crime Agency. His cases would have involved drug and human trafficking, armed robbery and murder. There would have been enough candidates for the Sussex police to check on in

cooperation with their colleagues at the Met – but had they? And
if Grainger had been killed because he was about to reveal something
about Esther Shannon, then Marvik knew he was also in danger, a
fact that Crowder had pointed out. Did Duncan Ross also know the
truth behind Esther's death? Was he in danger? He'd survived for
seventeen years after Blackerman had been sentenced, so perhaps
he knew nothing.

Marvik left the library, bought some sandwiches and ate them
on the waterfront thinking over his conversation with Ross. There
was no need for Ross to have lied to him, but equally there had
been no need for him to tell him what he had about the Blackerman
case. Marvik could put that down to his clever questioning tech-
nique and acting skills but surely a copper would know when he
was being pumped for information. But perhaps Ross had just told
him what he might have been able to find out if he'd applied to
see the files under the Freedom of Information Act. He wondered
what would be in those files. Perhaps he should make a request
to see them, except that it would take far too long, and he didn't
have the luxury of time on his side if he wanted to find Charlotte
alive.

He called Strathen using his own mobile phone again. Strathen
told him that Charlotte was on the usual clutch of social networks
where she'd posted about her work and friends, but there was nothing
to give him any indication of where she might be.

'The police must be checking out her friends and relatives,'
Strathen added, clearly as worried as Marvik judging by his tone.
'I can't find her having any connection with Palmer. Can't you tell
me more?'

'I will tomorrow. I'm heading back.'

'From where?'

'I'll tell you when I see you.'

He rose. There was nothing more he could glean about Esther
Shannon and her death here from Ross because he had the feeling
that Ross wasn't about to return. It was time to talk to Helen
Shannon.

SIX

Sunday

I t wasn't until Sunday afternoon though that Marvik was finally driving the Land Rover towards Locks Heath and the address he'd been given for Helen Shannon. The weather had closed in on Saturday afternoon and gale-force winds and heavy rain had persisted throughout the night, preventing him from leaving Littlehampton until Sunday morning. When he'd arrived on the island just after midday his cottage was how he had left it. There was no sign of an intrusion.

Several times during the night and on the crossing to the Isle of Wight he'd considered calling Crowder to report in and then decided against it. He had nothing new to tell him and although Crowder might be able to give him more details about Grainger's accident, Marvik doubted he would. Crowder would claim that going through official channels would alert the killer. Marvik guessed he'd already done that by talking to Ross but then he was the bait. He had no evidence that Ross would go running to the killer, but a nagging feeling, born out of what he'd seen and heard yesterday, told him that there was something not right about the man, and about their earlier exchange.

He'd caught the three o'clock Red Funnel sailing from East Cowes to Southampton and on the hour-long crossing had speculated what Helen Shannon might be like. He didn't even know if she was older or younger than Esther. Maybe he wouldn't find her at home. She might be on holiday or working. But he knew that however he found her, and when he did, his questions would bring back painful memories for her. Perhaps she wouldn't want to talk about her sister's murder. He couldn't blame her if she didn't.

It was just after four thirty and raining heavily when he turned into a modern estate a few miles south of the motorway. Earlier he'd stopped off at a garage and bought a street map. The area had been built up so much over the years that without a map he could waste a lot of time going around in circles. He had satnav on his mobile phone but didn't want to risk using it in case he was being tracked, and besides there was no substitute for maps for giving him a better all-round view of the terrain.

The three-storey modern house was the last in a row of identical properties. It faced another row of the same style of properties across a road where cars were parked at an angle separated by a line of bare-branched trees and street lighting. It being Sunday most spaces were taken despite the fact that the properties had garages with cars parked in front of them. But Marvik found a space almost opposite Helen Shannon's house and next to a street light which flickered intermittently in the gathering dark and rain. He climbed out and studied Helen Shannon's house. There was a light showing on the first floor and an old Fiat was parked in front of the garage. Someone was at home but it might not be the woman he was hoping to talk to.

He pressed his finger on the bell and waited under the porch out of the rain. He hadn't heard the bell sound inside the house and as no one came to answer it he tried again, and lifted the knocker.

'OK. I'm coming,' a woman testily cried out. He could hear footsteps on the wooden flooring.

The door opened and Marvik found himself confronted by a thin woman in her early thirties. She was about five foot five and dressed head to toe in black with long, bright purple hair and heavy dark eye make-up. Despite that he found her attractive.

'Helen Shannon?' he asked.

'Yes?' she answered cagily. Her wary brown eyes flicked over his face. He wondered what she saw – a scarred stranger dressed casually – and what she thought, that he was about to sell her cavity wall insulation or con his way into the house to steal from her?

He hastily apologized for disturbing her and added, 'I'd like to talk to you about your sister.'

He watched her visibly start before fury swept across her face. 'Oh yeah, and who the hell are you? You're a bloody journalist, aren't you? Well you can sod off.' She made to slam the door on him.

Marvik thought he hadn't handled that very well. He could see there was no bullshitting her. Placing his hand firmly on the door to prevent it being slammed on him he quickly said, 'I'm a friend of Charlotte Churley who has gone missing after visiting the man who killed your sister in prison. I'm trying to find Charlotte before someone kills her and I think they will because somehow she's stirred up interest in your sister's death and someone doesn't want that, which makes me wonder why.'

'Crap!'

'Charlotte visited Terence Blackerman in prison on Wednesday. He told her he didn't kill your sister.'

She snorted. 'And you've fallen for that! Of course he killed her. He followed her to the lift, chatted her up, followed her to her room and then raped and killed her.'

'There was no evidence of rape.'

Her expression held contempt. 'You don't have to use physical violence to get what you want. *Threats* of physical violence are enough and as Esther's not alive to say any different he would say she was willing, wouldn't he?'

It was a good point. He said, 'It was out of character for her then, to sleep with a man she'd only just met?'

'Fuck off.'

His hand came solidly on the door again. That had been clumsy of him and harsh. He desperately needed her cooperation. He took an inner breath and said urgently, 'Helen, please. I need your help. I'm sorry for offending you.'

She looked about to repeat her previous instructions, then hesitated. Perhaps she'd caught the despair in his voice or saw it on his face because after a moment she stepped back and reluctantly, still with suspicion said, 'You can have five minutes. And the clock starts ticking now.' She consulted the large watch on her bony wrist.

Relieved he entered the narrow hall and made to close the door behind him but she said, 'Leave it.' Clearly she didn't trust him. He didn't blame her.

Swiftly he continued. 'Charlotte's a nurse in the Royal Navy, she's seen a lot of wounded personnel and been into combat zones. The police believe that nursing Paul Williamson, who was Terence Blackerman's son, who died as a result of his wounds incurred while in action, and then visiting Blackerman in prison to tell him of his son's death could have pushed her over the edge and has nothing to do with the fact that Blackerman maintains his innocence.' Or rather the police with the exception of Crowder believed that. 'I don't agree. Charlotte came to me worried that someone was following her. She was obviously right.'

'Maybe she imagined it, stress and all that.'

'No. Charlotte's not like that.'

'But why should someone abduct her because of my sister's death?'

'That's what I'm trying to find out. I thought you might talk to me about what happened, and that it might throw up something that could help me find her.'

'I can't see how,' she said warily, still eyeing him with suspicion.

'I have to try. I can't ignore the fact that she's disappeared straight after talking to Terence Blackerman.'

'What does that scum bag say about it?'

'I'm not being allowed to question him.'

She narrowed her eyes, obviously not sure whether to trust him. 'How come you found me?'

She was smarter than he'd given her credit for. He could lie and say he'd found her through his own research but he knew that would just get him thrown out.

'The police told me where you lived.' She looked about to explode. Hastily Marvik continued. 'When I say police, it was one officer, working alone. And he, like me, believes that Charlotte's abduction is connected with what happened in 1997.'

'Then send this copper here.' She stepped forward, as though to evict him.

Marvik had to prevent that. 'There isn't time.' Swiftly he pressed on. 'Every minute counts if I'm to find Charlotte alive, and if what Blackerman claims is true and he didn't kill your sister then the person who did is still at liberty and might be willing to kill another innocent woman in order to protect himself. He will certainly try and kill me if I get close to him. But I couldn't give a shit about that as long as I can find Charlotte and make sure she's safe first.'

She was still eyeing him guardedly.

'Please, Helen, five minutes, just a few questions. I know it will be painful for you but it could help me find Charlotte. Then I'll leave you in peace.'

She gave a heavy sigh, then shrugged. 'Might as well. I've got sod all else to do. But I still say he killed her.' She closed the door and made for the stairs opposite. 'The kitchen's on the second floor,' she said by way of explanation. 'Crap place to put it but the architect obviously thought it would be good exercise for the occupier who has to lug all the shopping up there, and the washing from the garden, not that you can call a postage stamp a garden.'

'You don't like living here?' he said to her rear, clad in a tight short black skirt.

'Would you?' she tossed over her shoulder.

'No,' he answered instantly. 'Then why stay?'

'Because I've got a crap job in a crap company which pays me just enough to continue with the rent on this crap house for another month until the lease expires since my even crappier partner decided he'd have more fun with a blonde twice his age, with three kids in tow.'

He smiled, taking care not to let her see it. He rather liked her style.

She turned into the modern kitchen at the front of the house. 'Coffee?'

'Thanks,' he said, taken aback by the unexpected offer. She'd mellowed. He wasn't sure why and he wasn't going to ask or quibble over it. He was just glad. It would make his delicate task that much easier. And by drinking coffee he was going to get a lot longer than five minutes. He peered out of the window. The street was deserted. The rain bounced off the pavements and ran off the pitched roof of the porch below him.

'It'll have to be instant.'

'That's fine,' he said, turning back. 'Where will you go when the lease runs out?' he asked as she flicked on the kettle.

'Anywhere away from here and the shit job I've got.'

'What do you do?'

'I work in a call centre, answering calls from irate customers who have been fucked around by the company who really couldn't give a toss about them anyway. It was all I could get and better than being on benefit, which I add I have never been on in my life,' she declared as though he was going to accuse her of that.

He didn't ask why she wasn't taking calls today. Perhaps she didn't work Sundays anyway, or perhaps the call centre was closed at weekends, although that was unlikely these days. 'What would you like to do?' he said, watching her heap a large spoon of coffee into a mug. Good job he liked it strong. She did the same in her own mug.

'Not what I'm doing now.' She sloshed hot water into the mugs, not noticing she'd spilt some on the work surface or if she did she wasn't going to bother mopping it up. She pushed a hand through her long straight purple hair and studied him again with her penetrating eyes but they weren't quite as hostile as previously. 'And what do you do when you're not looking for your girlfriend or working for the police?'

He hadn't said Charlotte was his girlfriend: maybe she was fishing to see if she was, or perhaps she'd just assumed it.

'I'm between jobs,' he answered evasively. He didn't see there was any need to tell her about his past or that he worked for Drayles.

She raised her black eyebrows and opened the fridge. Retrieving a carton of milk she poured some in her own mug and did the same to his without asking him whether he wanted it. Tossing the empty packet in the bin she said, 'Was Blackerman's son in the army?'

'Marines.'

She handed him his mug and picked up her own. 'Well I'm sorry for him and his mother, but not for his father.' She walked away assuming Marvik would follow her and he did into the lounge which gave off from the tiny kitchen. Here she plonked herself on to the L-shaped sofa, tucked her long legs under her and clutched her coffee mug with both hands. Marvik sat and turned to face her across the low table on which was a laptop with the lid down and a mobile phone.

She said, 'Have you any idea of what Esther's death did to my family?'

'Yes,' said Marvik, recalling his reaction to his parents' death. It fucked you up. He'd joined the Marines to get as far away as possible and to become absorbed in a life so different from the one he'd known that he no longer had to think of it. And maybe that was what Paul had done, except he hadn't known about his father's crime until he'd enlisted. After that perhaps he'd placed himself in as much danger as possible as a way of goading fate into trying to kill him. With Paul fate had succeeded. And how had Helen coped, he wondered. How old had she been when her sister had been killed? In her teens he thought.

'How can you know?' she scoffed, but there was an edge of sadness to her tone.

'I understand that your father was killed in the Falklands War.'

'I was a year old, so I have no idea what he was like except what I was told when I was growing up, that he was funny, kind and brave.'

That made her thirty-three.

'There was a big gap between me and Esther; she was eight years old when I was born, so she looked after me a lot as a kid, especially when she was a teenager and mum's condition got worse. Mum had MS.'

'Did Esther always attend the Remembrance Service at the Albert Hall?' Ross had told him it was Esther's first time but no harm in checking.

'No. She'd never been before but Mum died in 1996 so Esther wanted to do something to remember them both. And she was involved with the Royal British Legion.'

'Did you offer to go with her?'

She shook her head. 'No. I thought it would be boring. I wish to God I had gone. She might still be . . . Well I didn't and that's that.' Her head came up and her eyes flashed anger as though he might be about to accuse her of neglect.

'Did she go alone?'

'I don't know. I can't remember the details. I know the tickets were issued through the Royal British Legion so she might have arranged to meet up with some of the members there.'

Marvik needed to check that out.

'When did she go up to London?'

'On the Friday before the Remembrance Service – look you must know all this.' The suspicion was back in her voice and in her eyes. 'This police officer you mentioned must have told you, it's all in the files.' She put down her mug and made to move, obviously with the intention of throwing him out.

'I haven't had access to the files or the trial notes. Intentionally. I don't want to be prejudiced by what is in them.'

She eyed him sceptically and slightly puzzled. 'But wouldn't it help you find Charlotte quicker?'

'Not if this killer has friends in high places. He mustn't think the authorities are on to him or he'll kill Charlotte and cover his tracks. No one's found him for seventeen years. He's very clever and very powerful.'

'So what makes you think you'll find him now?'

'Because he's abducted Charlotte and that's a big mistake.' She considered this. Marvik caught the beeping sound of a vehicle reversing. He added, 'I know you don't believe Blackerman's innocent, that's fair enough, but he knows something and he's kept quiet about it and he'd only do that if his family were being threatened and I believe they were.'

'But his son's dead.'

'Yes, and his wife, but Charlotte's missing, so she's now become the threat to keep him silent.'

She studied him for a moment, then nodded. He took that as assent to continue his questions. 'Do you know where she stayed on the Friday night?'

'In the Union Services Club.'

'Did she?' Ross hadn't said but then why should he have done, and Marvik could hardly have pumped him for all the information.

'No, hold on, the police said she didn't. She only stayed at the club on the Saturday night. They asked me where she stayed Friday and I said I didn't know and I still don't unless the police found out.'

'Did it come up at the trial?'

'I don't think so but it's all a bit of a haze and I was only sixteen.'

It was something that Marvik would need to check with Crowder or Blackerman's defence lawyer and he wondered who that had been. He couldn't remember seeing the name in the reports he'd read on the Internet on Wednesday night.

'Did Esther keep a diary?'

She shrugged. 'The police didn't find one.'

But *had* Grainger found it and suppressed it? If he had was that because it cocked up his case against Blackerman and he didn't want that, or perhaps Blackerman had taken it from Esther's room. But if he had then why not hand it over if it exonerated him? Unless he was mentioned in it. Perhaps their relationship was more than a one-night stand.

'Did Esther have a boyfriend?'

'Not at that time. She'd had boyfriends, but Esther wasn't very lucky on that score. Neither am I,' she added with bitterness. 'But not in the same way. Esther was too trusting, I'm not trusting enough.' She fiddled with the ends of her hair. Marvik noticed her bitten nails were painted a deep purple that almost matched her hair colour. He could see she'd been hurt but how, why and by whom he didn't know and wasn't going to ask. It was nothing to do with him or with finding Charlotte.

'Esther was the opposite of me,' she continued. 'Gentle, quiet, romantic. I think she was looking for her knight on the white charger, only they don't exist, do they?' she challenged.

'No,' he replied with conviction and at last got a smile from her. He thought she should do it more often. 'What was her mood like immediately before she was killed?'

She appeared momentarily stunned but Marvik knew it wasn't because of his question but his choice of words. Esther hadn't *died* she'd been *killed* and that made a world of difference.

'I can't really remember. I didn't take much notice. I was still angry and hurt at Mum's death. I was sick of school, and keen to get out into the big wide world of work. We were living in a rented flat in Marchwood, great view across the river to the docks,' she added with a slight sneer. 'I spent as much time as I could out of the place, with friends or just hanging around the shops.'

'Was she at work the Friday before the Remembrance Service?'

'I suppose so. She must have been. Everything is a bit of a blur. And I've tried very hard not to think of it, until now,' she added with bitterness, narrowing her eyes at him.

Marvik wasn't sure he could press her further but there were a couple more things he still needed to ask because he didn't think he'd get a second chance at this.

'Esther's personal belongings? Do you have them?'

'How the hell's that going to help you find your girlfriend?' she flashed.

'I've no idea,' he answered with a touch of frustration, and it was the truth.

She seemed to regret her outburst. 'Look, I'm sorry she's missing but I can't see how what I've told you can help you find her. There was nothing in Esther's personal belongings except clothes, toiletries and jewellery, and no I don't have them. I got rid of everything.'

'Everything?' he said quietly.

Her green eyes flinched. She had kept something but he understood that it was too personal to share with anyone, particularly a stranger. He tossed back the remainder of his coffee and made as though to rise but didn't. 'I'm sorry for dragging up such painful memories.'

She opened her mouth to reply then closed it. Perhaps she'd heard the sincerity in his voice that stemmed the sarcastic reply she'd been forming. Their eyes connected. Hers were questioning and anxious, but there was also sadness. She looked away first.

'It seems such a long time ago now that I sometimes wonder if it ever happened,' she said sorrowfully. 'Then I hear a tune on the radio or watch a serviceman being brought home in a coffin on the TV and bingo I'm back there in November 1997 wondering what the hell is going on, why there are so many people in our flat.'

She swallowed her coffee. 'I have to look at her photograph to remind myself that I had a sister once.' She sprang forward and put her coffee mug on the table. 'Would you like to see her?'

He would, very much, and said so. There had been no pictures of Esther in the media reports he'd read, which he now considered unusual. But the press would have been kept away from Helen and perhaps Esther's employers had refused to give them a photograph. Maybe they didn't have one. The media would have tried Esther's friends but maybe she didn't have many and the ones she'd had were protective of her. And the police hadn't issued a plea to ask if anyone had seen Esther on the Friday before her death because as far as they were concerned there was no need. They had the killer.

Helen handed him her phone. Esther Shannon was not how Marvik had imagined. For a start she was blonde and very pretty in a delicate way, with an oval face, clear pale skin and a slightly shy smile. She also had very blue eyes much like Charlotte's and he thought there was quite a striking resemblance between the two women, but not the two sisters. He said as much.

'Esther favoured Dad. That picture was taken on her twenty-first birthday. And three years later she was dead.'

It was pointless and unnecessary saying how sorry he was. After a moment he said, 'Could you send that to my phone?' He wondered if she'd tell him to get lost but she asked for his number. He gave her the number of the phone he'd been given by Crowder and a few seconds later it was there.

She led him down the stairs but before opening the front door, she said, 'What will you do now?'

He'd been considering that. 'I'd like to know where Esther went and where she stayed on Friday night.'

'You think she was with someone?'

'Don't you?'

'Yes. But it can't have anything to do with her death.'

'It might not but why didn't whoever she stayed with come forward?'

'Maybe they did and it wasn't thought necessary to mention it at the trial.'

That was possible. 'I'd still like to know why it wasn't thought necessary.' Now for a delicate question. 'Do you know if your sister was on the Pill or practised any other birth-control methods?'

'No idea. And before you ask I don't remember that coming up at the trial either.'

But Esther's medical records must have been checked by the police. Would Crowder know? Not if he hadn't accessed the file as he said for fear of alerting the killer. And Marvik knew Esther's doctor wouldn't disclose that kind of confidential information to him.

She said, 'I don't remember seeing any pills or any other birth-control devices in her belongings.'

But they could have been removed along with anything else that might have been incriminating. Maybe Terence Blackerman would know: he'd had sex with her after all. Perhaps he'd used a condom, though Marvik found it hard to believe a chaplain would have carried them around on the off chance of a casual relationship. But again he wondered, perhaps it hadn't been so casual after all.

He left wanting to ask if he could talk to her again. There was so much he didn't know and which she might be able to tell him if only he knew what questions to ask. But he could see how traumatic it was for her. Her sister's death had cast her adrift. He didn't know if she had other relatives but even if she had he sensed that, like him, she'd shut them out. How could they possibly understand? And she, like him, didn't want their banal, although probably well meaning, condolences.

Climbing into the Land Rover he thought how hopeless was his quest in trying to find Charlotte by uncovering the truth behind Esther's murder. It would take forever. Crowder had spun him a line and he'd fallen for it. He was stumbling about blindfold with no authority and no bloody clue where he was going. For Christ's sake this needed a whole team of police officers working on it, not a lone bloody ranger. He had no chance of ever finding Charlotte this way. It was time he told Crowder that, and he would once he reached Strathen's apartment. There he would call him and ask for a meeting. He'd tell him the deal was off and if he didn't pull out all the stops on finding Charlotte then Marvik would go to a higher authority. And yet even as he thought that he had a sinking feeling that Crowder would block him. He was caught between a rock and a hard place and there seemed no way out of this. He had to do as Crowder asked. But Crowder's plan had failed. There had to be another way. He only wished he knew what that was.

SEVEN

Marvik looked in his rear-view mirror. The dark coloured van was still behind him. He frowned. He'd seen the same van parked not far from Helen's house. Or rather the same type of van. He hadn't noted the vehicle registration number.

He slowed and the van slowed. He pushed his foot down on the accelerator and the van kept pace but always just far enough back for him not to be able to see the driver or the registration number. The rain and spray from the motorway made visibility difficult and there were no lights on this stretch of road. But even if he could see the number it wouldn't have helped him much, not unless he asked Crowder to check it out.

It struck him that this could be one of Crowder's men following him, perhaps to protect him. Or maybe Crowder didn't trust him – a thought that had already occurred to Marvik. Maybe Crowder believed he *had* abducted Charlotte and possibly killed her and was stringing him out with this tale about Blackerman in the hope he'd make a mistake and lead them to Charlotte. Perhaps Crowder thought he'd had a brainstorm, had sexually assaulted Charlotte and killed her. Was Esther's murder really about sex? Possibly, but Marvik didn't think Blackerman had killed her in a sexual frenzy.

The van was still there.

Could DI Feeny and DS Howe be on his trail? he wondered as he crossed the River Hamble. Perhaps Feeny had set officers to follow him in the hope he'd lead them to Ashley Palmer. But if whoever was following him wasn't Crowder or Feeny then it had to be someone connected with Esther's death. And that meant the killer had taken the bait.

He indicated off the motorway heading towards the Hamble. He expected the van to do the same and was surprised when it didn't. He'd been wrong; no one was following him. He was getting paranoid. Or was he, he thought, glancing in his mirrors. There was a black saloon car with tinted windows behind him and it was sticking to him as though it was being pulled by an invisible traction beam.

The van had ducked out and this vehicle had taken up the trail. Well, not for much longer.

Marvik waited for his chance. It came as a bus indicated to pull out in front of him. He flashed at it to let it go, staying a distance behind it that gave him a clear view of the road ahead. After half a mile the bus signalled to pull up at another bus stop. Rapidly Marvik calculated there was just enough time for him to get around it before the car heading towards him on the other side of the road drew level. He pressed his foot on the accelerator and sped around it with barely feet to spare and immediately swung into a side street on his left just ahead of the bus, then another while checking the saloon car wasn't behind him. It wasn't.

Marvik scoured the residential roads. There was a narrow lane ahead, leading into a small field and to the right of it a building that looked like stables. A final glance in his mirrors told him nothing was behind him. He swung left into the lane, pulled up behind the building, doused the lights and silenced the engine. He waited for a couple of minutes and consulted his street map by the light of a small torch. All was silent.

Pushing the map and torch back into his pocket he climbed out, locked the car, pulled up his collar against the wet night and walked briskly to the front of the stable block minus any horses. By its air of neglect it appeared to have been abandoned some time ago. Good – that suited him even better. No one would come to enquire about the Land Rover parked there. There was no sign of the dark saloon. Marvik hurried back towards the main road by a different route. No one followed him.

He broke into a run and twenty minutes later he was turning into Coach Road and running past the units where Strathen worked, then along Westfield Lane with Southampton Water on his left. The tree-lined road was deserted. There were no houses and nothing down here to attract visitors except for the dinghy park and slipway, but nobody would be there on a dark, wet February evening. The road culminated in a large house in front of which Marvik halted and pressed the intercom to the right of the electronic gates. The Grade II listed whitewashed house, built in 1809, had once been occupied by the US Marines during the Second World War. It had also been a sports and social club, an apprentice training school and owned by a corporation before being converted to luxury flats.

Strathen answered and pressed the buzzer to let Marvik in. By the time he reached the front door it was open and standing on the threshold was a well-built man in his early thirties with powerful muscular shoulders, cropped dark hair and a puzzled expression on his broad-jawed face.

'What's going on?' Strathen asked, stepping back to let Marvik enter.

'I had to ditch the Land Rover. Someone's tailing me. It could be Feeny.'

'Why?'

'Because he thinks I've kidnapped Palmer and I'll eventually lead them to him or his body.'

'Did he say that?'

'No, but he didn't believe I went there just because you asked me to.'

Strathen's grey eyes looked troubled. 'I'm sorry I got you into this.'

'It's OK,' Marvik hastily dismissed, following Strathen to his ground-floor flat on the left, thinking he'd got Strathen into worse. There was no time for regrets though. 'Any news on Palmer?'

Strathen swivelled round to close the door behind them. 'No, but I have been talking to some of his past colleagues who worked with him at the university. They've no idea where he is. They haven't seen or heard from him for the last year and none of them say he's ever done this sort of thing before. What about Charlotte, any news on her?' he asked anxiously, but before Marvik could answer his pay-as-you-go phone trilled. Only Crowder had the number. It had to be him. Correction: both Crowder and Helen had the number and it turned out to be the latter. He quickly answered it.

'The house has been trashed,' she said before he could speak.

Marvik's heart stalled as he rapidly thought. She sounded irate rather than scared, understandably so.

'I only went out for a few moments and I've come back to this.'

'Anything taken?'

'No bloody idea; the place is a total mess.'

'Have you called the police?'

'No, I called you,' she stressed as though it was his fault – and it was. But who had done that? Surely not the police. And not whoever had followed him in the dark coloured van, unless they'd doubled back. But even then it was quick work. Perhaps he'd been wrong about being tailed, but he wasn't wrong when he believed that Helen was in danger.

Strathen was eyeing him with curiosity.

'Move to the window and look out, but don't let anyone see you.'

'Why the hell should I?' Helen demanded.

'Just do it,' he commanded. He heard her shoes clumping on the wooden floor. 'See anyone there who isn't usually there?'

'No. Yes, hang on. There's a van, no lettering on it and I can't see anyone in it.'

Marvik cursed. It *had* doubled back when the saloon car had taken over tailing him. He calculated there had been two men in that van and one of them must have stayed behind outside Helen's house waiting for the chance to enter it. 'OK. Now do what I tell you. Ask no questions.'

'Why the—?'

'Just do it,' he roughly interjected. 'I'm heading back to you. Helen, you must do exactly as I say otherwise your life could be in danger.'

'That's rubbish.'

'Is it?'

There was a moment's pause. 'How can I—?'

'Trust me? You have to. It'll take me about twenty minutes to reach you.' He wished he could get there sooner. Would they try anything before he got to her? Would she be bundled into that van and spirited away as Charlotte had been? He hoped to God she wouldn't. How long would it take for the police to arrive? It might be hours. There was no point in calling them.

'Don't change your clothes. Put some things into a bag but not your phone or any computer device. Be ready to leave. Don't answer the door or the phone. When you receive my call, on this phone number, leave the house with your bag. When you answer my call I'll ring off. Walk calmly but quickly to the corner of the road. Don't look back. I'll be in a black Volvo.' He glanced at Strathen who nodded before saying into the phone, 'Is that understood?'

'Yes.'

'You'll do it?'

'All right.'

Marvik rang off and turned to Strathen. 'I need to borrow your car, your boat and a jacket.'

Strathen was already reaching for a navy-blue sailing jacket from the peg in the hall. 'This hasn't anything to do with Ashley Palmer, has it?'

'No. I can't explain now but I think the woman I've just been to see, who was on the phone, is in danger and it's connected with Charlotte's disappearance.' Marvik hastily pulled on Strathen's jacket and transferred the contents of his jacket pockets to Strathen's. 'I need you to find out whatever you can about a man called Terence Blackerman who murdered a girl called Esther Shannon in 1997.' Telling Crowder to go it alone was no longer an option.

Strathen nodded. He was curious but he'd know there was no time for questions. Marvik handed him the Land Rover keys. 'I had to abandon it in a field.' He took the keys to the Volvo from Strathen, thankful that the vehicle was fitted with dual controls.

'My spare boat key is on there,' Strathen said. 'You know where to find it.'

Marvik did. 'I'll call you later. Don't ring me on your mobile. It might be hacked.'

'I'll check that too. I wish to God I didn't have this bloody leg,' Strathen declared vehemently. 'I could have collected your Land Rover and driven it to decoy whoever it is.'

'It doesn't matter,' Marvik dismissed lightly, seeing the frustration on his friend's face and feeling for him but taking care not to show it. 'I need all the information you can get me on Esther Shannon, and as soon as you can get it. But Shaun . . .' Marvik paused as he was about to leave. 'They might come looking for you if my phone is hacked, because I've called you on it. I'm not sure if they know there's a connection between us. I can't see them trying any rough stuff, not yet anyway, but—'

'I'll be ready for them.'

Marvik didn't ask how. Strathen, a clever, resourceful and fearless man, would find a way.

He found Strathen's Volvo parked at the rear of the house and headed back towards Locks Heath. He could have told Helen to leave by the property's back door into an alleyway he'd noticed earlier on arriving at the estate, but that would have made it easier for her to be snatched. There was still the possibility that they'd get to her before he did or that they'd take her as she walked along that road. As he pressed his foot on the accelerator and swung on to the motorway he prayed that he'd make it in time and that Helen would do exactly as he had asked.

EIGHT

She was striding towards him, a large black rucksack over her
shoulder. He could see the van she'd mentioned parked in the
corner of the small car park at the far end of the road. It was
the same van that had followed him on to the motorway. Silently,
with the engine running, first gear engaged, Marvik urged her to
hurry.

She climbed in. 'Now perhaps you can tell me what the hell—'

'Not now,' he said sharply, pulling quickly away. He sensed her
shock but didn't have time to look at her or acknowledge it. His
eyes darted to his rear-view mirror as he rapidly and expertly navi-
gated the residential streets. The van wasn't behind them but a car
was, dark coloured, but not the same one that had followed him
earlier. It kept a short distance behind. Perhaps it was just coincidence. And perhaps it was coincidence that it followed him on to
the main road and in the direction of the waterside village of Warsash,
but he wasn't taking any chances.

He scoured the road ahead looking for a suitable turning and,
spotting a gap in the housing on his left, without decreasing his
speed, he wrenched the wheel to his left and veered into the lane
with a squeal of rubber on the wet road. The wheels spun into a
skid; he steered into it. Helen cried out but he had no time to explain.
He was speeding down the narrow lane, his eyes darting between
the mirror and the road ahead. There was no sign of the vehicle
following him. The car bucked as it hit the potholed road. Then
he spotted a track ahead on his right. He spun the wheel round. The
car slewed into the track in a flurry of gravel and tyre screeching.
The trees and shrubs either side of them closed in. Marvik slammed
his foot on the brake. Helen shot forward with a cry of alarm and
fear, saved by the seat belt from crashing into the window. He
rammed the gears into reverse and sped the car back between the
trees where it came to rest. He silenced the engine.

'What the hell—?'

'Quiet,' he shouted. Not that anyone could hear them. Or rather
he didn't think they could but he couldn't be certain.

She snapped her lips shut, glaring at him, her face flushed with fury. No one came after them. No lights of a vehicle appeared on the lane ahead. There was no sound of an engine but Marvik waited a full two minutes before breathing a little more easily. It seemed an age and he sensed her restlessness beside him, along with her alarm. Indicating for her to keep quiet he took hold of the rucksack that she'd placed on the floor by her feet.

He opened the rear door and strewed the contents of it on the seat, causing a small cry of surprise and annoyance from her. Carefully he went through her belongings. He removed her make-up and toiletries from the small bag and studied them before putting them back. He indicated for her to hand over the coat that she was wearing. With a roll of her eyes, to hide her panic, she shrugged her shoulders out of it. She was wearing exactly what she'd been dressed in earlier that afternoon: black boots and tights, a short black skirt and black T-shirt under a black loose-fitting V-necked jumper. But had she been wearing that coat when she'd left the house at the time it had been ransacked? He couldn't ask her now. And he couldn't take any chances.

Leaving everything where it was he climbed back into the driver's seat and restarted the engine, quickly consulting the street map. The lane came out on to another that would eventually take them to a road leading to Warsash. He didn't know if the lane was passable by car and he wished he had his Land Rover, but the Volvo was a sturdy vehicle and would cope. He put a finger to his lips urging her to remain silent.

He pulled out and turned right on to the rutted lane. With only the side lights on, they jolted their way along it heading south for a mile. Nothing followed them. He spotted the lane on their right and swung into it. It was barely wide enough to take a car. After half a mile there was a gate. Marvik climbed out, opened it and drove on to a tarmacked road. Quickly consulting the street map again he swung left and soon they were passing fields and ahead he could see the lights of houses. Before he reached them he turned left. Again they were passing fields, but after half a mile, Marvik swung right and drew to a halt. Ahead of them was the sea. Helen stared at him, clearly puzzled. Marvik climbed out, retrieved the coat and rucksack from the back seat and walked down towards the shore. He was now standing on the Solent Way and across the water he could see the lights of Fawley oil refinery.

He placed the coat and rucksack on the ground and quickly returned to the car.

'Hey, that was the only warm coat I've got.'

'I'll buy you another. For now you can have mine.' He pulled off Strathen's jacket and handed it to her. Then he started the car and turned up the heater. She was shivering but not from cold. He pulled away and this time swung right and then left into the lane and then, bearing right, headed northwards towards the main road.

'It's OK, we can talk now.'

'Was all that James Bond stuff really necessary?' she snapped.

'Your bag was carrying a tracking device and probably a listening device.'

'You're kidding.'

He threw her a glance. Her complexion paled a little. She pulled Strathen's jacket a little tighter around her.

'I'm sorry about the coat but I didn't know if you were wearing it when you left the house and I couldn't take the chance of asking you.'

'I wasn't. I just jumped in my car to go to the shop.'

Then he was right. It could have been bugged. He hadn't found one in the pockets but a small device could easily have been slipped into a torn seam or the hem. He hadn't had time to feel all over it. Her car could also contain a tracking device which could have been fitted earlier in the day. But a tracking device would have been the least of his worries: her brakes might have been tampered with, causing an accident at some stage, and that would be very convenient for the killer.

Marvik continued. 'When you left the house you gave them the perfect excuse to get in. They're keen to monitor who you'd get in touch with after my visit. Where did you go by the way?'

'To buy some milk. I'd run out. I gave you the last drop I had.'

Marvik recalled her opening the fridge and retrieving the carton. He'd watched her empty it into his mug. He hadn't seen any other milk bottles or cartons inside the fridge. There could have been one in the kitchen cabinets, but he didn't think she was lying.

'They took the opportunity of planting a device in your coat, assuming that was the one you wear the most, although they had probably seen you wearing it earlier.'

'Just who the hell are you – some kind of secret agent?' she blazed.

'No, just a guy who has started asking questions about your sister because a friend has gone missing and is probably dead.'

She said nothing for a while. Marvik headed east and was soon once again crossing the River Hamble and winding his way through the streets towards the marina where Strathen moored his boat.

'How did they know that's the bag I usually carry?' she finally asked.

He didn't reply.

'You can't be serious. You are. You think I've been watched.'

'I'm not sure for how long though.' Before Charlotte had visited Blackerman? Before Blackerman's son had died? Or since he had started asking questions and Crowder had stuck his nose in? Could that telephone call he'd witnessed DI Duncan Ross making have been to put a watch on Helen?

After a short pause she said, 'So Blackerman didn't kill her.'

'No, but he knows who did and he's too scared to say who and why.' And Marvik was beginning to understand that. Whoever it was had muscle and Blackerman must have known that any threats to him and his family would be carried out. He added, 'And until I find out who Esther's killer is it's not safe for you.'

'Suppose you never find out,' she said quietly.

'I will,' he firmly replied. He thought she looked a little reassured. He added, 'I'm sorry I've put your life in danger.'

'But I don't know anything about Esther's death.'

'Perhaps you do and don't realize it, or perhaps they think you do.'

'Who the fuck are *they*?' she cried, her exasperation tinged with fear.

'I don't know, but I'll find out.'

She took a breath. 'Can't we just go to the police?'

'They might be involved.'

'Jesus, you've been reading too many thrillers!' Her humour was used to disguise her terror.

He turned off down Hamble Lane, only this time he continued along it instead of branching off for Strathen's place. Strathen's boat would be a good base for tonight but tomorrow he'd have to sort out something else and he didn't think he could risk returning to his cottage or collecting his own boat from the pontoon – both would be watched and possibly bugged.

'Hope you like boats,' he said.

'In this weather? It's freezing.'

'It's got a heater.'

'Great!'

'And it's got two cabins.'

'Fantastic, can't wait,' she said with heavy sarcasm.

He gave a brief smile. It also had a powerful engine and that meant they could make a quick getaway if needed. He checked his mirrors as he had done constantly on the journey. There was nothing behind them. The car that had tailed them – if it had been – might now be heading for the Solent Way and the beach where Helen's coat and rucksack lay. Or perhaps the driver of the van was. There had been no need to follow them; all they had to do was follow the tracking device.

The lights of a petrol station appeared ahead. Marvik swung into it and pulled up outside the shop. Strathen *might* have food on board but he wasn't going to chance it. He told Helen they needed to buy something to eat for that night and the morning. Further ahead he hadn't yet planned, although he had ideas. He bought tins of soup, baked beans, eggs, bread and milk. He also purchased tea and coffee and added a couple of tins of tuna, bananas and a packet of biscuits. He asked for a couple of extra carrier bags and handed them to Helen.

'You can put your things in these.'

He pulled away. Everything was clear. A few minutes later he was driving into Hamble Point Marina car park where he parked as close to the pontoons as he could but it still meant a trek to where Strathen's boat was moored. All was quiet. There was no one about. The marina office and the café were closed.

The blustery wind caught at them and drove the rain into their faces as they hurried down the wooden pontoon. Marvik's polo shirt and trousers were wet but that didn't bother him. He'd experienced worse. Helen looked swamped in Strathen's jacket and she also looked cold and scared though he could see she was doing her best to put on a brave face.

'Hope you don't get seasick,' he said, stopping at the large motor cruiser and unzipping the canvas awning.

'We're not going out to sea, are we?' she cried, alarmed.

He nodded and jumped on board holding out a helping hand. But she pulled herself up and declined it. 'I'm quite capable of getting on a boat. This yours?'

'No, it's a friend's.'

'Pity. I was hoping to be sick all over it.'

He smiled and opened up the hatch. He nodded her down the spiral staircase to the main saloon and cabins and watched as she took in her surroundings, noting that she seemed suitably impressed by the opulent interior, the leather seating, mahogany cabinets. 'I thought you said it had heaters.' She shivered and drew the jacket tighter around her.

'I'll run the engine. Decide which cabin you want to sleep in. There are two.'

He climbed back on deck and at the helm inserted the key. The engine started first time, as he knew it would in a modern boat of this calibre. It was newer than his boat and larger with a quieter engine, though not a more powerful one. He left it ticking over and climbed back into the cabin, leaving the hatch open just a fraction. She'd taken the cabin in the aft with the en-suite, leaving him the one for'ard with adjoining heads. He called out to say that it would soon be warm.

He washed his hands in the small shower cubicle then opened the cabinet to find soap, toothpaste, a toothbrush and battery operated shaver. In the cabin he also found a T-shirt, jumper and sailing jacket. Strathen was a similar build. Marvik exchanged his wet polo shirt for Strathen's T-shirt and pulled on the jumper. There was also a double duvet and two pillows.

Helen appeared in the doorway. 'Looks cosy,' she said as he threw the duvet on to the bed.

'Have you got bedding?'

She nodded. 'Can we eat? I'm starving.'

But Marvik said, 'Not yet.'

He made to step past her but she didn't move. 'What now?' she said with weary exasperation.

'We get under way.'

'You still think they'll find us.'

'Out there they can't,' he said, pointing in the direction of the Solent, except they could if they looked at the shipping movements via satellite tracking on the Internet. Anyone could tap into that but not anyone would know they were on a boat, let alone which one. Besides, Marvik had no intention of staying 'out there'. All he'd done was buy them some time, and he intended to buy them some more.

He brushed past her, catching the hint of her perfume. It smelt spicy and reminded him of Charlotte. He called up the GPS navigator. Strathen had many routes loaded and as Marvik touched the screen to find where he wanted to head his hand froze. There was a course set for the Isle of Wight. Nothing unusual in that – Strathen often motored across to the island – only this one was set for the bay where Marvik had been on Wednesday night in his search for Ashley Palmer in that derelict coastguard cottage. He checked the log but there was nothing recorded for that day or evening. That didn't mean that Strathen hadn't gone there, just that he hadn't recorded his trip on that day, *if* he had been there.

He set aside the thought and cast off. Jumping back on board he released the throttle and with the aid of the bow thrusters eased the craft from its mooring. Visibility was poor because of the rain and the night, and the sea state was choppy. He had radar and knew the Solent like the back of his hand but he still didn't want to travel too far. He didn't know how good a sailor Helen was and he wondered if the best course of action was to head for the cottage or rather close to it. His house and boat might possibly be under surveillance but if both were that meant their pursuers had been able to find out where he lived. And that narrowed down who could be after them. DI Feeny and Crowder knew where he lived, and so too he thought would Duncan Ross who would have got his name from Littlehampton Marina. Then all he'd had to do was run it through the databases available to the police, such as Her Majesty's Revenue and Customs. If Ross was in league with whoever had killed Esther then he would pass on the information. Perhaps he'd already done that because someone had been waiting for him outside Helen's house. Several thoughts occurred to him but he postponed them for the time being and manoeuvred the boat out of the River Hamble into Southampton Water.

Soon he was in the Solent and motoring across to the Isle of Wight. They'd pick up a buoy in the Newtown River entrance for the night. At this time of year they would have the place to themselves.

Peering into the darkness memories of his missions in the Special Boat Services came to him. It had been a career he'd loved and had only reluctantly relinquished to be replaced with another on the sea – not quite as dangerous, he'd originally thought, but he'd been wrong. But even before the death of Harry Salcombe he'd found the job unrewarding and tedious, and perhaps that was why he'd let down his guard. He had made the fatal error of not getting to know his fellow crewman and the boat's owner. His colleagues in the Commandos and in the Special Boat Services had received the same training and shared the same experiences as him. They had been schooled to obey commands without question. Lee Addington had been out of the armed forces for some time and Salcombe had never been in the services. They were civilians. Just as he now was.

'Thought you might like this.' Helen appeared with a large mug of coffee which she handed to him. 'Don't want you falling asleep at the wheel.'

'Helm. Never done that before.'

'No, I don't expect you have,' she answered seriously. She sipped her coffee. 'Where are we going?'

'Somewhere quiet and deserted.'

'Sounds romantic, or rather it would if it wasn't so cold and some maniac wasn't after us. What do I call you?'

'Marvik.'

'No, what's your first name?'

'Art.'

'Short for Arthur?'

'No, just Art.'

'Suits you.'

He wasn't sure what that meant and he didn't ask. He sipped his coffee, watching her scan the dark sea ahead.

'How long will it take to get there?' she said, finally breaking the silence.

'About half an hour.'

She looked as though she was going to say something; he thought it was to ask questions about him but she took a breath and swallowed some coffee. Perhaps his body language had communicated to her that personal questions as far as he was concerned were off limits.

His thoughts slipped back to Charlotte and the night he'd spent with her. Where was she now? Was her body somewhere out here in the Solent? Would she be washed up along the shore in a few days, or maybe never? Or was she being held against her will, cold and terrified? The thought filled him with dread. If she'd been taken by Esther Shannon's killer then Marvik knew she had to be dead. Two innocent people killed and another incarcerated for most of his life – how many more lives had this killer destroyed? Grainger's? And now he'd destroy Helen's.

Marvik briefly studied Helen. She looked bewildered and vulnerable. Then there was Blackerman's wife and his son, Paul. Marvik's resolve hardened. This was one man he wanted to meet face to face. But would Crowder get justice? Somehow Marvik doubted it. So perhaps he'd make the killer pay for what he'd done, when he found him.

The lights of East Cowes drew closer. Marvik piloted the craft west and Helen slipped below as they neared the entrance to Newtown River. Marvik scoured the darkness for a buoy to pick up. Soon he was letting down the anchor and he could smell food coming from the galley. He made certain the boat was secure and went below to find soup and bread on the galley table. The cabin was warm and they ate in silence. The soup was followed by an omelette, which he cooked, with baked beans and more coffee. Marvik didn't think the caffeine would keep him awake because he didn't think he'd get much sleep anyway, although he knew it would be safe to do so here. For tonight at least. Helen ate hungrily. Fear and adrenalin gave you an appetite. It was after they'd cleared away and were drinking their coffee that she finally spoke.

'I've been thinking about the night Esther was killed and if there was anything I'd heard or been told that might help to find out why these people are following us. I can't remember much. Maybe it will come back to me but there was the fact she was stuck in the lift with her . . . with Blackerman.'

DI Duncan Ross had told him that.

Helen added, 'And that would really have freaked Esther out. She was terrified of being shut in; she hated confined spaces and she never got into a lift unless she really had to.'

'Her room was on the thirteenth floor. That's a lot of stairs to climb.'

'I've known her climb more.'

So why get in it that night? He said, 'Do you think she knew Terence Blackerman and he persuaded her into the lift?'

Helen lifted a shoulder in response. 'Nobody mentioned that at the trial.'

Marvik examined this new information. 'So Blackerman would have tried to calm her if she was in a panic at being trapped.'

Helen nodded. 'Which made me think he then took advantage of her fear and vulnerability.'

And it was no doubt what a jury had been told.

Helen continued. 'Maybe after that she didn't want to be alone and one thing led to another. But why would she sleep with him?'

'Because she was afraid.'

'Then why the hell did he leave her alone in her room in the early hours of the morning?'

'Something he has no doubt regretted.'

There was a long silence between them, during which Marvik heard the wind whistling around the boat as it gently rocked on the tide. Finally he said, 'Can you remember who she went to the Remembrance Service with?'

'I've been thinking about that too since you mentioned it earlier. John Stisford organized the tickets. He always went and he was a friend of Mum's. He knew Dad, served with him in the Falklands. He used to speak about Dad.' Her expression clouded over. 'I remember thinking why doesn't he shut up and why isn't my dad still alive and not him?'

'Was he married?'

'Divorced. I wondered if he'd end up marrying Mum, and I didn't much care for that, but then her health got worse and perhaps he didn't want to be saddled with an invalid. Esther seemed to get on with him though. I used to moan about him and call him Mister Boring and she'd stick up for him and say he was kind.'

'Do you know where he is now?'

'No, but I can find out. I'll call the British Legion branch in Marchwood. They'll tell me. Only I'll need to get their number; it was on my mobile phone.'

'Call directory enquiries in the morning. We'll find a pay phone.' He didn't want to run the risk of his number being traced from the Legion's call log. Perhaps the killer was already trawling through Helen's mobile phone numbers and had found the British Legion number but if he had then he could hardly make anything of that. Would Stisford be able to tell him anything relevant about the final day of Esther's life? He had to try.

'Did the police question him?'

'They must have done.'

'Did he appear at the trial?'

'Not in the stand if that's what you mean, but he came with me and my aunt, my mum's sister, and before you ask she's dead. And even if she wasn't you wouldn't get anything out of her except that Esther brought it on herself by sleeping with Blackerman. I hated her for saying that. She was one of those God-fearing, always-right type of women. After the trial I had nothing more to do with her. I only found out she'd died because it was in the announcement column in the local paper.'

Marvik could see her mind flitting back to the ordeal of the trial. 'Can you remember who they called to give evidence? Or who Blackerman's defence barrister was?'

'No. It's all a bit of a muddle in my head. I remember them saying the lift had broken down, as I told you, and that the fire service were called. And that apart from the chambermaid and a previous occupant of the room only Blackerman's fingerprints and DNA were in the room. It was so obvious he'd done it. I just remember thinking why doesn't the bastard own up? How dare he put me through this? See, I was only thinking of myself, not poor bloody Esther.'

'Don't be so hard on yourself, you were only sixteen.'

'Yeah, well.'

And Marvik could see the anger was still there. 'Do you remember a police officer called Grainger?'

'Yes. Big fellow. Gruff. Hard.'

'He's dead. Killed in a hit and run in Brighton nine months after retiring in 2004. No one was ever caught for it.'

'That's grim.' Then her eyes narrowed. 'Hey, you can't think . . .'

'Perhaps he was writing his memoirs.'

'But he was convinced Blackerman was the killer.'

'Do you remember a police officer called Duncan Ross?'

'Don't tell me he's dead too!'

'No. I spoke to him yesterday about Esther, only he didn't know why I was interested.' Or rather he pretended he didn't. 'He has doubts about the conviction.'

'Then why didn't he say?'

Marvik shrugged. 'Perhaps he didn't have doubts at the time.'

'What are you going to do next?'

'Talk to a few people, see what I can ferret out.'

'I guess I ought to phone work tomorrow and report sick.'

She was planning on being with him and there was some advantage to that. But it was too risky for her to remain with him. He'd need somewhere safe for her to stay until this was over, and he had no idea when that would be.

'Let's turn in.'

He lay on his bunk, fully clothed with the duvet over him, just as Helen lay on hers in the other cabin. He needed to call Strathen. He wondered what he'd managed to find out. He'd do that in the morning. He let his thoughts return to the course he'd seen on the navigation plotter. When had Strathen been in that bay the other side of the island? Was it on the day that Palmer had disappeared? He hated this feeling of mistrust creeping in. Strathen was one of his oldest friends, in fact his only friend. If he couldn't trust Strathen who could he trust? The answer was no one.

The boat rocked and a few seconds later Helen appeared in the doorway of his cabin, still fully dressed but without her boots. She was carrying her duvet.

'I'm freezing.'

He switched on the cabin light. 'You can have this one,' he said, sitting up and holding out his duvet for her.

'But you'll freeze to death.'

'I've survived worse.'

She entered the cabin and climbed in beside him. 'No point in us both being cold. But no funny business, right?'

'Right.'

She spread her duvet over the top of his and lay down beside him. Marvik turned off the light. The wind was slapping the water against the boat. He was used to the sound but Helen wasn't and he wondered if she'd be able to sleep. After a while she said, 'What was Esther scared of?'

Despite all her quips Marvik knew she was frightened. He didn't blame her. Charlotte too had been scared.

'That's what I intend to find out.' He just hoped he would be in time to save Charlotte's life.

'But will the police believe you when you do find out the truth?'

He liked the way she said *when* rather than *if*. 'That's a different question.'

She said nothing. He thought she might try and get some sleep but some minutes later she said, 'For years I've wished that man dead. I've thought of him with nothing but hatred, and all this time my hatred has been focused on the wrong man. Who is this killer? Why did he kill her? Why did he let another man go to prison for it?'

'Try and get some sleep.'

'Will you?' But she answered her own question. 'No, I don't expect you will. What happens tomorrow?'

'I'll tell you tomorrow.'

NINE

Monday

'**N**ot bloody likely,' she said, sitting bolt upright in bed in his cabin. It wasn't yet daylight but the anger in her eyes blazed brighter than the glow of the cabin light. It was just after four thirty a.m. 'You're not dumping me,' she insisted.

'It's not safe for you to be with me,' Marvik repeated.

'It's not safe for me to be on my own either. My house was trashed in case you've forgotten. And, if what you say is true and they did plant a bug on me, even though you got rid of it, I reckon they'll still find me.'

'They won't.'

'Oh yeah, you sure about that?' she said with heavy scepticism.

No, he wasn't, and that was the trouble. He didn't like the idea of leaving her in a hotel any more than she fancied being dumped in one but there was an alternative and that meant he needed to talk to Crowder.

She added, 'I don't want to end up like my sister, or your girl-friend Charlotte. I'm sticking to you like glue.'

'It's dangerous, Helen.'

'Yes and that goes for whether I'm with you or alone. And Esther was *my* sister.'

Marvik held her determined gaze. He could see she was resolute and he didn't have time to argue. There were dark circles under her eyes which were bloodshot and her make-up had smeared. She'd slept. He'd heard her steady breathing next to him but it had been a fragmented troubled sleep, like his. He knew they were safe from intruders out here in the middle of the river but that didn't stop him being alert to any. During the early hours of the morning his thoughts had veered from Charlotte's whereabouts to Blackerman's claims of innocence and then back to Esther and the woman sleeping beside him. But no matter how many times he ran through what he had learned, which was precious little, he could get no closer to who had taken Charlotte and where she might be.

She said, 'People will answer *my* questions because Esther was *my* sister. I could help you.'

There was that. He'd considered it himself. 'OK, but you do everything I tell you to.'

She nodded.

'Pack your things and the food we bought yesterday into that holdall,' he said as he headed for the helm.

He started the engine and pressed the switch to release the anchor. He'd decided during the night that he would transfer to his boat. He was curious to know if his cottage and boat were being watched. He'd have preferred to have been alone so that he'd have the chance to confront whoever was waiting – *if* they were waiting. He didn't like the fact he also had to take care of Helen, but she was right. She could help him get to the truth much more quickly. He was turning the boat around when she appeared on deck huddled in Strathen's jacket, yawning, Strathen's holdall beside her.

'Where are we going?' she asked.

'Further up the river.'

She must have sensed that conversation was out of bounds. She said no more. The dark was to their advantage. That and the unexpectedness of his return, if someone was waiting for them.

He motored slowly ahead. There were no lights here. The darkness of the shore enveloped them. She threw him an apprehensive glance. He'd already decided not to enter the cottage. He could buy what he needed elsewhere and he had clothes and toiletries on his boat. The pontoon was twenty-five yards from the house but it would take him time to moor alongside it, tie off the boat and make it up before transferring to his own boat. If the killer wanted to strike he'd have plenty of time to do so.

After a few minutes he said, 'There's a pontoon just a little ahead and to the left. We're going to moor this boat up and take the boat on the pontoon, but we need to do it quickly. As I come alongside, jump off with that line up forward. Hold on to it while I shut off the engine. I'll throw you your bag. While I tie off run to my boat and get the cover off. If anyone comes along or they start shooting—'

'Shooting?' she cried, alarmed.

'Run away from the house and pontoon, not towards it, get down and stay down and call the police. Take my phone. Don't come back to see how I am or what I'm doing. Understood?'

'You said it would be dangerous, but you didn't say . . . you don't think . . .'

'Just do it and let's hope we're quicker than they are, if they're there.'

She swallowed and nodded, her face ashen, her eyes full of fear, but he recognized determination when he saw it. It reminded him for a moment of Charlotte before he quickly blotted it out.

Marvik scanned the dark horizon as he swung the cruiser in; they were too exposed and there was too much time. They could be killed at any second.

She did exactly as he had told her. His eyes were trained eagerly on the horizon and his ears strained for the slightest sound. As swiftly as he could he made the transition, all the while his eyes darting around him but there was nothing and no one. They were safe. Soon they were heading out into the Solent. She was trembling.

'There's drink below.'

'I'll make some tea.'

He hadn't meant that and she knew it. But tea would be good.

Marvik watched the grey horizon gradually grow lighter as his mind worked out his game plan.

Helen appeared on deck five minutes later and handed him a mug of tea. She seemed to have recovered. 'It's not as posh as that last boat, but I like it. It's got more character. It has a lived-in appeal. Is it yours?'

'Yes.'

'What now?'

'We head for Southampton.'

'About Esther . . .'

But he sharply interjected: 'We'll talk about that later.'

Her puzzlement quickly turned to disbelief as she caught his meaning. And the shadow of fear was back in her eyes. He needed to check out the boat. Crowder had been on board it on Thursday and Duncan Ross or the person Ross had telephoned could have got on board on Saturday while he'd been in Littlehampton library. It had also been lying unguarded on his pontoon since Sunday afternoon. No one had needed to physically watch his cottage when they could do it – and probably were doing it – electronically. He'd deal with that at Southampton.

They fell silent as they crossed the Solent. They had the grey sea almost to themselves apart from a container ship heading out of Southampton and a Red Jet ferry.

It was light when they made the marina where only a few days ago he'd been talking to Crowder. Helen went off to the showers carrying a towel he kept on the boat. There was a shower on board but it wasn't anything like as efficient as the ones in the marina.

Marvik began his sweep of the boat, starting with the cockpit. He found the tracking device at the helm. He descended into the cabin. The listening device was under the galley table where Crowder had placed it. There were no other devices on board that he could find but it was possible one or more were carefully hidden and he was meant to find the two that were strategically placed where he would locate them.

He threw a change of clothes into his holdall along with shower gel and a razor and locked the boat. He took his time walking down the pontoon studying the boats around him. His was the only one on the visitors' berth and the marina was too large, with over three hundred yachts, to remember all of the boats moored in it, but he noted those around him and the fact there was no one on board.

He needed to call Strathen but in order to do so he needed a public pay phone. That wouldn't be tapped but as he'd said to Strathen his phone could be. He entered the marina office and paid the visitor's fee to the receptionist, a woman in her mid-twenties with blonde hair scraped back in a pony tail off her round, friendly face.

'I was hoping to meet a couple of friends but got held up. Can you tell me if they've been and gone? Philip Crowder was one of them.'

She checked the lists in front of her on the counter. 'Mr Crowder left on Saturday afternoon.'

After Marvik had been recruited. What guarantee did Marvik have that Charlotte hadn't been on Crowder's boat? None. But if she had been then who *was* Crowder? Was Charlotte's disappearance a charade, something agreed with the navy and designed to do what? Suck him in and flush out Esther Shannon's killer? But why? Why not use an undercover cop? And if Crowder was corrupt and had lured Charlotte to that boat with the purpose of silencing her, then he'd do the same with him. But first Crowder wanted something from him – was that Helen? Was he being set up here? Just let him try, thought Marvik with vigour.

'Apart from Mr Crowder there's only been Mr Duggan who came in from Poole, but he left yesterday.'

'I must have got it wrong. I'll call Philip. I might not stay here long.'

'Stay as long as you like, Mr Marvik.'

He smiled his thanks. He hadn't seen that it would serve any purpose giving a false name, not with a GPS tracking device on the boat. Crowder knew he was here. And Crowder knew he had gone to Littlehampton and returned to the island on Sunday where he'd collected his car. And he was guessing that there had also been a tracking device on the Land Rover, which had probably been planted on the same day someone had entered his house, on Thursday when he had taken Charlotte to Southampton. Crowder had denied that was down to him, but then he would. But Crowder was the only person who had been in the cabin. The boat hadn't been broken into and entered by anyone else. Marvik was certain on that score.

Outside he surveyed the car park and those vehicles parked in the Royal Southampton Yacht Club spaces. There was no one loitering, but then there was unlikely to be. However, mentally he stored away what he saw.

Crossing to the showers he waited for Helen to emerge with a pretence of looking irritated at having to be kept waiting, glancing impatiently at his watch every so often, just in case someone was watching him. As soon as she came out he said, 'Go back inside and if you can get a signal, call the British Legion and see if you can get hold of John Stisford.' He handed her the pay-as-you-go mobile phone, wondering if Crowder would be able to listen into her call there. He took the towel from her. It was damp but that didn't bother him; the smell of her body fresh from the shower did.

He punched the code into the keypad and pushed open the door to the men's shower room where he let a hot jet of water cascade over his naked body easing the aches, pains and scars, sloughing off the fatigue. Helen was waiting for him when he stepped outside.

'He's moved to Weymouth but I managed to speak to him.'

'They gave you his telephone number just like that?' Marvik asked, surprised and cautious. 'They're very trusting.'

'Only because I was speaking to someone I knew, Rosie Chandler.

She's been with the Legion since the year dot – and before you ask, no she didn't go to the Remembrance Service in 1997. She was in hospital giving birth. John said he'd be at home all afternoon and that he'd be delighted to see me. I didn't mention you.'

Marvik quickly weighed up their options. Weymouth was a small seaside town on the Dorset coast about sixty miles west from where they now were. By car, if they'd had one, it would take them about ninety minutes, but Marvik wasn't going to risk going back to Locks Heath to get Helen's Fiat or retrieve his Land Rover from behind that abandoned stable block. Hiring a car would be traceable and take too long and taking a taxi meant relying on someone else. They could catch a train from Southampton Central station but there was a much better way to reach Weymouth.

'Come on,' he said, striking out towards the pontoon.

'We're going by boat!' she cried incredulously, hurrying after him.

'Weymouth has a perfectly good marina and it will only take an hour, ninety minutes at the most.'

'But what about breakfast?'

'We'll grab something on the way.'

'And you expect me to cook it for you!' she complained.

'Unless you want to pilot the boat. I can show you how.'

'No. I'll cook breakfast,' she said hastily. 'But I'm warning you, don't make a habit of it.'

'I wouldn't dream of it.'

'And if you end up with egg all over your kitchen—'

'Galley,' he corrected.

'It's tough shit.'

'Toast and coffee will be fine.'

'Maybe but don't blame me if I bring it up again.'

He smiled. 'You've managed all right so far.'

'Yeah, but it looks stormy out there,' she said warily, climbing on to the boat.

Marvik studied the dark clouds gathering over a choppy water. The Solent and beyond would be rougher. Still, they could hug the coast as much as possible as far as Bournemouth and Poole, then around the tip of Swanage, along the Dorset coast, and into the sheltered bay of Weymouth.

'Don't worry, it will be perfectly calm,' he lied.

'Oh, yeah.'

He set a course for Weymouth Marina while Helen went below.

Once out on Southampton Water he called Crowder. He answered promptly. Marvik gave him a sanitized version of events, leaving out the fact that DI Duncan Ross had called someone immediately after his visit to him, and that Marvik believed he had been followed and watched at Littlehampton. He also said nothing about his visit from DI Feeny and DS Howe but he told Crowder about his interview with Helen, the fact that her house had been searched, and that he'd got her out but they'd been followed.

'I shook them off, but they'll be back,' Marvik added, hoping she would stay below for a little longer. 'She's with me now but she can't stay with me, it's not safe for her.'

'You've obviously got him worried.'

'Yes, but whoever he is, he has clout enough to have me followed.'

'That's not surprising, is it?' Crowder answered.

Marvik didn't need to consider that for long. 'No.' This man had protected his own back for seventeen years and had managed to threaten Blackerman into keeping quiet. 'Do you know who he is?'

'No.'

Was that a lie? Could the killer be a top-level police officer? It would certainly explain Crowder's caution. But there was another possibility and one that had been buzzing around Marvik's brain ever since that van had tailed him. It would also explain Crowder's reluctance to use the official channels. This had all the hallmarks of the intelligence services and perhaps they had been detailed to cover up something connected with the navy. Blackerman had been navy and so too was Charlotte.

'We're getting close,' Crowder said.

And close meant the risks increased.

'Has Helen given you any new leads?' Crowder asked.

'No. Until her house was broken into she firmly believed Blackerman was guilty, but now she's not so sure and that puts her at risk. I can't protect her all the time. If the killer comes for me that's fine but I don't want her hurt. I want her somewhere safe.'

'I'll get it sorted.'

Marvik relayed what he'd discovered about Grainger's hit and run and what DI Ross had intimated. 'Maybe Grainger wanted to blow the whistle or was looking for a financial contribution to top up his pension. Is there any mention of Brighton in the Esther case?'

'If there is I don't know about it. Like I told you I haven't requested the file, which means I haven't read it, and you know why that is. And before you say wouldn't it be quicker and better bringing this out in the open and re-investigating it, remember what I said on Friday and what you've just experienced with Helen. The moment there is any hint of this being officially investigated this killer will make sure all routes to him are firmly closed. And he can do it.'

Marvik squinted at the horizon, frowning. 'I'd like to talk to Grainger's next of kin, his sister.'

'Her name is Amelia Snow and she lives at flat twelve Esplanade Mews, Bognor Regis.'

That was a small seaside town on the coast of West Sussex, fifty miles from London and about a hundred miles to the east of Weymouth. It was also about seven miles to the west of Littlehampton. Marvik didn't ask how Crowder knew Amelia Snow's address without reading the file. But then it would have been easy enough for Crowder to have accessed Grainger's police record under some other pretext.

'Don't forget we need somewhere safe for Helen.' Marvik rang off, noting that Crowder hadn't asked where he was heading. He didn't need to. He knew.

'Who were you talking to?' Helen asked, appearing on deck with a mug of coffee and a plate of toast.

'A police officer.'

'Well you can forget about locking me up in some dive with a bodyguard.'

'It wouldn't be like that.'

'How do you know?'

He didn't and he didn't know if he could trust Crowder. He postponed the thought. He was keen to speak to Strathen, which would have to wait until they reached Weymouth. He'd take a chance on Strathen's phone being tapped. If it was though Shaun would warn him before he spoke too freely.

By eleven o'clock they were on the pontoon waiting for the town bridge to lift so that they could enter Weymouth Marina. Marvik had radioed up to request the lift as they were heading past the Condor Channel Island ferry terminal. It was winter and he knew from previous visits that an hour's notice was required and that the bridge would be lifted at midday and after that not until two p.m. They had an hour to wait. He used the time to discuss with Helen how he wanted to play the interview with John Stisford.

'You lead the questioning. He expects that. Introduce me as a friend. Don't say how we arrived, let him assume it's by train. And if he asks why you're asking questions—'

'I'll tell him I'm looking for closure,' she interjected with heavy cynicism. 'Isn't that what all the psychiatrists say?'

It was, Marvik agreed. He'd been told it too but he'd decided closure wasn't an option. He didn't *want* to know more about his parents' death because there was nothing more to know. Helen had believed she'd had the answers and that she'd had closure until he'd shown up and shattered the foundations on which that belief had been built. He was forcing her to face her past. Perhaps someone would one day force him to face his. Until then he'd forget about it.

He watched her studying the boats in the narrow strip of water of the harbour and the apartments and buildings on either side. He wondered what she was thinking. Was it her sister and the memories they'd shared as children and teenagers? Or was she still trying to come to terms with the fact that her sister's killer had never been caught? And him? Where did his thoughts take him as he waited for the bridge to lift? His concerns for Charlotte were uppermost and every minute spent waiting here could be a minute taken off her life. Was pursuing this line of questioning a waste of time? Perhaps he should contact Charlotte's commanding officer and tell him what he knew. Perhaps he should approach DI Feeny and Sergeant Howe and ask them about Crowder. Crowder had the kind of clout to mount the operation he had witnessed last night.

The radio crackled into life, the bridge slowly divided and opened up and soon they were mooring up. He'd intended heading straight for somewhere to eat but Helen forestalled him.

'I can't walk around dressed in your friend's jacket for ever. I might look like a sexy waif swamped by a gigantic waterproof jacket but it is not the height of fashion this winter, and I'm beginning to get some weird looks.'

'I thought that might be because of your purple hair. Why that colour?'

'I like purple. I need to buy a coat and you did promise me one.'

She wanted to head for the town centre but Marvik prevented that by entering the nearest shop that sold sailing jackets where he bought one with a hood and fleece lining which happened to be her favourite colour, purple.

They returned to the quayside and to the Ship Inn on Custom House Quay overlooking the water for something to eat. Stisford was expecting them early afternoon. The marina office staff had told him that Stisford's address was about three miles to the east of the town, not far from the college and hospital.

Marvik hadn't seen anyone following them and none of the dozen or so people in the pub looked as though they were remotely interested in them, although the colour of Helen's hair and his scarred face drew some curious looks. He guessed they did look a rather unusual couple. They certainly didn't blend in. If anyone came asking after them they'd be remembered, but perhaps not found. By then they would have left Weymouth but he knew that it wouldn't take long for whoever was monitoring their movements to get here by car.

Helen's appetite was healthy. Marvik watched her tuck into battered cod, chips and peas. 'What do you remember of Stisford?' he asked, forking a piece of steak and Tanglefoot ale pie into his mouth. It was good.

'Creepy.'

'In what way?'

'Like I said before, he was always hanging around, volunteering his opinion even though no one wanted it.'

'Your mum might have done.'

She shrugged a reply.

'What did he do after leaving the army?'

Her brow furrowed in thought. 'I can't remember. I took as little notice of him as possible. It couldn't have been anything special otherwise he'd have banged on about it.'

Marvik would be interested to find out.

She pushed away her empty plate. 'I can't see what Stisford can tell us that can help.'

'He was with your sister the last time anyone saw her alive.'

Her expression clouded over.

Marvik continued. 'I want to know exactly when that was, how she was behaving, what she talked about, when exactly he last saw her. Anything, Helen, that might help us find out who really killed her.'

'You're sure it's not Blackerman? I mean all that stuff last night, the house could have been ransacked by drug addicts after money for a quick fix.'

'It wasn't and you know it.' He held her gaze.

She held her hands in capitulation. 'We got time for a pudding?'

He nodded.

She ordered jam sponge with custard while Marvik declined dessert. 'I'm making the most of it,' she said with her mouth full. 'It's not every day someone buys me lunch and with you I'm not sure when we'll next get to eat.'

'I'll pay the bill.' He headed for the bar and after settling up asked where he could call for a taxi. He was directed to a pay phone outside the customer toilets. He ordered a taxi and then called Strathen.

'Is it OK to talk?'

'Yes. Are you all right?' Strathen asked, concerned.

'Yes. Your car is parked at Hamble Point Marina.'

'And my boat?'

'On my pontoon on the Isle of Wight.'

'Which is where?'

'Didn't the police tell you?'

'They're not telling me anything and Professor Shelley is avoiding my phone calls. His sister, Beatrice, had the pleasure of telling me this morning that my contract has been terminated. Some of Palmer's research has shown up at a German competitor.'

'Perhaps they were just working along the same lines as Palmer.'

'Shelley claims not and that it could only have come from Palmer. It's exactly what he's been developing over the last year. It's an intelligence software programme that can help those suffering from Parkinson's disease using electrodes to record signals from the brain to the muscles. Chiron was about to register a patent for it but the German company did that yesterday.'

'That could still be just coincidence. Any sign that Palmer is in Germany?'

'Not so far but I've put that on hold to work on Charlotte's disappearance, which is far more important, and the Esther Shannon murder. It makes very interesting reading. Blackerman seems to have been convicted on the flimsiest of evidence and no appeal against the sentence has ever been lodged. His lawyer was a guy called Vince Wycombe. Blackerman had an exemplary service record. No hint of playing away from home and he saw combat in the Gulf War. I'm still digging. Where are you?'

Marvik hesitated for a fraction. Even if Strathen had gone out to meet Ashley Palmer on his boat, Marvik couldn't see him having anything to do with Palmer's disappearance or Charlotte's. He'd trusted him implicitly in combat and he had to now. A course plotted on a navigation chart to that bay on the Isle of Wight meant nothing and yet Strathen had found Palmer's note. Marvik pushed aside his suspicions with irritation. 'In Weymouth. I'll tell you why later.'

'OK.'

He returned to find Helen had finished her pudding and the taxi had arrived.

Time to see what Stisford could tell them, thought Marvik eagerly.

TEN

The man standing on the threshold of the dilapidated bungalow could have been any age from mid-fifties to late-sixties. He was bald and slight, with yellowing lined skin. He was also an alcoholic, or bordering on one, thought Marvik, smelling the booze on his breath and registering his bloodshot eyes behind small rimless spectacles. Stisford's surprise at finding Helen accompanied swiftly gave way to suspicion. Clearly he was dubious that she was the same person he remembered from fifteen years ago. If Helen was startled at the change in Stisford, she didn't show it.

'It's so good of you to see us, Mr Stisford,' she said brightly, forcing him to step back to admit them. The narrow hallway smelled of eggs, tobacco and alcohol. The orange and brown patterned carpet was well worn and the geometric green and yellow wallpaper faded. The interior was as shabby as the exterior where Marvik had seen grubby net curtains covering the two small bay windows either side of a weather-beaten door. The small square of a front garden was weed-strewn and the iron gate rusted and creaking.

'John, please,' he said with an attempt at lightness but Marvik caught the edge of apprehension in his throaty high-pitched voice.

Stisford led them through the narrow passageway to a cluttered, dishevelled, musty lounge that faced on to a square of overgrown weeds that couldn't by any stretch of imagination be called a garden. Marvik noted the cigarettes and an almost empty bottle of whisky on a small table beside one of the four armchairs. On the dusty brick mantelpiece were grimy photographs of a young man in army uniform, alone and with colleagues. They had to be of Stisford but there was very little left of the once fit and lean soldier from those pictures.

'Would you like a tea, coffee? Or something stronger?' Stisford asked.

They both refused. They'd agreed that in the taxi. Marvik wanted to get down to business and so too did Helen, and the clock was ticking fast. He could also see into the kitchen to their right and thought their decision a wise one given the filthy state of it.

Stisford waved them into seats and took the chair beside the whisky bottle. His glass was empty.

Helen perched on the edge of a threadbare armchair with shiny arms which were black from grime and sweat. She showed no signs of revulsion; in fact her expression betrayed nothing but keen interest and for that Marvik secretly admired her.

'As I said on the phone I want to talk about the last time you saw my sister,' she began as Marvik took the chair beside her.

Stisford looked solemn and sorrowful, only Marvik thought it was a little contrived.

Helen continued. 'It was in the bar of the Union Services Club at Waterloo, wasn't it?'

'Yes. It was after the evening Remembrance Service. We were all feeling a little relieved and light headed. It's a bit like after a funeral at the wake when everyone is happy for a while. I'm sorry if that sounds callous after what happened.'

'What time was this?' Marvik interjected, seeing Helen's frown.

Stisford threw him a doubtful look before answering hesitantly. 'The performance began at seven and ended just before nine p.m. . . . It was about half past nine or just after that when we arrived back at the club from the Albert Hall.'

'You bought the ticket for her?' Marvik again asked. Helen flashed him a hostile look which he interpreted as *I thought I was supposed to be asking the questions.*

'You know the system?' Stisford said, surprised.

Marvik did. 'I'm ex services.'

'Which branch?' Stisford brightened up and thawed towards Marvik.

'Marines.'

'Commandos? You look like one'

'Yes.'

Stisford nodded his approval. 'I worked with you lot, well the Royal Marines Amphibious Task Group. I was Army, 17 Port and Maritime Regiment Royal Logistic Corp based at Marchwood, near Southampton. I've seen a lot of action in my time and learnt many things, some of which no man should. You seen action?'

'Some.'

'I was in the Falklands, that's where your dad was killed,' he said to Helen, who looked as though she was about to scream *I bloody know that.* Marvik quickly interceded.

'So, as a member of the British Legion you bought a ticket for Esther who wasn't a member.'

'Her mum, Jean, was. Your mum,' Stisford corrected. 'But Esther didn't join, had too much on her plate to think of that, but I knew she'd want to go in place of Jean. And although she could have got tickets for the afternoon performance because some are made available to the public, I didn't see why she should, not when I organize a party every year and that year I offered a place to Esther and she grabbed it. I only wish now she hadn't.'

Helen took over. 'So how many of you were there that night?'

'From our party, there was me, Gary Holman, Jack Harriman and Esther. We were the only ones staying over at the club. Gary and Jack were coming with me to the Cenotaph the next day.'

'So why did Esther stay? She could easily have travelled home. It's only just over an hour by train.'

'She would have done but that's down to me again.' Stisford wriggled and pulled at his right ear. 'I'd booked a twin-bedded room on the thirteenth floor for Esther and Irene Withers. Irene went every year to remember the death of her husband, Archie. He was a pilot, got shot down in the last days of the Second World War. Esther said she'd be quite happy to stay over and help Mrs Withers. She didn't have good health and she was nearly eighty. Unfortunately Mrs Withers passed away two weeks before the Remembrance Service, all the other rooms were booked so Esther said she'd stay over alone.'

Why? wondered Marvik. Was it because the room had been paid for that she thought she might as well use it, or had there been another reason?

Helen said, 'Who left the bar first?'

'Esther did. She said she was tired and she looked it. It was a sad occasion. She remembered her dad. You were too young, Helen, to have known him. He was a fine man and a good friend. I remember—'

'Why didn't you see Esther to her room?' Helen sharply interjected, abandoning the neutral air she'd originally adopted. Marvik now saw the disgust on her face. Maybe Stisford saw it too because he squirmed. Marvik didn't blame her for letting her emotions show. She'd done well until now. It seemed that mention of her father goaded her more than thoughts and talk of her sister and her mother. And he knew why. She was resentful for never having known him because it made her feel excluded from an inner circle who sang his praises and talked of his experiences.

'I wish to God I'd gone up in that lift with her,' Stisford answered. 'You don't know how many times I've regretted it. But I stayed down with Gary and Jack, drinking and talking over old times. Esther must have found us boring although she was too polite and too kind to ever say that. I don't know what time she left exactly, and I told the police that, but it must have been some time after ten o'clock because she only had one drink with us.'

'Would the other two know?' Helen asked eagerly.

'They're both dead.'

Helen looked annoyed.

'Gary died four years ago, cancer, and Jack last year. Motor neurone disease, bloody awful way to go.'

So no suspicious deaths there, thought Marvik.

'She said she wasn't going to the Remembrance Service parade the next morning, so I didn't think anything of her not showing at breakfast. I thought she might already have left or was having a lie in.'

Marvik said, 'Apart from being tired, what was her mood like in the bar after the service?'

Stisford answered hesitantly. 'OK.'

'You don't know!' Helen picked up, her tone hostile.

He wriggled uncomfortably. 'We were all talking and drinking. I didn't really notice anything different. Esther was always quiet.'

'She probably couldn't get a word in edgeways with you all gabbing on about how many people you've killed.'

'It wasn't like that, Helen.'

'No?' she challenged, infuriated.

Marvik interjected. 'How was she during the service?'

'Reflective, proud, sad, the same as we all were.'

'You had seats together?'

'Yes.'

'And she met you at the Union Services Club before the service?'

'No, at the Albert Hall. I don't know where she was before then or on Friday night. The police asked me but I couldn't help them. I asked her if she wanted to travel up to London with me, Gary and Jack but she said she was working on Friday.'

'Where?' Marvik hadn't asked Helen that.

'I don't know where exactly but she worked for Danavere Medical on the Solent Business Park.'

Marvik knew it. It was a large modern business park and housing estate just off the M27 between Portsmouth and Southampton and not far to the north from where Helen lived. He had no idea what Danavere did but the word 'medical' connected in his brain with both Charlotte and Ashley Palmer.

'Esther said she'd make her own way to the Albert Hall on Saturday.'

'Is that exactly what she said?' asked Marvik.

Stisford looked puzzled and then his face screwed up in thought. Helen sniffed impatiently. After a moment he said, 'I'm sorry, I don't remember her exact words.' He addressed Helen. 'Didn't she say anything to you?'

'No.'

Stisford continued. 'Maybe she just wanted time alone to remember your dad.' His eyes flicked to Helen and then back to Marvik. 'I came out three years after the Falklands War and decided to help those who had suffered as a result of it through my voluntary work with the Royal British Legion. I also did what I could for the widows and mothers who had lost loved ones during the conflict but it's never enough.'

No, it wasn't, reflected Marvik, recalling those he'd known who had been killed and the loved ones left behind. His thoughts shifted back to Terence Blackerman and he wondered how he was feeling, after learning that his only son had died as a result of wounds inflicted in action. A son he had hardly known and one he had sacrificed his freedom for as a result of that night in November seventeen years ago.

'You did voluntary work, but what was your job after the army?' Marvik asked.

'I worked in the stores for Ford in Southampton,' Stisford answered a little uneasily, probably, Marvik thought, because the job lacked prestige and perhaps the voluntary work gave Stisford back some kudos.

He said, 'Did you see anyone leave the bar at the same time or just after her?'

'I wasn't really taking any notice. And I didn't know the lift had broken down until the police told me.'

'When did they tell you?' Marvik jumped in before Helen could say anything.

Stisford was beginning to look frazzled and Marvik could see his right hand trembling, which was either the symptom of an illness, the sign of strain or the need of a drink. And Marvik thought it was the latter two.

'Monday morning. I was at home at Marchwood. I didn't even know Esther was dead. You didn't tell me.' He threw Helen a hurt and puzzled look.

'It wasn't top of my list of things to do,' she said caustically. But Marvik hadn't asked her how the police had broken the news to her, or when. Or what had happened next. He would, but later.

'It came as a great shock.'

Marvik felt Helen's body go rigid, with anger he thought at Stisford's rather obsequious manner more than distress at the memory. He threw her what he hoped was an understanding and pleading look but she wasn't looking at him. If he put a hand on her arm he knew she'd shake it off.

Quickly he said, 'Can you remember what they said? I know this must be as difficult for you as it is for Helen, which is why I'm here to help her.'

She flashed him a furious look. He hoped his eyes said 'ease back, it won't be long, we need this information'. She obviously understood the message because she took a breath and forced a sad smile from her tight lips.

Stisford said, 'I'm not sure how I can help but I do understand that sometimes piecing together traumatic events can make towards a better understanding of what happened and assist some people in coming to terms with it.' He cast a sympathetic gaze on Helen. Marvik thought she might hit him, but again she smiled tightly and he saw her fists clench as they rested on her knees.

'I tried to do that with Jean to help her come to terms with Jim's death. We talked for ages about it and the past. I like to think it helped in some way. It certainly helped Esther but you, Helen, were too young of course.'

'What did the police tell you?' Marvik persisted. Stisford had avoided the question, but whether deliberately Marvik didn't know.

'That Esther had been found dead in the room and they were treating it as suspicious. They asked me more or less what you have and I couldn't help them.'

'Can you remember their names?'

'Yes. It was a DI Grainger and a DS Ross from the Metropolitan Police.'

'Did they return to question you?'

'No. I made a statement and that was it.'

'They didn't ask you if you knew Terence Blackerman?'

'No.'

'Did you?'

'No.'

A lie or the truth?

'I attended the trial. I found it hard to believe a navy chaplain could have committed murder and did wonder if he'd been suffering post-traumatic stress, but the medical people said he hadn't. Still, not everyone recognizes it and it can show up in different ways. Oh, I'm not excusing what he did,' he added hastily. 'But—'

'Did you see him in the bar that night?'

'No. But then it was very busy. He could have been there. He might have followed Esther into the lift.'

But he couldn't have known it would break down or that Esther would invite him to her bed, unless they had already known one another and were having an affair, which would explain why Esther had got in the lift in the first place. Perhaps that was the reason Esther had gone to London the day before and stayed over on Saturday night, and when Irene Withers had conveniently died they thought they'd make use of the double room, albeit with twin beds.

'Is he still in prison?' Stisford asked.

Helen answered. 'Yes.'

'I'm sorry, Helen. There's nothing I can tell you that can help. You must try to get on with your life. Esther wouldn't want you dwelling on it and going over it all again.'

Marvik thought it best to leave before Helen exploded. He rose and thanked Stisford by extending his hand. Stisford's grasp was firm but his palm moist. Hastily they extracted themselves from the dreary, dirty bungalow. Marvik gripped Helen firmly by the elbow and steered her down the road and around the corner before she could say anything. Only when they were out of sight he eased his grip and she shook him off.

'What a creep. I didn't like him in 1997 and I like him even less now. He stinks.'

'Of booze and sweat,' Marvik said.

'You know what I mean,' she flashed at him.

He did.

'I bet he was trying to get into Esther's knickers, she rejected him and he killed her. He *was* a soldier, trained to kill.'

'Then why weren't his DNA and fingerprints in that room?'

'Maybe he cleaned it up before leaving her.'

They began walking through the estate towards the main road.

'He wouldn't have been able to eliminate all trace of his DNA.'

'Then the police covered it up.'

'But why would they protect John Stisford? You saw him and that bungalow. He's not important enough.'

She scowled. 'Maybe he knows something about one of them and threatened to expose it.'

'If he did it's not made him rich.'

'He could have spent it all on booze and gambling.'

'Then he'd have gone back for more.'

'Not if the cop who covered up for him is dead. Grainger.'

'His death is too recent for Stisford to be living like that. Even if he had managed to squeeze more money out of Grainger, or Duncan Ross for that matter, Stisford couldn't have spent it that fast.'

'No? Just give me a few grand and I'll show you how quickly it can be spent.'

'It's not him, Helen.'

After a moment she said, dejectedly, 'I know.'

'But he's not telling us everything.' And Marvik would like to know what it was and why he felt the need to hold back.

'Do you think he knows Blackerman?'

It was what Marvik had been considering. 'It's possible. But I can't see Blackerman protecting Stisford, certainly not going to prison for him, and as I've already said Stisford's not Esther's killer. Do you remember seeing Stisford at the trial?'

'Yes, but I didn't sit with him. I couldn't bear him near me, not even then. He made my flesh crawl, still does.'

They turned on to the main road and began walking in the direction of the marina. It was at least three miles but Marvik made no attempt to volunteer to call a taxi and Helen didn't ask him to. It was as though they needed the fresh, cold March air to blow away the stench of that bungalow and to rid themselves of Stisford's sycophantic manner.

'When did the police break the news to you, Helen?'

'Sunday morning. It was just after eleven. I was in bed. I'd been at a nightclub until two, drinking and mucking about – yeah I know I was under age but no one bothered to ask me for my birth certificate and I took advantage of Esther being away. I had a hangover and I ignored the bell for as long as I could, hoping that whoever it was would go away but they didn't. Then I looked out of the window and saw the police car and I thought, shit, they've come after me because I lied about my age and got drunk. It put the fear of God in me. I staggered down and looked into this police woman's eyes and my . . . well I threw up all over her before she even told me. The rest is a blur.'

He reached a hand and took hers. She didn't recoil but gripped it firmly. They didn't speak for some moments but continued walking.

'The next thing I remember was being told by this fat copper, who was DI Grainger, that Esther had been murdered. He asked me if she had a boyfriend. I said no. They wanted to look around her room. They'd already done so once but they did it again. They went through her books, looking for letters I guess. She didn't have a mobile phone or computer – yeah, hard to believe now. She must have used a computer at work though. I guess they looked at that.'

And Marvik wondered what that had revealed. Probably not much given that the Internet and email were not as freely used then as now.

'They asked me about a diary, just as you did, but I said Esther didn't keep one or if she did then I hadn't found it. They also asked me what train she caught to London on Friday. I had no idea, only that she was going from work.' She withdrew her hand and pushed it through her hair.

'Do you know what she did at Danavere?'

'Secretary I think, something like that. I can't remember and I didn't bother to ask her about it. Like I told you I was a self-obsessed teenager with a bloody great chip on my shoulder.'

Marvik stopped outside a café. 'Fancy a drink?'

She nodded. When they were seated with teas in front of them, she said, 'I remember at the trial they said she left work at four. But no one knew where she went after that. I guess the police might have checked the hotels in London but that's a hell of a lot of hotels to check and nothing was mentioned about any money coming off her account. Now, come to think of it, there were no payments made out either that night or Saturday but then the room in the Union Services Club had been paid for earlier. So Esther must have stayed with someone Friday night.'

'Yes and he or she never came forward.'

'Do you think it's her killer?' she said eagerly.

'It's possible.'

'How the hell do we find out who that was? Unless it's Blackerman. Maybe Esther did know him and spent both Friday and Saturday night with him. She wanted to end the relationship and he flipped.'

'She might have known him but he didn't kill her. And if she had known him, why didn't he say?'

'Because it would make matters worse for him.'

'But that doesn't explain why someone is intent on preventing us from looking into it. And how would Esther have known him? He was navy and your father was army. I suppose he could have met your father in conflict or on a joint exercise.' Marvik thought he'd get Strathen on to that unless Crowder cared to give him that information, *if* he knew it.

Helen shrugged and sipped her tea. Marvik said, 'Apart from her job, how else did she spend her time?'

'Looking out for me. She didn't go out or have any hobbies or interests.'

'Did the police ask you this?'

'I don't remember. They must have done.'

Marvik stared out of the window, scrutinizing the busy road. 'Did Esther go to church?' He wondered if she'd met Blackerman there.

'Sometimes. Christmas, Easter, the anniversary of dad's death and then mum's.'

'Where?'

'Not locally,' she answered, eyeing him sharply. 'She liked the big services at the cathedrals, that's what appealed to her about the Remembrance Service at the Albert Hall.'

Perhaps she'd met Blackerman at one of these.

'This doesn't seem to have got us very far,' Helen said dejectedly. But Marvik thought it had got them another step forward.

'Finish your tea. I'm going to make a call.' He indicated the public pay phone opposite, from where he called Strathen. 'Esther Shannon worked for a company called Danavere Medical,' he said as soon as Strathen came on the line.

'Danavere!'

'Yes, why? Do you know it?'

'I should, they make prosthetic limbs.'

Marvik could almost hear Strathen's brain making the same connection as he'd done earlier when Stisford had mentioned it, a medical connection between Esther, Palmer and Charlotte. 'We need to know what Esther did at Danavere and whether she was working for them on Friday the seventh of November 1997. If so, where, doing what?'

'I've got contacts there. I'll get on to it right away.'

'Also see what you can dig up on John Stisford, especially his service record.'

Next Marvik rang Crowder on the pay-as-you-go mobile phone. 'Any news on a safe house for Helen?'

'Not yet.'

'Well hurry it up. I need information on Blackerman's defence lawyer, Vince Wycombe. Can you get it for me?'

Crowder said he could and rang off. He didn't ask where Marvik was or what he was doing and Marvik didn't volunteer the information because Crowder knew anyway.

'What now?' Helen asked on his return.

Marvik had been considering that. 'We talk to Grainger's sister tomorrow morning. In Bognor Regis.'

'We going there by boat?'

'Of course.'

'Thought you might say that. In the dark again?'

'No other way to travel.'

She rolled her eyes at him.

'And the sooner we start the better.' The nearest marina to Bognor Regis was Chichester. From there it was a twenty-minute drive across the flat arable countryside. He'd call for a taxi to take them. Chichester Marina was sixty-four nautical miles to the east of where they now were. He didn't tell Helen that the weather forecast for the next twelve hours wasn't good. It would take them about four hours. He hoped they could make it before the front closed in.

ELEVEN

It was just after ten thirty when Marvik moored up on the visitors' berths at Chichester Marina. The wind and rain had slowed them. The front had come in quicker than anticipated. It was still raining heavily, bouncing off the boat, and Marvik could see the lights of the yacht club blazing out a welcome. It would have been good to share a drink in the warmth and comfortable atmosphere of the club but Helen looked emotionally drained and slightly the worse for wear after a rough journey across Southsea Bay and Hayling Bay before they'd entered the relative shelter of Chichester Harbour. The ordeal of the last couple of days and the memories of her sister's death were beginning to take a toll on her, although she insisted it was the extra cream cake she'd indulged in while waiting for him to return from his phone call to Strathen.

He surveyed his surroundings. There was another boat several spaces along and close to the fuel pumps but apart from that it was quiet. The small car park in front of them was deserted. The café was in darkness and so too were the units beyond it.

'Are you up to eating?' he asked.

She shook her head. 'Think I'll go to bed.'

He made himself a coffee and a bacon sandwich, listening for sounds outside that would alert him that someone was drawing near, but he also listened for the rhythm of Helen's breathing that would tell him she was asleep. He thought about the day to come and his interview with Amelia Snow. Would she be in? For all he knew she could be on a Mediterranean cruise or touring Australia. And this could be a wasted journey. But he knew that Crowder would have told him if that were the case.

His mind went back to what he had considered earlier, about the intelligence services and the navy being mixed up in this. He wondered if Crowder was from MI5 and their suspect was someone high up in one of those organizations.

He tossed back the remainder of his coffee, made sure that Helen was asleep, then climbed off the boat and headed along the pontoon. He stopped at the only other boat moored there and climbed on board.

Crowder looked up from his seat in the cabin. 'Did John Stisford give you any new information?' he asked.

So Crowder had known that Stisford was mentioned in the original investigation and that he lived in Weymouth, which clearly indicated he knew a great deal more about Esther Shannon's murder than he was telling him and that he had no concerns about showing it. What else was he withholding? And why feed him this stuff piecemeal?

Well two could play at that game. 'No.' Marvik didn't mention Danavere. Not yet. He wanted to know what Shaun discovered first. 'Have you the information on Wycombe?'

'Yes.' Crowder nodded him into a seat but Marvik declined.

'Can we discuss this in the cockpit?'

Crowder rose. He didn't need to ask why. He'd know that Marvik would want to keep a watchful eye on his boat to make sure that Helen was safe. Crowder followed him up on deck where they stood under the shelter of the helm. Marvik studied Crowder. Behind the inscrutable expression and calm manner was a man of intelligence and cunning. And possibly a dangerous man.

Crowder said, 'Vince Wycombe is Head of Chambers at Six Blights Court, Chancery Lane, London.'

'So Wycombe's risen to the top since failing to get Terence Blackerman off a murder charge.'

'It seems that way. He's a criminal barrister specializing in complex and high-profile cases: murder, manslaughter, serious violence, sexual offences. The Chambers acts for both defence and prosecution across the UK and they also handle white-collar crime, serious fraud and have a military practice group.'

Marvik's ears pricked up.

'They didn't have it in 1997,' Crowder said, reading Marvik's thoughts.

'But perhaps that was what kick-started it, although I'd hardly have thought a failure would inspire the military to engage them.'

'Perhaps it wasn't a failure as far as they were concerned.'

And that connected with Marvik's own earlier thoughts that the navy were behind this in some way. 'You mean they wanted Blackerman convicted.' But what the hell was happening in 1997 to make the navy so jittery? He'd consider that later.

'It's one theory,' Crowder answered. 'The military practice group was set up in 1999 and the Chambers now has barristers who have served in the military. They deal with Court Martial work and represent military personnel here, in Germany and elsewhere. Wycombe has an apartment in London and a house not far from here, at Itchenor.'

'Expensive and exclusive,' Marvik said, recalling the small sailing village on the eastern shores of Chichester Harbour. A small ferry crossed to the peninsula of the ancient village of Bosham on the opposite side of the harbour in summer. It was, Marvik mentally calculated, about four miles from the marina on foot. He asked if Wycombe was a sailor.

'He keeps a motor boat on a pontoon bordering his property. He's married with two daughters, aged thirty-one and twenty-eight. The eldest daughter, Kimberly Wycombe, is following in her father's footsteps but at different Chambers in London. She's already made a name for herself representing some tough criminals. The latest was Steven Preston whom she managed to extricate from a charge of armed robbery, despite the fact the National Crime Agency know he did it. Vince Wycombe's youngest daughter lives in America with her television producer husband and three children. Wycombe is fifty-seven, married to Sophie Allingby, daughter of Roger Allingby, deceased, who was the MEP for South Hampshire and chairman of a technology company. Wycombe's currently sitting at a criminal trial in Portsmouth, the murder of an air hostess by her boyfriend who claims he had left her alive and well two hours before she went missing and who was found strangled in West Wood, two and half miles to the west of Winchester.'

'How long is the trial set to run?'

'It's only just started.'

'So the likelihood is he'd come home to Itchenor in the evenings.'

'I'll give you the address.'

Crowder relayed it. He didn't say that Wycombe was unlikely to see him, let alone talk to him about the trial of Terence Blackerman, because as Crowder had previously said, Marvik would find a way. He asked if there was any news of Charlotte.

'Hampshire police have questioned all the shopkeepers and office workers at Town Quay and circulated her picture. The delivery driver has been traced and interviewed but claims not to have noticed her. And his van has been examined for fingerprints and DNA and both are being matched against items taken from Charlotte's room in Birmingham.' Crowder paused. Marvik knew there was more and whatever Crowder had to say he didn't think he was going to like it.

'Charlotte's laptop computer has also been taken away and is being examined. The Computer Crime Squad are trawling through her social networks for any indication that she was being groomed by someone for sexual exploitation or has been lured away through an online romance. There is no evidence that she used an online dating service but they have found her emails to the prison authority requesting details on Blackerman's whereabouts and her request being granted to visit him in Parkhurst. They also found an email to you.'

Marvik eyed him with scepticism. 'What does it say?'

'It was sent the night before she travelled from Birmingham to the Isle of Wight, telling you that she wanted to come and see you.'

'And my reply?'

'That you'd love to see her. Here is a transcript of it.'

Marvik took the piece of paper Crowder was holding out and read while his mind rapidly tried to make sense of this new twist. Apparently he'd replied: 'It will be lovely to see you again. Come any time. You know where to find me.'

'Where was it sent from?'

'Your IP address.'

'Which means you think it was sent from my computer.' He remembered how his cottage had been illegally entered and that someone had looked at his laptop. But that had been after this had been sent.

'Not necessarily, but it implies that you sent it. The police will want to question you.'

'And that means a delay. Can't you keep them off my back?'

'Not without letting on what you're doing and if I do that, it will alert the killer that the police are involved.'

'Do you know DI Feeny and DS Howe?' Marvik studied Crowder's reaction carefully. He showed no sign of recognition at the names but then he hadn't expected a man as experienced as Crowder to betray himself in that way.

'No.'

So who was investigating Charlotte's disappearance if not them? He said, 'They're investigating the disappearance of Ashley Palmer. Does he feature in this anywhere?'

'I don't know the name.'

But Marvik couldn't believe him. He nodded towards his boat. 'Have you found somewhere safe for Helen to stay?'

'No, and I'm not going to. You know why.'

'For God's sake, can't you make up some plausible story?'

'The fact that she is Esther Shannon's sister will send alarm bells ringing, and alert our killer. He's already running scared, which is good. He'll make mistakes and that means we can catch him.'

'Not if the mistake is my death and Helen's,' Marvik said tautly. 'Or perhaps you don't care. We're expendable. Perhaps our deaths will give you more information about him and you can get someone else to take this up.'

'You know we're tracking you. We'll do our best to keep you safe.'

'Short of finding somewhere for Helen, yes, I know,' Marvik said wearily. 'Who have you got sitting at the monitor?'

'You don't need to know that.'

'How certain are you of them? They could be in league with the killer.'

'They're not. Call me anytime and especially if you or Helen are in danger.'

With that Marvik had to be satisfied but he felt deeply concerned, not for himself but for Helen. If they were in danger what guarantee did he have that Crowder and his resources would reach them in time? None. He understood Crowder's logic but that didn't make it any easier to accept. He scanned the marina and the area around the car park and business units: everything was quiet.

He considered what Crowder had told him about the email. Was he bullshitting him? As he'd suggested, his account could have been hacked into and used to send this email but Marvik had no proof that an email had actually been sent. He stared at the piece of paper Crowder had given him. It had his email address and what he supposed was Charlotte's at the top of the printed page but that didn't mean it was genuine. This could have been fabricated by Crowder and the only reason he could think of for that was to increase the pressure on him to act more quickly. But if it *had* been

planted on Charlotte's computer, just as that text had been sent to
her, but not from him, then why did someone wish to implicate him
in Charlotte's disappearance? The only reason he could think of
was the same as he'd previously considered – because Charlotte
had to be eliminated in case she'd discovered something from
Blackerman about the real killer, and whoever was responsible knew
of their past affair, making him the perfect fall guy.

He stuffed the paper in his pocket and checked on Helen. She
was sleeping. She had the coat he'd bought her spread out over the
duvet in an attempt to keep warm and was wearing one of his
sweatshirts over her clothes. He could rough it on the boat in winter
but he didn't think it fair that she should and as Crowder wasn't
going to find somewhere for her to stay he would need to and soon.
And without telling Crowder where that was.

He showered quickly in the cold and then turned in. The rain
stopped just after three twenty and he slept fitfully until the sound
of a boat motoring slowly past roused him into full wakefulness.
On deck he saw it was Crowder's boat. It was an hour before dawn.
He washed and changed and ran the engine to get the heaters going,
wondering if it would wake Helen, but it didn't. He made them
both some toast and tea. He had to shake her to wake her.

'Breakfast in bed, you certainly know how to spoil a girl,' she
joked, shivering. 'What time is it?'

'Just after six o' clock.'

'Christ, is there such a time!'

He walked her to the ladies' shower block, where he waited
outside. He still couldn't trust Crowder. Even though his boat
had left the marina he wasn't sure that he and Helen weren't
being watched and that someone wasn't waiting for the chance
to snatch Helen. There was no one around. But he couldn't watch
her forever.

They walked to the marina office by the lock where Marvik asked
a member of staff to call a taxi for them. Outside Helen turned
towards the harbour. 'It's nice here,' she said, leaning on the railings
and gazing out across the lake-like water and the surrounding flat
countryside in the distance. The wide channel to their right led up
to the small hamlet of Dell Quay, barely a handful of houses and
a pub. Further northwards the water narrowed to a creek and then a
stream and beyond that the South Downs.

'Quiet too except for those noisy seagulls.' She squinted up at them. Then she looked despondent. 'I should have phoned in sick yesterday. I'll need a job to go back to, even though I hate it.'

'We'll find a pay phone in Bognor.'

'Never been to Bognor,' she said, making an effort to brighten up.

'There's a first time for everything.'

She smiled. 'Isn't there a saying, "Bugger Bognor", by some king or other?'

'King George V who died in 1936. The legend has it that they were his last words and there are a couple of versions on why he said that. One is that he was in Bognor in 1928 recovering from a chest infection at a wealthy friend's house and when he was leaving and was petitioned to rename it Bognor Regis, as a mark of his visit, he said "Bugger Bognor!" Another is that on his deathbed it was suggested that he'd soon be well enough to return for another spell of convalescence at Bognor, to which he replied—'

'Bugger Bognor.'

'And promptly died.'

'So what did he actually say on his deathbed?'

'No idea.'

She laughed. Marvik wished he could prolong the moment but soon they'd be sucked back into the more immediate past, and her past, and the wounds would start hurting again.

Staring back out to the harbour, she said, 'I hope Amelia Snow is an early riser.'

Marvik just hoped she was at home.

TWELVE

Tuesday

'Can I help you?' A bright, musical female voice answered Marvik's summons on the intercom of an Edwardian house which had been converted into apartments on the Bognor seafront. He flashed Helen a relieved look and quickly introduced himself, apologizing for disturbing her so early. It was just on nine o'clock and he and Helen had spent an hour kicking their heels along a wind-blown, tired and dejected Bognor promenade on a cold, damp early-March morning. The only coffee shop that would normally have been open, one of the large national chains, was closed for refurbishment. So it seemed was Bognor – although not for refurbishment, judging by its appearance – and there was hardly a sign of any of the sixty thousand inhabitants.

Helen had remarked, 'Now I know why King George said "Bugger Bognor".'

Marvik had replied, 'We're not seeing it at its best.' Into the intercom he said, 'I'd like to talk to you about your brother, Mrs Snow. I understand it might be painful for you but it is very important. I'm happy to explain outside if you prefer.'

'Are you from the police?'

'No.' There was no reason for her to admit him or to agree to speak to him but she said, 'Third floor,' and the door release buzzed. He pushed it open. The hall was spacious, clean and well decorated, albeit blandly in magnolia with a beige carpet.

'Needs a splash of colour,' Helen muttered as they climbed the stairs. Her tone was light but he could hear and sense her tension.

The door of flat twelve was open before they reached it and standing on the threshold was a short, plump woman with curly white hair wearing red voluminous trousers and a loose-fitting hip-length green and blue top with sequins. She more than made up for the lack of colour in the hall. Beside her was a small West Highland terrier.

'I apologize for disturbing you,' Marvik began. She was studying them curiously but not warily. Marvik suddenly saw what she must, a muscular, broad-shouldered man with a scarred face and a scruffy woman with heavy, dark eye make-up, black tights, big black boots with a purple coat and purple hair. He thought they were enough to make Amelia Snow slam the door on them and call the police but her fleshy face broke into a broad grin.

'It's not often I get such interesting callers. Come in. You look frozen to the bone. That wind off the sea at this time of the year can cut right through you.'

He stepped in, exchanging a quick glance with Helen, who seemed as surprised as he was by their welcome and by the warmth and trusting nature of Amelia Snow. It boded well for their mission.

They followed her into a well-proportioned, high-ceilinged room partly decorated in Helen's favourite colour, purple, contrasting with green. It should have been hideous but somehow it wasn't. In front of Marvik were two sets of long French windows that gave on to small verandas each with black iron balustrades and a view of the grey sea. The room was comfortably furnished with an assortment of easy chairs covered in bright fabrics and throws and an untidiness that was homely rather than slovenly. It was also extremely cluttered and very warm.

'You look as though you could do with a coffee.'

Helen nodded eagerly. She unfolded her arms and stopped shivering. Marvik unzipped his jacket.

'Take your coats off. The heating's on full pelt. Life's too short to be cold,' she called out as she entered a room on the right giving off the lounge. The little dog followed her.

'Thank you,' Marvik replied, as the rattle of cups reached them. He shrugged out of his jacket and looked for a suitable place to put it.

She popped her head out of the kitchen. 'Just sling it where you like.'

He draped it over one of the easy chairs. Helen raised her eyebrows at him, wrenched off her coat and threw it on top of his before sauntering to an open door on their left.

Marvik turned to study the photographs on the cabinets. There were several of her dog and a few of her with her dog, taken, by the look of the settings, on various holidays, but there was one of her taken several years ago standing beside a sturdily built man who Marvik thought might be Bryan Grainger. There was a similarity between them in build and around the eyes. But whereas Amelia Snow's face had lost its shape because of the excess flesh around it, this man's still retained its square-jawed ruggedness. He was about late-forties and confident looking and when Marvik's eyes travelled up to the numerous paintings on the walls he saw one of the same man, this time looking thoughtful and preoccupied, perhaps even troubled. The other paintings were a mixture of people undertaking various activities: a man behind a market stall selling oranges; a fisherman huddled in the cold and rain on the beach; a woman pushing a child on a swing in the park. They were good.

Helen's voice came from the distant room, 'You're a painter,' she called out. Marvik joined her in what was clearly Amelia's studio. It was as chaotic as her lounge and there were two further French windows looking out to sea.

'I dabble,' came the distant reply.

It looked more than dabbling to Marvik.

She appeared in the doorway.

'They're really good,' Helen said with genuine admiration. 'I used to love art at school but never got to take it seriously.'

'Maybe you should. You obviously have a taste for the dramatic.' She nodded at her hair.

Marvik wondered if Helen would be insulted but she smiled with real warmth.

Amelia Snow added, 'Although that purple sailing jacket rather lets the side down.'

'I had to buy it very quickly and at the last moment. My other coat got thrown away,' she added pointedly with a glance at Marvik.

'Come and have coffee.'

Marvik was glad to find Amelia Snow so open and friendly; it made his task of questioning her much easier. But it didn't mean he would get the answers he was seeking. A coffee pot, three mugs, a plate of chocolate biscuits, milk and sugar was waiting for them on a tray on a circular table in front of the big marble fireplace. The dog settled itself at Amelia Snow's feet.

'Is that your brother, Bryan?' Marvik asked, indicating the painting he'd been studying earlier.

'Yes. I finished that two months before he died.'

Marvik took the coffee mug from her. He said, 'This is Helen Shannon.' He watched for her reaction. He could feel Helen holding her breath. But Amelia Snow showed no recognition of the name.

'Help yourself to biscuits.'

Helen picked up one. 'My sister was Esther Shannon, she was murdered in 1997 and your brother investigated the case.'

Amelia Snow looked sympathetic. 'And that's why you're here to ask me if he discussed it with me. I'm sorry, dear, but Bryan never talked about work. He was a very self-contained man, dedicated to his job, too dedicated I often thought, and he considered me too flighty, but we rubbed along well enough for brother and sister although we were never what you would call close.'

Marvik felt the disappointment keenly. Another wasted morning. But they couldn't just leave and besides, even if Bryan Grainger had never talked about his work, there was still his death and she could give them more information about that. But first he asked her about the painting.

'What did you talk about while you painted him?'

'We didn't, that's probably why he looks reflective.'

'Or puzzled.'

She studied it. 'Maybe he does.'

'And rather sad,' added Marvik, ignoring Helen shifting impatiently beside him. 'Perhaps he was thinking through his old cases or wondering what to do with the rest of his life.' Was that Bryan Grainger he was describing, or himself? But he had a job to go to in a week's time and one he knew he felt no enthusiasm for. Perhaps he would once this was over, *if* it was over. And if it wasn't then he'd have to tell Drayle that he needed to postpone his start date.

Amelia said, 'Bryan loved his job and he didn't really want to retire but he had no option – you had to go then, once you'd done your thirty years, although I believe it's different now and police officers can rejoin as civilians.'

And was that what Duncan Ross was going to do? Marvik wondered. He'd said not but maybe he'd miss it too much to sail away into the sunset on his refurbished boat.

She continued. 'Bryan had decided to set up on his own.'

'A private detective?' Helen asked with her mouth full of biscuit.

'Not divorces, husbands spying on wives and vice versa, but something more substantial or rather meatier, so he said, but don't ask me what because I have no idea. It wasn't long before he was killed and I never had the opportunity to question him further about it. He didn't intend staying in the area though. He told me he was going to sell his flat. He said it had been a mistake to buy it and I agreed with him; the gentility of Chichester didn't suit him. I'm sorry about your sister, dear,' she said to Helen. 'Bryan's death was sudden and shocking. I felt very angry that his life had been cut short in so cruel and callous a manner but I can't even begin to imagine how you must have felt when you must have been nothing but a teenager and your sister much younger than Bryan. I won't ask you how she died because I'm sure you don't want to dredge it all up, but did my brother get her killer?'

'He thought he had and so did I but . . .'

'Now you're not certain.' Her eyes flicked between them. 'Something has happened to doubt that conviction. You think my brother made a mistake?' she said, disturbed.

Marvik hastily answered. 'Not necessarily. It might have been the only decision he could make given the evidence, but other information has come to light since then to throw doubt on it.'

She sipped her coffee and scrutinized him closely. 'Are the police re-investigating it?'

'No.'

'You're a private detective?'

What did he say to that? If he said yes, perhaps she'd ask for some kind of identification and that would catch him out in a lie. He didn't think she deserved that. She'd trusted them. 'Sort of. I'm looking into the background of the murder unofficially, but with Helen's approval.' Perhaps she'd think they were lovers. It didn't worry Marvik if she did. She seemed to accept his explanation.

'And you're wondering if he ever expressed doubts about the case? Well he didn't. Not to me.'

'Did he ever talk about DI Duncan Ross? He worked with Bryan on the investigation.'

'No. I don't recall the name.'

Marvik left a short pause before saying, 'What was your brother doing in Brighton on the day he was killed?'

'I don't know. He might have been there looking for somewhere to live and work.'

Marvik thought that unlikely at eight thirty at night.

'I'd assumed he'd return to London though. The police have never said why he was there and they've never apprehended who killed him.'

'When did you last see him?'

'A week before he died. And that was the last time I spoke to him.'

'How did he seem?'

'Very cheerful, elated almost, because he'd made a decision about his life and the future.'

Or because he'd discovered something connected with Esther Shannon's murder, Marvik wondered. He couldn't see how any of this helped them. 'I suppose the police asked you these questions.'

'They didn't actually. They just told me that Bryan had been killed, they were very sorry but they were doing all they could to find the driver. They put out appeals for witnesses and for the driver to come forward but no one did.'

'But the case is still open?'

'As far as I'm aware. No one's been back to tell me anything more.'

Helen interjected. 'Aren't you cross about that? Surely they can do something.'

'I'm disappointed, but getting het up about it would be a wasted emotion. It would only hurt me. It can't do Bryan any good. And the driver who killed him can't have any conscience so getting angry and letting it eat into me would destroy my life and no one else's.'

Helen frowned as she considered this.

Amelia Snow continued. 'Wailing and moaning about it and badgering the police won't achieve anything, so I get on with my life as best I can. It's certainly what Bryan would have wanted.'

But Marvik thought Bryan would have wanted more than that. He would have wanted his killer found and punished. He recalled what he'd read in the newspaper articles when he'd visited Littlehampton library. Grainger had been walking towards the seafront. There had been only one witness, Linda Hannam, but she'd only seen Bryan's body on the wet road.

'Did the witness reveal anything that could help the police?'

'If she did they didn't tell me, and I think they would have done. The post-mortem found that Bryan wasn't drunk, there was no alcohol or any other drug in his system. He was just in the wrong place at the wrong time.'

Marvik swallowed his coffee. He half expected Helen to jump in with a question but perhaps she was thinking of her sister being in the wrong place at the wrong time – only Marvik didn't believe that for either Esther or Bryan Grainger. They had both been targeted.

He said, 'What happened to your brother's belongings?' Could Grainger have left some note or indication of what he was doing? But if he had then the police hadn't found it. Or had they, and passed it on to the person who had killed or organized the killing of Bryan Grainger?

'There was very little on him when he was killed, just his wallet with credit cards intact and some money.'

'No mobile phone?' asked Marvik, suddenly more alert.

'No. I gave the police the number and they tried it but it had been disabled. They thought it must have fallen from Bryan's pocket when he was struck by the car and someone picked it up from the gutter, or wherever it had landed, and walked off with it.'

That was possible but Marvik was beginning to wonder if the driver had stopped and quickly searched Grainger and removed anything incriminating.

'What about the keys to his flat?'

'It's funny you should ask that,' she said, stroking the dog before looking up at Marvik. 'I didn't even think about them when the police handed me Bryan's belongings. I didn't go to the hospital because he was already dead. I just accepted his personal items without really registering what they were. But when I went to his flat, two days after his death, there had been a break-in.'

Marvik's nape hairs pricked. Helen almost choked on her biscuit.

'The front door was locked, so I had no idea what I was about to see until I let myself in.'

'How?' Marvik sharply interjected.

She looked puzzled, before her expression cleared and she smiled. 'I had a key and Bryan had one for my flat, in case we lost it or anything happened to one of us. I thought his keys had been lost in the accident but when I saw his flat had been entered I wondered if someone had picked them up along with his mobile phone and got hold of the address, and had come looking for valuables. That really hurt. To think that someone could do something so despicable.'

But would a former copper keep his address with his house keys? Unlikely, thought Marvik, and the address wouldn't have been on his mobile phone, not unless he'd given his address in an email sent from it or on something ordered over the Internet. If so that meant whoever had stolen the keys and phone could have hacked into his email and web accounts, just as someone appeared to have hacked into his.

'Was anything taken?' he asked.

'I don't really know because I didn't know what Bryan kept there.'

This was frustrating but relevant and Marvik pressed on. 'Did you report it to the police?'

'Of course. And before you ask they didn't catch who did that either,' she answered, looking bewildered. 'I don't see how this is helping you.'

It wasn't. Not in the way she meant. Did he tell her that he thought her brother could have been deliberately targeted to silence him? If he did he didn't think she'd believe it anyway. She wasn't stupid, just very trusting and a bit too innocent.

He said, 'I just wondered if Bryan might have kept notes on his old cases and had jotted down something that might help us find out who killed Esther.'

'Well I didn't find any notebooks or diaries when I was clearing his flat. There were several of my mother's diaries but that was all.'

'No computer?'

'No.'

And Marvik thought that a little unusual. There didn't seem to be anything further she could tell them and Marvik again apologized for having brought back unpleasant and sad memories for her. He rose to indicate to Helen they were leaving. Amelia Snow pulled herself up and showed them to the door, the dog trotting at her heels.

At the door Marvik turned back. 'Where was your brother's funeral held?'

'At Chichester crematorium. Several of his colleagues came. I don't know who they are so I can't help you there but the undertaker might still have a list of them on file. Ryans in Bognor. I hope you get to the truth,' she said, looking at Helen. 'But if you don't, don't waste your life wondering or worrying about it. Easy enough to say, I know, far more difficult to carry out. I'd like to know how you get on.' She reached into the pocket of her trousers and pulled out a card.

Helen took it. 'I'll come and tell you.'

'That would be nice, dear.'

Helen thanked her for the coffee and biscuits. When outside the building she turned to Marvik. 'Do you think that whoever ran him down took his computer and any notes?'

'Sounds likely. I think he must have been re-investigating Esther's murder.'

'But why was he in Brighton? As far as I know Esther never went there. Maybe she did though and didn't tell me. We didn't confide in one another. Brighton is a notorious place for lovers, isn't it? Could she have gone to a hotel with a lover, the same man she met in London before she was killed? Or perhaps she went with Blackerman if they were having a fling.'

Marvik didn't know. 'Let's call on the undertakers.'

They found Ryans in a large building erected in the mid-1860s which, along with conducting funerals, boasted selling houses and household items, or so stated the ancient sign above the door. Marvik didn't know if they did either these days and he wasn't interested in finding out. He asked the elegant blonde in the plain black dress at reception if it was possible to have the list of mourners for Bryan Grainger's funeral in 2004.

The receptionist said she would call Mrs Snow for her permission to release it and if granted she would post or email him a copy. Marvik couldn't wait that long. He said he had just come from Mrs Snow's and if the receptionist could call her now and ask, they would wait or return to collect it.

Amelia Snow gave her permission and the receptionist asked if they could call back in an hour. They walked down to the beach and along the promenade after Marvik had called into a local stationers and consulted an ordnance survey map. He didn't buy it but replaced it on the shelf once he'd found what he was looking for. He also withdrew some money from the bank. Crowder knew he was in Bognor anyway and if anyone else was monitoring their movements they'd be long gone by the time they discovered that he and Helen were here.

Helen seemed rather preoccupied. Marvik didn't disturb her thoughts but focused on his own. Grainger had probably gathered many enemies in his career, villains who would like to see him dead, but he was convinced that he had been about to reveal something significant connected with Esther Shannon. The police's inability to find any leads on his hit and run and the break-in at his flat seemed to indicate even more strongly that behind this was someone very powerful in the police force, or the intelligence services.

They ate a very early lunch in a steamy café behind the seafront that seemed to specialize in serving baked beans with everything. Helen expressed the view that she liked Amelia Snow but said very little else. Marvik let her be. When they returned to the undertaker the list was waiting for them.

'It might not be a complete list of mourners,' the receptionist informed Marvik. 'We took the names of all those who entered the crematorium before the service, on Mrs Snow's instructions, as she wanted to write to them all and thank them for coming, but there could have been others who slipped in after the service had started.' He wondered why Amelia Snow hadn't given them the list of names and addresses if she'd written to them all, but perhaps she'd destroyed it or lost it, which wouldn't be difficult he thought given the chaos of her flat.

Marvik tucked the list into his jacket pocket. He found a taxi outside the railway station, and as the flat countryside sped past them he withdrew the list and scanned the names. Only one registered with him and that was Duncan Ross, whose address was simply given as Sussex Police. That wasn't unusual though because looking at Grainger's other former police colleagues they'd also done the same. There were a few from the Met who might be worth speaking to. He handed the list to Helen and asked if she recognized any of the names on it. She studied it for a moment then shook her head. As they neared the marina Marvik leaned forward and asked the driver to divert to Copse Lane, Itchenor.

'Why there?' Helen asked.

'Something I want to see,' he answered with a glance that indicated he wasn't about to expand on that.

It was a five-mile detour from Chichester Marina by road and about the same distance on foot. The map he'd consulted earlier had shown him there was a public footpath from the marina, skirting Birdham Pool and then following the coastline before crossing some farmland and into Copse Lane.

The taxi turned into Itchenor Road then indicated right into Copse Lane. Marvik asked the driver to slow down. As they drove past the select, large and very expensive houses Helen raised her eyebrows. 'There's a lot of money here; you got rich friends?'

He didn't answer.

He found the house he was looking for. It was on his left and the last in the cul-de-sac, which culminated in woods. It backed on to Chichester Harbour and opposite it he could see a footpath leading into the woods. The entrance to the house was secured by electronic gates behind which was a long sweeping driveway to a large sprawling brick built property under a slate roof surrounded on either side by shrubs and trees. He gave instructions for the driver to head for Chichester Marina. After he'd paid him off, Helen said, 'So who lives there?'

'Vince Wycombe. Blackerman's barrister.'

Her eyebrows shot up. 'He's done well for himself. You going to see him?'

'Later, maybe.' And without her tagging along. 'First I want to get this list to Shaun and ask him to check out the names. I also need to know if he's got anything further on Esther's employment with Danavere.'

'Who's Shaun?'

'A friend of mine who's helping us.'

'The one with the boat?'

'Yes.'

Helen halted on the pontoon. 'I've been thinking about what Amelia said about her brother having his mother's diaries. Esther didn't keep a diary, as far as I know, but she did keep hold of mum's. When Esther died and I had to clear her things, I found them in her room in a shoe box. There were no other notes or any letters or postcards. I've never looked at them. I just wondered . . . It's a bit of a long shot, but they meant a lot to Esther; do you think she might have written something in them?'

If she had then Marvik doubted they would have remained in that shoe box in Esther's room. 'Where are they?'

'At the house.'

Or perhaps they weren't. Perhaps they'd been taken long ago or had been what the intruder had been after when he'd trashed Helen's house on Sunday. There was only one way to find out. But first he said, 'Let's get back to the Hamble.'

THIRTEEN

Tuesday

It was late afternoon when Strathen admitted them to his apartment. The day was drawing in early because of the gathering clouds that heralded more rain. They had walked from the marina where Marvik had moored up on Strathen's berth. He'd obviously collected his car because there was no sign of it where Marvik had parked it. No one had followed them on the twenty-minute walk. He placed Helen's bag on the floor and introduced her.

'What happened to your leg?' she asked Strathen as she shrugged out of her jacket.

'It got blown off.'

'In Afghanistan.'

He nodded, exchanging a smile with Marvik who quickly interpreted it. Strathen welcomed her directness. Most people avoided asking or skirted around the subject, as they did on seeing Marvik's scars. Strange that Helen hadn't asked about them. Although he hadn't exactly been encouraging.

'What have you found out?' Marvik asked Strathen.

'Follow me.'

He led them into a large room directly opposite. Through the wide windows at the far end of it Marvik could see the dull grey sea of Southampton Water and beyond it the lights on the tall metal chimneys of Fawley refinery. The room was packed with computers and monitors. There was also a large whiteboard on the right-hand wall. On one half was a circle with the name Ashley Palmer in the centre; on the other a circle containing the name Charlotte Churley.

'Looks like mission control,' Helen said, throwing herself into one of the vacant chairs.

'Any news on Palmer?' asked Marvik.

'His passport's not gone through Border Control yet. It might not ever. But there are some interesting developments. I'm glad you're here because I was just about to update the board.' He crossed to it and erased Charlotte's circle then drew two new circles. Inside one he wrote 'Charlotte Churley' and in the other 'Esther Shannon'. Marvik sat forward eagerly. Helen eyed Strathen keenly.

Strathen began. 'Danavere, Esther's employers, started life in the 1970s as a medical supplies company, mainly specializing in prosthetic limbs but its remit over the last fifteen years has expanded. It now provides innovative trauma and casualty care, and rehabilitation programmes to amputees, including service personnel, veterans and civilians.'

He drew a line from Esther's circle and wrote 'Danavere' at the end of it. 'Danavere are involved in programmes in all specialist hospitals in the UK including the Queen Elizabeth Hospital Birmingham, the Royal Centre for Defence Medicine, Critical Care Unit where Charlotte works.' He drew another line from Charlotte's circle and joined it up to the word 'Danavere'. 'The company also works closely with Chiron on the development of new technology that can aid patients. I thought that might make you sit up,' he tossed at Marvik. He extended a line from Palmer's circle to 'Danavere' and wrote along it 'Chiron'. 'So now we have a connection. Not that it necessarily means anything but it's very interesting.'

'Who's this Ashley Palmer?' Helen asked.

Marvik explained, 'He's a computer research scientist for Chiron and he went missing the night Charlotte showed up at my cottage and the day before she went missing.'

She looked thoughtful.

Strathen resumed. 'The relationship between the hospitals, Chiron and Danavere is three-fold. Physiotherapists, consultants, doctors, nurses and patients give feedback to the Head of Research at Danavere, a Dr Lester Medway, who then liaises with Professor John Shelley at Chiron on the development of new technology to aid patients. Once certain innovations have been developed Danavere trial them and a joint patent is filed. This leaves Danavere to continue to develop trauma and casualty care, and rehabilitation programmes to amputees rather than developing software applications.'

'Could Charlotte have been giving feedback to Danavere?' Marvik asked.

'It's possible, and if she was then she might have done so to Medway. Palmer might also have been liaising directly with Medway. And Lester Medway was a director at Danavere in 1997 when Esther worked there.' Strathen drew three more lines on the whiteboard extending from each circle and connected them by writing above them, 'Medway'.

Helen pursued her lips and narrowed her eyes as she thought. 'I don't remember hearing Esther talk about anyone called Medway, but even if she did I don't think I'd have taken any notice. Could he have been the man she saw on the Friday before she was killed?'

Strathen put a question mark beside Medway's name and wrote, 'Esther's lover?' He continued. 'As well as Dr Medway there are three other directors who were around in 1997: James Marningham, Managing Director, Peter Inchcup, Finance Director, and Roger Witley, Commercial Director.' He wrote the names on the white board to the right of 'Medway'.

'Many of Chiron's projects are funded by DRTI, the Defence Research and Technology Institute, under its remit for the development of human and medical sciences. It's an executive agency of the Ministry of Defence. It has a huge turnover and commercial and financial flexibility. As well as being responsible for funding human and medical sciences, DRTI is also responsible for maritime safety and security and defence research. It works with the brainiest people from niche start-ups to the giant listed defence companies. Its funding comes from the government, private investment companies, charitable organizations and the European Commission.'

Marvik said, 'So Danavere and Chiron receive funding to develop applications and then apply for a patent so they commercially benefit if anyone else wants to buy their inventions and equipment.'

'Yes. But there's nothing illegal or wrong in that. DRTI award contracts to many providers who all have to bid for funding. For every Chiron there are several other technology companies bidding for the money. It's fiercely competitive and a missing computer research scientist is not good for business and future funding, especially when something they've been working on shows up in Germany. And both Chiron and Danavere probably spend a great deal of time and money on developing projects that come to nothing.'

'Go on.'

'DRTI came into being in 2000, so has no connection with Esther's murder. Its first chairman was Sir Edgar Rebury who, before being appointed, was Permanent Secretary at the Ministry of Defence. He stepped down from DRTI in 2010. The current chairman is Rodney Dearman, as I mentioned to you before, Art. The other members of the board are a mixture of people from academia, the medical profession, defence and those working in allied defence areas. Chiron was established in 1996.'

Marvik studied the board as his mind grappled with the information Strathen was giving them. It still didn't explain why Esther had been killed but Strathen had more.

'I contacted Vera Pedlowe, she's been Dr Lester Medway's secretary for years. I know her well. She was working for Danavere in 1997 and she remembered Esther not only because of the tragic way she was killed but also because she was very good at her job.' He addressed Helen. 'Your sister began working there as an administration clerk but was very quickly transferred to Vera to assist her with organizing conferences, medical seminars, fund-raising dinners and charity events. Danavere support a number of charities including the Royal British Legion, Combat Stress, the ex-services Mental Welfare Society, the Association for Limbless Service Personnel – although they changed the S and P around to make it ALPS, aspiring to the top, scaling the heights, nothing's impossible, that sort of thing, proving that there is life after amputation – Blind Veterans, Wings Away and many other medical and service charities as well as fronting cutting-edge medical seminars and conferences in the UK.'

'Esther's job was to liaise with the venues, make sure everything was in order, book the accommodation for speakers and VIPs, help to pull together the programme or brochure for the event, and drum up support from the businesses, the VIPs and the celebrities to donate items that could be auctioned to raise funds for the chosen charities.'

Helen looked dejected. 'I didn't know. She never spoke about it. But then I never asked her.'

'Was she at work the Friday before she was killed?' asked Marvik.

'Yes, but she left early, at four o'clock. She didn't say where she was going or what she was doing except Vera told me that Esther said she was attending the Remembrance Service at the Albert Hall on Saturday evening because her father – your father,' he directed at Helen, 'was killed in the Falklands War. I'm sorry about that.'

'Why should you be? You didn't start it.'

'Did Danavere send representatives to it?' asked Marvik.

'I'll ask.'

'Any hints or talk of a boyfriend?'

'None that Vera can remember but she says they didn't really discuss personal things. I'll ask her if Esther organized an event to take place in one of the conference rooms at the Union Services Club and for a list of all the events Esther organized and the names of those who attended. But it might take a while.'

Marvik pulled out the list the undertaker had given him and handed it across to Strathen. 'I also need you to check out these people.' Strathen ran his eye down it as Marvik continued. 'I'd like to know if anyone who attended Grainger's funeral, aside from Duncan Ross, was on the original investigation and if anyone has a connection with Chiron or Danavere.'

'The latter I can do, the former is more difficult.'

Marvik knew that Crowder would be the best person to ask for that but he'd probably shoot him the line that he was unable to find out because he couldn't access the files. Perhaps Marvik would ask Ross that question.

'Did you get anything on Terence Blackerman?'

'Only what was in the press reports at the time. But I'm tracking down those who served with him who can hopefully help. It's proving tricky.'

Marvik told Strathen about their interview with Amelia Snow and filled him in with the background that he and Helen had gleaned about Esther from their interview with John Stisford. Strathen quickly came to the same conclusion as Marvik.

'So Grainger was following up his own leads on the case and was killed because of it.'

'Or because he'd withheld something and was blackmailing someone regarding it. His flat was searched for any notes he'd made. His computer taken, if he had one. It's my guess he'd arranged to meet someone in Brighton and was killed coming away from that meeting.'

'By DI Duncan Ross?'

'I'm not sure. He might know nothing but I'm certain he was primed about me when I met him on his boat. He was very forthcoming, too informative.'

'Crowder could have told him.'

'Which is why we're not telling him this.'

'I'll see what I can find out about Crowder,' Strathen said. 'I'm also looking into John Stisford as you asked.'

'Helen will help you,' Marvik said, rising.

'Oh will I? You're not dumping me here.'

Strathen said, 'There are worse places to be – or is it just my company you object to?'

'No. Look, I—'

'I'm going to fetch your mother's diaries,' Marvik said, adding silently, *if* they're still there.

'But there's probably nothing in them that can help us with Esther's murder.'

'It's worth checking though. Where are they kept?'

She sighed resignedly. 'In the bottom of my wardrobe, third floor, the room that faces the front.'

'Give me your house keys.'

She handed them over.

'Shaun, can I take your car?' Marvik knew he could return to where he'd parked the Land Rover but if Helen's house was still being watched then he'd need a quick getaway and his Land Rover was too slow for that. It was probably also bugged.

Strathen thrust his hand in his trouser pocket and threw Marvik the keys.

'If I'm not back within two hours call Crowder.' Marvik handed Strathen the pay-as-you-go phone. 'His is the only number in the address book. You should be safe here, but if you see or hear anything suspicious don't take any chances. Get out and stay out. Send me a warning on my normal phone.'

Strathen nodded.

Marvik left without a backward glance. He found Strathen's car in its space behind the house. As he swung out of the electronic gates and along the lane he wondered if someone would still be watching Helen's place, waiting for her return.

No one followed him. He parked four streets away and made his way quickly on foot to the corner of Helen's road. It was dark now and the rain was helping to keep people inside. Only a few cars swept past him, people returning home late from work. He moved quickly to the alleyway that ran along the rear of the properties, his hands rammed in the pockets of his dark jacket, his collar up against the rain, his senses on full alert. It was possible that someone was watching the property, not physically, but via a surveillance device placed on the rear gate or on the back door.

He halted outside the house next door to Helen. It was in darkness. Good. He tried the gate. It opened easily and he stepped into the small square of back garden where a child's slide and trampoline filled the space. A light flicked on in a third-floor room and he pressed himself back between the fence and the slide. Curtains were pulled. The light dimmed. He waited a few seconds then nimbly climbed the slide, reached for the top of the fence and grasped it with both hands before propelling himself up and over in one fluid movement, landing in a crouch on the other side. He froze for a moment. He could hear only the sound of the wind and rain.

The street lights in the alley were bright enough for him to study the back entrance from where he stood. He couldn't see a surveillance device on the back door or the patio doors but he was assuming there was one. It would be focused at mid height and above.

Dropping to his stomach he crawled along the soaking wet grass until he reached the edge of the house. There was a concrete path bordering the patio doors and the back door; carefully he eased along it. When he reached the back door he extracted the keys Helen had given him and found the one that would open it. Would the door be alarmed? Not necessarily with a sound alert but an infrared one, which would notify those watching the monitors that the property was being entered. It was a chance he had to take and if that was the case he would have minutes, maybe just seconds, to get in and out. He could move swiftly but not that swiftly.

There was no time to waste. He stood up, unlocked the rear door, hoping that whatever surveillance device was being used was still looking beyond him into the garden, and slowly pushed open the door, again dropping low on to the floor. He spotted the device on top of the bookshelves on the opposite wall. It would have registered that the rear door was opening but it wouldn't see him. He sprang up and raced up the stairs to the front bedroom and threw open the doors of the wardrobe. The box was where Helen had said he would find it. There were five books in total and he stuffed them into his jacket pockets. Marvik froze as he caught the hint of a soft footfall below. Perhaps he'd sensed it rather than heard it because no other sound followed. He wasn't going to hang around and find out. And he wasn't going to exit the property from the front or the rear.

Within seconds he had the front bedroom window open, thanking God and Helen that she hadn't locked it. Below him was the apex of the porch above the front door but the roof was angled in such a way that there was a small flat space rather than a sharp point on the apex. That was obliging of the builders, he thought with a wry smile. Without hesitating he climbed out, grabbing the window ledge with both hands. He was now dangling from the front bedroom window and there was about a two-foot drop to the top of the porch and from there an eight-foot drop to the ground. As he looked up he saw the shadow of a dark figure. There was no time to lose. With a spilt-second glance down, he judged the distance, then he let go, bending his knees, bringing his hands up, landing on the flat part of the porch before swiftly springing forward into the air, legs bent, hands coming forward. He landed on his toes, touching the ground with his strong right hand, bracing his arms to take the full impact, rolling over and up. He didn't look back.

He sprinted down the road and around the corner until he came to the car. Throwing himself inside he started the engine, thrust it into gear and pulled away, stepping on the accelerator when he was clear of the houses and on the main road. Then he permitted himself a smile and let out a long exhalation. No one had followed him. Whether or not the activity had been worth it only Helen would be able to tell, but even if Esther hadn't written anything in her mother's diaries which could help them find her killer, it had been worth it purely for the sheer exhilaration he'd felt at the activity and the danger that had set his nerves on fire, his heart pumping and the adrenalin surging. It had been a good fix. And he knew that providing consultancy to Drayle's clients was never going to give him that.

FOURTEEN

'Did you get them?' Helen asked eagerly, looking up from a computer screen.

Marvik pulled the diaries from the inside of his jacket and handed them to her. She opened one. Then her hands froze and a shadow darkened her face. 'I'd forgotten what Mum's handwriting looked like . . .' Her voice trailed off. Suddenly the tears sprang from her eyes. 'Shit.' She sprang up, clutching the diaries, and ran from the room.

Marvik let her go. He was glad to get Strathen on his own. He wanted to trust him. He *did* trust him otherwise he wouldn't be here. And he wouldn't have brought Helen here but there was something that had to be cleared up.

Without preamble he said, 'Why were you in the bay below that coastguard cottage the day Ashley Palmer disappeared?' He saw Strathen's surprise. 'The course is set on your helm.'

Strathen took a breath and slowly nodded. He wasn't going to deny it.

'I was hoping to find out what the hell Palmer was doing, and persuade him he was making an idiot of himself and wrecking his career into the bargain if he thought he could sell information and get away with it. I thought I could also get him to tell me who was paying him for company information and catch the bastard who was buying the stuff. Yeah, I thought I could recapture my commando days even with a gammy leg and it was this fucking leg that stopped me.'

'Why didn't you tell me?'

'Because I was ashamed, angry and pissed off. I tried to get up that cliff.' He ran a hand over his closely cropped dark hair and sighed heavily. 'We could scale anything, Art. I thought I was OK. I thought I could do it – after all there are men and women in a worse state than me. For Christ's sake some of them are winning medals in the Paralympics. Well I failed. No matter how many times I tried I couldn't climb that cliff. So I called you.'

Marvik could see instantly that it was the truth. But he could also see there was more. Strathen's eyes clouded over with anguish and frustration.

'I lost it. I suddenly ran out of all the things we had stood for, Art: the sense of humour even in adversity, endurance, courage. The mission mindset was completely blown. I'd kept it up through all the pain, the hospitalization, the rehabilitation. I suddenly thought "sod it". I turned the boat around and went out into the channel. I wasn't sure what I was going to do. I thought . . .'

Marvik made damn sure not to show any sympathy or pity in his expression. He didn't even express empathy. He just said solemnly, 'What stopped you?'

Strathen took a breath. 'You've got to be tough to do that.'

'You're tough all right.'

A silence fell between them. Marvik didn't say anything as fatuous as 'it's early days yet', or remind Shaun of what he'd told him when they'd met up at East Cowes, that he was awaiting two different types of prosthetic limbs to be fitted, one for running, the other for swimming. Sometimes facts made no difference to how you felt.

Strathen pulled himself up. 'Then I'd better prove I'm tough,' he said grittily. 'I'm going to return to that cliff and ruddy well scale it, but after we find Charlotte, and alive.'

'Right. So let's get on with it.' Marvik sat down. 'Someone was waiting for me at the house. I didn't hang around to see who it was, maybe I should have done. It might have helped speed things up.'

'Could be just the monkey and not the organ grinder and the monkey might not have spoken up.'

'Or know who is behind this and what the hell's going on. So have you and Helen managed to unearth anything in my absence?'

'I spoke to Vera again, managing to catch her before she went home. She can't remember the company using the Union Services Club conference rooms during 1997 or before then but she said she'd check tomorrow and get me a list of the events that Esther organized and the guest lists. She says that one of the directors attends the Remembrance Service every year depending on who is available at the time. She'll let me know who went in 1997.'

'Has she asked why you want to know all this?'

'I told her it has nothing to do with Palmer's disappearance and that I'd been asked to look into Esther's death by a friend. She didn't ask who.'

'But she could alert one of the directors.'

'She could, even though I asked her to keep it to herself. It's a risk we have to take. She gave me one piece of interesting information though: Roger Witley is in Germany on business.'

Marvik's thoughts ran along the same lines as Strathen's. Germany was where the application Palmer was working on had just been patented. 'Could he be involved in Ashley Palmer's disappearance?'

Strathen shrugged. 'Witley's got a high profile in the business world. He's very well respected and has a reputation for spotting talent and applications that will be commercially viable; maybe he spotted Palmer. But why hand it over to a competitor when his own company would benefit? It can't be for money because although he has an expensive lifestyle – a large house in the posh part of Winchester, two kids, one at Cambridge, the other at Durham University, and a wife who is big on the charity circuit – he'd rake in more money if his company patented and manufactured anything Palmer came up with. He's in demand as a keynote speaker at seminars and conferences worldwide and he's ex-army, served in the Falklands War, although he was then only twenty.'

'Could he have known Esther's father?'

'I'm checking. Witley left the army after six years aged twenty-five and went to work for Danavere, where he very quickly scaled the company heights to become a director in 1998, aged thirty-six, and has been prospering ever since.'

'What about Professor Shelley and his sister, Beatrice? How flush are they?'

'You're wondering if they're siphoning off funding from DRTI and sharing it with Witley or the other directors?'

'Perhaps that's what Palmer discovered and he threatened to blow the whistle. Although that shoots to pieces the theory that Palmer, Charlotte and Esther are connected because DRTI weren't around in 1997. Perhaps either Witley or the Shelleys met Palmer at Cowes. Shelley could have got hold of Palmer's mobile phone, after he'd been disposed of, and set up the text message, or Witley could have sent it to Shelley to divert suspicion from them.'

'I'll check if Witley owns a boat. The Shelleys wouldn't know their starboard from their port or their aft from their for'ard. From the research I've already done on the Shelleys I'd be amazed if they had their fingers in the till. Their credit checks are good both for the business and for them personally. They live together in an old rambling house that their mother left them just outside Fareham. But they could have money stashed away in foreign bank accounts. If Shelley is siphoning off funds though he's not the materialistic or socially ambitious kind but he could be using it to fund some invention or application of his own. And if Palmer's vanishing act isn't linked to Charlotte's disappearance or Esther's death then maybe we should rule out anything connected with Danavere.'

'Except Lester Medway and a possible affair, or perhaps Witley *was* having an affair with Esther and does have his hands in the DRTI till.'

'Beer?'

Marvik nodded and followed Strathen into the modern galley kitchen. There was no sign of Helen but the door to one of the bedrooms was closed and Strathen indicated by the nod of his head that she was inside.

Opening the large fridge Strathen handed Marvik a beer and grabbed one for himself. 'I'll cook something for us to eat. Pasta be OK?'

Marvik nodded and took a welcome swallow of beer. As Strathen began to prepare the meal Marvik said, 'We know that Blackerman didn't kill Esther so whoever did managed to get into the Union Services Club and we know that security there is very strict. You can't just walk in off the street. IDs and membership cards have to be shown, which means Esther's killer was either a service man, a veteran, someone working for the emergency services or retired from the emergency services – who are also eligible for membership – or an employee.'

'That's still a hell of a lot of people. And they won't still have records of who stayed that night but the police should have a copy of it.'

'And Crowder won't give me that in case accessing the files alerts whoever it is he's after.'

'They're already alerted.'

'Yes, but the killer doesn't know the police are involved.'

'Unless the police *are* involved. I can't find anything on Crowder. Admittedly I haven't had time to look very deeply and he could be active on serious crime or intelligence, which is the reason why I can't find him.'

Or perhaps he wasn't from the police at all, thought Marvik again. 'If there is a list on file of those who stayed at the club that night then it might have been sanitized by Bryan Grainger or Duncan Ross, or someone higher up the food chain. But Witley could have been a member then, and still might be. He could have been there that night.' Marvik took another swig of beer.

'There is another alternative,' Strathen said, flicking on the cooker. 'While members have to show a form of ID, visitors of members don't, and neither do they have to sign in. The killer might not be a member but was meeting a member there. The member would have met him at the door and vouched for him. He kills Esther and slips away again.'

'And is his accomplice aware of his murderous intention?'

'Probably.'

Marvik left a short pause before continuing. 'So we're looking for someone who could have access to the Union Services Club or knew someone who did. I think we can rule out a staff member because they wouldn't have had the clout to keep this investigation low key and I can't see why someone from the fire or ambulance service would want to kill Esther or have the means to pull weight with the police, and that goes for the fire fighters who turned up to free Esther and Blackerman from the lift. Dr Lester Medway could have arranged it so that he could get into the club.'

'I've met him and I can't see him as a killer.'

'Perhaps he got someone else to do it.'

'Whoever it was, Esther let him into her room.'

'Which means she must have known him.'

'She did.' A voice came from the doorway and they turned to see Helen, pale faced and red-eyed, holding one of her mother's diaries. 'It's that slimy bastard John Stisford.'

'It can't be him, Helen,' Marvik said after a moment. 'He just doesn't have the kind of pull we've experienced these last few days, and he can't have kidnapped or ordered the abduction of Charlotte.'

'Then read this.' She thrust the diary at him. Strathen moved the saucepan of pasta off the hob and waited while Marvik quickly skimmed the pages of neat small handwriting in black ink.

Hotly she said, 'I told you he was trying to get into Esther's knickers, and I was right. Mum found him trying it on. How the hell could Esther have gone with him to the Remembrance Service?'

Marvik didn't know but he intended finding out. He stretched the diary across to Strathen and said, 'That was written in 1995.'

'And before that Mum talks about how marvellous he's been,

what a comfort, always being there for her, supportive and reliable. And how she knew he had a soft spot for her but that she'd made it clear at the outset there could be no one else, only my dad.' Helen took a breath. 'How she loved him and couldn't come to terms with his death. Fuck that war.' She turned away. Marvik watched as she pulled herself up and swung back trying desperately to control her emotions. She took a breath and continued. 'Then she talks about her illness, and how, even if she wanted another relationship, which she didn't, she wouldn't be able to have one. She just hoped she could live long enough for her daughters to be able to manage on their own.' She swallowed hard. 'Then she found that slime ball trying it on with Esther. She threw him out and told him never to come near them again. Esther said she could handle him, not to worry, nothing happened. He was just a pathetic sad creature. But Mum writes that Esther was only saying that because she didn't want to upset her. Well you've read it. Then nothing. Mum stopped writing. He followed Esther to her room and killed her.'

'No.'

'You're so bloody sure of yourself, aren't you?' she raged.

'Not really,' he quietly replied. 'But I don't think he's played straight with us and I'm going to ask him why.'

'Then I'm coming with you.'

'No.'

'It was my sister that he killed,' she blazed.

'He didn't kill her,' Marvik repeated quietly. 'But I'll do whatever I need to do to get the truth out of him and I need to do that alone. I can't have you there,' he insisted. 'I need you here working with Shaun. Time is running out. Please let me handle this my way.'

She opened her mouth to protest, eyeing him coldly, but Marvik held her hostile stare. After a moment she sighed and held up her hands. Grudgingly, she said, 'OK, but if you come back with nothing more from that sleaze bag I'll go there myself.'

Steadily Marvik said, 'I won't come back empty handed.'

There was a pause then Strathen said, 'Let's eat.'

'I . . .' Helen began.

'Eat,' Strathen ordered.

And she did, picking at her pasta at first then devouring it hungrily. Marvik watched the colour come back into her face and the tension ease from her slender body. He knew that Strathen noted it too. None of them spoke during the meal. By the time they'd finished and cleared away it was almost ten. Helen was looking drained and tired. Catching sight of his reflection, Marvik thought he didn't look too bright himself. Strathen had already offered the spare bedroom to Helen. Now over coffee he said, 'Take my bedroom, Art. I'll kip down on the couch in the lounge when I'm ready. I want to get cracking on some of that research tonight.'

Helen looked up. 'I'll help you,' she said, trying desperately to stifle a yawn.

But Strathen shook his head. 'You're no good to me tired. I need fresh eyes, tomorrow morning will do.'

She didn't put up much of a protest. 'Mind if I have a shower?'

'Be my guest.'

'Then I'll turn in. Art, I . . .'

'I'll see you in the morning,' he cut in with a smile but he was already planning to leave long before she woke and Strathen would know that. Marvik waited until he could hear Helen in the bathroom. He crossed to the window in the lounge and gazed out across Southampton Water to the lights in the distance. Tomorrow he would put pressure on Stisford. And hopefully Vera, at Danavere, would come back with more information.

He turned to Strathen. 'We've got to protect Helen.' It was too late to protect Charlotte.

'She's very strong willed and unless one of us stays with her then she'll either make a mistake and let on where she is, or she'll make a bolt for it. She can stay here but this leg means I can't protect her if it gets rough.'

'I think you can. No, listen, you might not be able to physically run away as fast as they'd come after you, but when did you ever run away, Shaun?'

'Wednesday.'

'But you knew that was wrong. You weren't thinking – or rather you were and you thought of another way around the problem. It just happened to be me. And both you and I have got out of worse jams than this. If they show up here, you'll think of a way to deal with them. I'll leave early in the morning. Can I take your car?'

'Of course.'

Marvik turned in, leaving Strathen to continue working. It was four a.m. when Marvik heard him go to bed. Marvik rose an hour later. In the kitchen he found a note from Strathen: 'Roger Witley served in the same regiment as Jim Shannon and John Stisford. And all three served in the Falklands War.'

Now Marvik had something else to talk to John Stisford about. He stuffed the note in his pocket, sliced off a hunk of bread and slapped some ham inside it. Grabbing the car keys he headed for Weymouth. There was a great deal to do and not much time to do it. Maybe no time at all.

FIFTEEN

Wednesday

It was just on seven a.m. when Marvik hammered on Stisford's door.

'All right, keep your hair on, I'm coming. No need to break the ruddy door down,' a slurred voice called out. Stisford's lined, sallow face registered shock which swiftly gave way to alarm as Marvik forced his way in and pinned Stisford against the wall with a firm hand on his chest. Stisford's eyes widened, petrified.

Thrusting his face close to Stisford, not bothering to disguise the loathing he felt for the cowering man in front of him who smelled of sweat, sleep and alcohol, Marvik said menacingly, keeping his voice low, 'I suggest you start telling me the truth about what really happened on the eighth of November 1997 or—'

'I don't know what happened,' Stisford stammered.

'Did you kill her?' Marvik demanded, raising his voice.

Stisford flinched. 'No. I loved her.'

'Loved!' spat Marvik contemptuously. 'You don't even know the meaning of the word. You lusted after her.'

'No! I thought she was wonderful. I wouldn't—'

'You went into her room and tried to rape her?'

'No!' Stisford cried.

'Just like you tried once before, forcing yourself on her, only her mother came in and stopped you.'

'That's not true.' Stisford ran a tongue around his cracked lips. Beads of sweat were breaking out on his forehead and upper lip.

'I have evidence to prove it and when I show that to the police—'

'No. Please, you must believe me. I wouldn't harm Esther. I worshipped her.'

'Oh, come on, we're both men of the world,' Marvik sneered. 'An attractive, vulnerable girl, good-natured, innocent . . .'

'She wasn't that innocent,' Stisford quipped.

'You would say that to justify trying it on with her,' Marvik snarled but he took a step back and removed his hand.

Stisford shuffled his feet. The smell of his sweat was stronger. 'She was an adult,' he declared, emboldened. 'She'd been with men.'

'How do you know that?'

'She'd had boyfriends.'

'And that's your excuse for trying to force yourself on her?' Marvik snarled, disgusted. 'You followed her to her room hoping to take advantage of her. She was alone. You thought you were in with a chance. You must have been mad to think a woman like Esther would go with a creep like you.'

Stisford flinched at the harsh words and the contempt in them.

'You knocked on her door under the pretext of asking if she was OK. She let you in and then you killed her when she wouldn't let you have sex with her.'

'No!'

Marvik stepped forward again. He could see the veins on Stisford's nose and the rough bristles sprouting from the dirty open pores on his unshaven chin. The smell of his odious breath sickened him. Stisford cowered back in fright. Marvik continued in a threatening tone. 'She'd already had sex with Blackerman and you thought she was easy prey. You forced yourself on her but she managed to shake you off. She told you to get out but you weren't having that so you strangled her. You were furious and jealous; you didn't want anyone else to have her. She was yours.'

'You've got to believe me. I never touched her,' Stisford whined. 'I didn't even go into her room. OK, look, so I did follow her when she left the bar. I saw her get into the lift with Blackerman. I waited for the other lift to arrive, one was already out of order, but it was taking ages, so I used the family lift, or the service lift as it's called, at the rear.' Stisford couldn't get the words out quick enough.

Marvik eased back, his brain racing as he recalled the layout of the club. The service lift and the stairs could be accessed from a corridor behind the reception area. The killer – and he knew Stisford wasn't the killer – would still have had to show his pass to get into the club, but instead of crossing to reception and heading in the direction of the restaurant, bars and main lifts he could have turned left and made towards the baggage room before turning sharply right, down the narrow corridor that ran behind reception to the service lift without anyone seeing him.

Stisford quickly added, 'I went up in the service lift and knocked on her door but there was no answer. It was only then that someone told me the lift she and Blackerman were in was stuck. I hung around on the staircase where I would be able to hear the lift open and see her come out. She was ages. I almost gave up. Then I saw her, but Blackerman came out with her and went into her room.'

'How did she seem?' Marvik quickly interjected.

'OK.'

'You can do better than that,' Marvik said, looming forward.

'She looked pale and shaken. They both looked serious.'

'Was he comforting her in any way? Did they look like lovers?'

'He didn't have his arm around her and they weren't holding hands, if that's what you mean. She opened the door and I expected her to turn round and thank him or say good night or something but she stepped inside and he went in after her. I thought he'd be out again within minutes but he wasn't. I waited for a while.'

'How long?'

'Half an hour, forty minutes.' Stisford shrugged.

'Getting angrier all the time, imagining what they were doing, so that when he did eventually appear you went in and killed her,' snarled Marvik.

'No! I left. I went back to my room. I couldn't believe she'd slept with someone she'd just met.'

'How did you know that?' Marvik asked sharply.

'I didn't. It's what they said at the trial.'

'But you knew Terence Blackerman?' Marvik said. Stisford looked about to deny it then saw there was no point.

'Only briefly.'

'But you didn't tell the police this.'

'How could I? It meant I'd have to admit I followed her to her room. They'd assume I was involved in her death.'

Marvik despised the creep.

'Besides, I didn't really *know* him. I'd met him a few times, that's all. Said "hello", nothing more.'

'Where?'

'He'd visit injured veterans.'

'In their homes?'

'No, at the armed forces residential care and nursing homes. I used to visit them regularly myself, as part of my voluntary work.'

'Where?'

'St Vincent's on the Isle of Wight and Queen Alexandra Hospital Home at Worthing.'

That was a seaside town in Sussex between Chichester and Brighton, about ten miles to the west of Brighton.

'I went to my room and the next thing I know she's dead. I thought Blackerman had killed her when he couldn't get what he wanted from her.'

'But you'd no indication having met him that he was that type of man.'

'I didn't *know* him,' Stisford repeated whiningly. 'He could have been sex mad or sexually depraved for all I know.'

'Like you,' Marvik scoffed with a sneer.

Stisford flushed.

Marvik said, 'He was a chaplain.'

'Yeah, but he was a man.'

Marvik eyed him with disgust. He knew how Helen felt. He just wanted to get away from the despicable little shit. But there were a few more questions he had to ask first. 'Were any of his colleagues, or the people he helped, called to give character references at his trial?'

'No. I wondered why they weren't. It made me think there was a dark side to him.'

Oh yeah! Bloody convenient, thought Marvik. Wycombe hadn't done his job very well, or perhaps he'd done it too well and possibly just as he'd been instructed. Would Blackerman have insisted that witnesses be called? If so Wycombe had wriggled out of that. It was a question he was very keen to put to Wycombe.

'Do you remember a guy called Roger Witley?'

'Witley?' Stisford screwed up his face as he tried to recall the name. Then he brightened up. 'Yes, he was in the same regiment as me and Jim Shannon, 17 Port and Maritime Regiment.'

'When was the last time you saw him?'

'God knows. When I left the army. Why?'

'Was he at the Remembrance Service or at the Union Services Club that night?'

'Not that I know of. I didn't see him.'

Stisford looked puzzled. Marvik thought it was the truth. He said, 'Have you had any connection with a company called Danavere?'

'They donate to the British Legion and other service charities. But I don't know anyone from there and I didn't in 1997 except for Esther who worked for them.'

'Was there anyone from the company at that Remembrance Service in 1997 or did you see anyone from that company at the club that night?'

'There might have been but there was no one I knew and Esther never said.'

Was there anything more that Stisford could tell him? Marvik looked long and hard at the dishevelled man shrinking in front of him, his back pressed against the wall. He didn't think so. He wrenched open the door. Turning back he saw relief flood Stisford's face. 'If I find you've lied to me I'll be back,' Marvik threatened.

'I haven't lied,' Stisford wailed. 'It's the truth as God is my witness.'

'I doubt God will be bothered with a shit like you.'

Marvik slammed the door and marched to the car. He remained sitting in it for some time before starting the engine. He knew that Stisford was watching from the window. He just wanted to worry him.

After a few minutes he drove to the seafront where he parked close to the pleasure pier. He climbed out and crossed to the railings where he stared across the sandy bay to the cream-coloured washed Georgian houses lining it and opposite him, across the pale silver sea, the chalk downs of the Jurassic coastline of Dorset. The morning was dawning bright with a fresh, crisp wind bringing with it the smell of the sea. He considered what Stisford had told him. It was the truth. But was there more? Had he scared him enough for him to tell all? Probably. So what now? Or rather *where* now? He could call Strathen and relay what Stisford had said but there didn't seem much point because he'd told him nothing that could help them discover who had knocked on Esther's door, who she'd admitted and who had killed her. Witley was still a possibility, and Stisford could be protecting him or maybe he'd just not seen Witley, but they needed more than a possibility.

He began walking towards the seafront, but veered off left and along the old quayside, where on Monday he and Helen had been moored up waiting for the bridge to the marina to lift to permit them entry. It was still early and deserted. Later the tourists would arrive. He could return to help Strathen but he was too restless and impatient for that, and besides his skills lay in taking action not in tapping into a computer. Vince Wycombe was the answer but he would be in court until later that afternoon. He wished he could talk to Blackerman. He wondered if he should try. But that would mean a further delay because he'd have to cross to the Isle of Wight and then would probably only get a refusal, especially if Crowder had given orders that he was not to be permitted access to the prisoner.

The Isle of Wight conjured up thoughts of Ashley Palmer. Strathen had found a connection between Palmer, Charlotte and Esther and even though that might have nothing to do with any of this, as he and Strathen had discussed, there was someone who might be able to give him more information about Palmer, which might lead somewhere, he thought with desperation. It was worth a try and it would pass the time until he could confront Wycombe.

He spun round, hastened back to the car and made for a small army town in Hampshire.

SIXTEEN

The contemporary building proclaimed it was Woodlands Primary School, Bordon. It was aptly named, he thought, because he'd found it situated in a large wooded area half a mile along a turn off from the main road between Liss and Farnham just before the army base and married quarters at Bordon.

It had taken him longer to reach the small Hampshire town than he'd expected because of heavy traffic on the motorway and an accident at the service station near the Winchester turn off. It was mid-morning, and as he approached the building, he thought that Louise Tournbury, Palmer's former girlfriend, would be teaching and he'd have to hang around for another hour and a half before being able to catch her over lunch. She might not even be there, he thought, pressing the security buzzer at the door. She might be off sick or upset over her former boyfriend's disappearance, or she might have no desire to talk to him. He was pleased therefore when, after asking for her and stating that he'd like to talk to her about Ashley Palmer, she was fetched from her class and came eagerly to meet him.

'We can talk in the staff room,' she said, leading him along the corridor to a room that overlooked the playing field at the rear. The room was deserted and she informed him that no one would disturb them for another hour.

He said he hoped he wouldn't delay her that long but she waved that aside and gestured him into one of the many brightly coloured easy chairs in the slightly untidy room, and took the seat opposite across a low coffee able.

'My teaching assistant, Joanne, has taken over the class,' she said. 'It's art so the children will be happily engaged for some time and Joanne is very capable. Are you from the police?' She studied him keenly with very round dark eyes in an almost cherubic face that was open, friendly and worried. She wore no make-up or jewellery and was dressed tidily and fashionably in a knee-length skirt, dark tights and a jumper. Marvik put her about late twenties. She was a little younger than Ashley Palmer.

'No. I'm helping Shaun Strathen with his enquiries.'

'On behalf of Chiron?'

She remembered the name from when Strathen had called her earlier. Marvik nodded, thinking it was better than a lie, only it wasn't totally a lie. 'Have the police interviewed you?'

'Yes, three times. The first was a uniformed officer from the local station, the second and third were the same two detectives, DI Feeny and DS Howe. I couldn't tell them anything more on their third visit than I could on the second. Have they told you what I said?'

'No. They're keeping things pretty close to their chest.'

Her face fell. 'Because they think Ashley is a thief.' She leaned forward and said earnestly, 'I'm telling you, Mr Marvik, that is absolute rubbish.'

'Why? And it's Art.'

'Ashley is so honest that it hurts. If he found ten pence on the pavement he'd try and discover who had lost it and hand it back to them, and if he couldn't then he'd put it in a charity tin. And he loves his work. He wouldn't risk losing his job.'

'He might have been duped into giving information to someone he'd been told to meet.'

She considered this and sighed sadly. 'I suppose it is possible. He's very clever but he is rather innocent in the ways of people. But I can't see him being tricked into leaking valuable technical information; he'd know when he was being deceived in that respect.'

Not unless force was being used on him to betray that information, Marvik thought but didn't say. Witley was an ex-soldier; he knew how to use force, or perhaps he had others to do his dirty work for him.

'I understand you split up a while ago.'

'Yes, about two months after he went to work for Chiron.'

And that was a year ago. 'Can I ask why?'

She sat back and crossed her legs. 'The police asked me that. There's no big deal about it. We just drifted apart; he was very engrossed in his new job and I was, and am, in mine. Both our jobs are totally demanding, if you are committed to them, and we are. I work long hours, even though many people think teachers don't. Oh, I know we get lots of holidays,' she hastily added, as if he was going to question that as people obviously did judging by her defensive tone, 'but some of us put in a lot of extra work. I visit the children's parents, and run drama classes outside of school hours. I'm very keen to help build the children's confidence at a young age. And we run breakfast and after-school clubs as well as providing extra reading and maths classes. I'm also involved in the local forces community. Ash and I just ran out of time to be together, especially as I live in Petersfield and he lives in Southampton and he doesn't drive so for him it means taking two trains and for me a thirty-four-mile drive. Not that it would have mattered, you'd probably say, if we were really in love, but it became more and more awkward for us to spend time together. And we just sort of stopped. Neither of us was particularly upset. I think we were both rather relieved to have the time to concentrate on our jobs. He was very excited about the applications he was developing.'

'There was more than one?'

'Of course. There always is, so Ash says.'

And that bore out what Strathen had told him earlier.

'One application can have implications for other things, there is always a crossover, and Ash is always looking for that. His head is continually buzzing with ideas; he's a natural inventor. He was so pleased to work with Chiron on developing better movement for amputees and those suffering from neurological illnesses. His passion is to help others, and not commercial or military exploitation.'

'But his work will be commercially exploited. Whatever he develops will be sold.'

'I know but he didn't see it like that. As I told you he really isn't very commercially aware. I think he'd have been better suited working for a charity – but then a lot of charities, unless they are medical ones with considerable research funding, don't have the need or the money for the sort of work Ash specializes in. But Chiron work with charities.'

'Did Ashley tell you this?'

'Yes. I know he'd been in touch with some.'

'Did he mention which ones?'

'He might have done. I can't remember. We are both heavily involved with MPCU though – Marine Preservation and Clean Up,' she explained.

Marvik recalled the photograph that DS Howe had shown him of Palmer. He'd been wearing a baggy white T-shirt emblazoned with a logo and the words 'Caring for the Marine Environment' written underneath it. But that charity couldn't have any connection with Chiron or Danavere.

Louise Tournbury said, 'Ashley was always looking at ways to improve diving because that's where we see a lot of underwater pollution – under the sea. It's a huge dumping ground and we're doing immeasurable damage. People think it doesn't affect them but it does. The oceans provide food, transportation and oxygen for us to breathe.'

Marvik knew that from his own diving experiences, both with his parents on and around wrecks and in the Special Boat Services. In the latter case, some of those problems included dealing with underwater explosive devices planted in key and critical locations.

'Ashley hasn't dived with the club for over a year,' she added. 'He might have dived with someone else or another operator but he didn't mention it when I saw him at Christmas at the diving club.'

'I thought he was no longer a member,' Marvik said, recalling what Strathen had reported.

'He's not but I asked him if he'd like to come to the club's Christmas bash as my guest. It isn't usually Ash's style, he's not a natural socialiser, but he accepted and seemed to enjoy himself. In fact I was surprised because it was unlike him to be so sociable.'

Marvik wondered if her comment about the change in Palmer's

personality was significant. 'And he wasn't usually like that?' he probed.

'He's usually quiet, reserved, an introvert. The opposite to me.' She smiled and pushed her hair back from her face.

'Why do you think he was more outgoing the last time you saw him?'

'I don't know. He didn't say.'

'Do you think he could have a new girlfriend?'

'The police asked me that and I said no, and I still say no. I'm sure that Ash would have told me.'

'Perhaps he thought it would upset you.'

'He wouldn't think like that. We're very good friends. He wouldn't let me worry like this.'

Marvik couldn't see how questioning her further on that subject could get him anywhere. In fact he didn't think anything she was telling him could link with Charlotte's disappearance.

'Have you kept in touch?' Marvik could hear footsteps outside and voices. He hoped they weren't going to be disturbed. The sound of children's laughter came from a distant classroom.

'Only the occasional text,' she said. The voices and footsteps moved away.

'Not on the social networks?'

'No. Ash has nothing to do with them. He says they're an invasion of privacy and open to abuse. I'm afraid he's right. I try to tell the children that in a way they can understand.'

'Surely they're too young.' The oldest would only be about eleven, he thought.

'You wanna bet? Even if they are too young to register on the websites they are still exposed to them at home through parents and siblings. I suspect that some of them know how to fake their age and register. Ash is right, it's a minefield.' She sighed and looked troubled. 'I can't think what has happened to him or where he is. It's not like him. I can't believe he'd take off with confidential information. He seemed so happy, so energized by what he was doing.'

'Does he have any friends?'

'There were some from his university days, but that was years ago, and there's the diving club members, but apart from that no. I asked those detectives if they'd found anything in his house to help but if they did they didn't tell me. They asked me if he used a computer at home. I told them he had a laptop. They didn't find it, and as I haven't been to his house for a year I couldn't help them by telling them if anything was missing.'

She tried to take a surreptitious glance at her watch.

'I won't keep you much longer.'

'It's fine.' But she looked fretful. Marvik didn't think that was because he was keeping her from her class but because his questions had heightened her concern for her former boyfriend. She continued, 'The police also asked me about Ash's finances, whether he gambled or liked to drink. I said no on both counts. Material things don't matter to Ash. He's not into status symbols or accumulating wealth. If anyone offered him money for what he was working on then he'd only look bewildered by it.'

'And did he tell you what he was working on?'

Her face screwed up as she tried to recall. 'He talked about intelligent software that uses electrodes to record signals from the brain to the muscles and how it could help people with brain injuries, and send messages to prosthetic limbs to make people with them move more naturally and feel sensations. And he mentioned something about face-recognition software, object detection and analysis. I only remember that because he mentioned it in relation to diving, screening what's inside wrecks, but I'm afraid a lot of it went over my head.'

'And have you any idea why he would go to the Isle of Wight to a derelict coastguard cottage?'

'None. We've dived off the Isle of Wight though.'

And maybe that was what had been on offer: a dive.

'Is he in danger?' she asked, searching his face for an answer. She deserved a truthful one, not a fob off. 'I think so.'

'Because of his work?'

'It's linked to it but I don't know how. Did he ever mention a woman called Charlotte Churley?'

She shook her head.

Marvik decided to reveal something of the truth. 'It's why I'm here asking questions. I *am* working with Shaun Strathen as I told you, but we're both also trying to find the whereabouts of Charlotte who went missing the day after Ashley and we believe there's a link.'

'How?'

'We don't know except that she nursed service personnel amputees. I wondered if Ashley might have met her, if he'd visited the

Queen Elizabeth Hospital Birmingham in the course of his research for Chiron. Charlotte's a nurse there.'

'He never mentioned it.'

'Does the name Paul Williamson or Terence Blackerman mean anything to you?'

'No.'

'Or Esther Shannon?'

'No. I'm sorry, I've never heard of any of them.'

Which also meant that Feeny and Howe hadn't asked her about them. But then Marvik hadn't thought they would – not Esther Shannon or Terence Blackerman at any rate, they wouldn't know about that, but why hadn't they asked her about Charlotte? Had they dismissed any link between the two missing persons' cases on their patch, or perhaps, as he'd thought earlier, they weren't working on the case and another team had been briefed. Crowder's team could be handling Charlotte's disappearance; he had no idea how many officers Crowder had at his command. He rose, thanking her for her time.

She sprang up. 'I'll see you out.' As they walked along the corridor she said, 'Will you keep me informed? I'll give you my mobile number.'

'Of course. And if you remember anything that might help, it doesn't matter what it is, or how insignificant you think it might be, will you call me?'

She nodded. They halted outside the reception office. Marvik gave her his own personal mobile phone number. He switched it on and saw that Strathen had tried to contact him twice. In the car he rang him back.

'Where are you?' Strathen asked.

Marvik quickly told him and relayed the outcome of his meeting with John Stisford and Louise Tournbury. 'Have you got something?'

'Yes. Vera's come up trumps,' Strathen said excitedly. 'There are three fund-raising dinners that Esther organized for Danavere, an autumn celebrity dinner in 1996, a spring auction in 1997 and a summer ball in 1997, all in London. I have the guest lists. There are a handful of people who appear at every bash but one of the names jumps out and slaps you right in the face. Vince Wycombe.'

'So he knew Esther,' Marvik said contemplatively.

'He must have done.'

'And did he declare this interest at Blackerman's trial?'

'What do you think?' Strathen scoffed.

No. And that was another question in a long and growing list that he was very keen to put to Vince Wycombe QC – and the sooner the better.

SEVENTEEN

Portsmouth Crown Court had risen for lunch. Marvik was tempted to send in a message requesting an interview with Wycombe – the name Esther Shannon would guarantee him an audience – but he wanted to get the feel of the man first. And the best way to do that was to see him in action in court, even though he wasn't defending but sitting as a judge.

He bought some sandwiches and a can of drink and took both to the old fortifications in Old Portsmouth, built in the 1420s over-looking the narrow entrance to Portsmouth Harbour. The city's importance as a naval base meant that it was one of the most heavily defended in Europe. It made Marvik again think about the navy possibly being behind both Esther's death and the more recent developments. But how could they be involved? Certainly they would have no connection if this was related to a fraud that was being perpetuated.

The blustery cold wind meant he had the old tower to himself and his thoughts returned to his conversation with Louise Tournbury. According to her, Palmer was keen, intelligent, normally introverted but had displayed a sudden burst of uncharacteristic animation and sociability at Christmas. Why? Because there was a new woman in his life, despite what Louise thought? But if so then why hadn't the police found her or why hadn't she come forward? Perhaps she had and the police hadn't told Louise because they had no reason to.

Or perhaps, it suddenly occurred to Marvik, the new woman was Charlotte. He let his mind run along those lines. Charlotte was older than Ashley Palmer but that accounted for nothing, and normally he would have said that Ashley Palmer wasn't Charlotte's type but how did he know that for certain? Perhaps they had met at a medical seminar organized by Danavere. Charlotte might have been intending to meet up with Palmer on the island after visiting Blackerman, but no, she would have said if that was the case. But it was just possible that Palmer had been told he was meeting Charlotte. Perhaps Palmer had been sent a false text message, ostensibly from Charlotte, asking him to meet her.

He took a swig from his drink and watched the largest of the Wightlink Ferries, the St Clare, sail out of the harbour across the five-mile stretch of the Solent to the Isle of Wight. He could see the houses of Ryde rising on the hill slopes and the Downs beyond it stretching out to the west and east. The location of Palmer's supposed rendezvous was on the far eastern coast of the island and not visible from where Marvik was sitting. There was another reason for Palmer's heightened excitement just before Christmas, he thought. Palmer could have met someone who had promised him new and great things connected with funding his research and he'd been tricked into meeting this person on the island.

Marvik polished off his sandwiches. It was time he was heading back to court. He took a seat at the front of the public gallery and watched the court room assemble. Wycombe entered last. The court rose. As the session opened Marvik tuned out the lawyer speak and studied the tall, lean and distinguished looking man with an angular lined face and fair complexion. Crowder had told him that Wycombe was fifty-seven. He looked his age although he was well preserved. Marvik wondered what he'd looked like seventeen years ago. Then he'd have been a successful barrister, on the brink of being made Queen's Counsel, a mark of outstanding ability. Beneath the bench wig Marvik could see flecks of silver-grey hair. In 1997 it had probably been fair or light brown. Wycombe had a keen expression tinged with a slightly superior air. Marvik expected the session to last at least until four but as his concentration focused back on the barrister standing and speaking, he heard him say that his client had changed his plea. That was it. The jury was dismissed. The trial and the session was over. Wycombe left. The court emptied.

Outside Marvik called Strathen on the pay-as-you-go mobile and told him what had happened. He relayed his idea that Charlotte and Ashley might have met at a medical seminar or conference and Strathen said he'd get on to it. Marvik added, 'I'm heading for Wycombe's house at Itchenor. He'll show up there sooner or later.'

An hour later he was parking the car, not in Copse Road, but in the driveway of a house that led down to the quay. It had taken him a while to find the right property, a holiday home, which would have no possibility of being occupied on a damp day in early March. And it was perfect as it was almost opposite the entrance to Copse Road.

He climbed out, zapped the car shut and headed for Wycombe's house, his brain computing how long it would take to walk, or run if necessary, back to the car. There were no vehicles parked along the road, a fact he'd noted on his earlier exploration by taxi. And although there was nothing to stop anyone parking, no yellow lines prohibiting it, it wasn't the sort of road where casual visitors left their vehicles, not only because there was no reason to park here – there being no shops, offices or access to the sea – but because visitors and tradesmen would be admitted to the inner sanctum of the exclusive properties which lay behind the electronic gates, and that meant any parked vehicle would be noticed and probably noted and that was the last thing Marvik wanted.

When he reached Wycombe's house he didn't even look at it but turned right on to a narrow, muddy footpath surrounded on either side by woods. From here he scrambled into the wood, wishing it was any season but winter when the leaves would have given him better protection. But the day had turned overcast and the night would draw in quicker because of it. The twilight, then darkness, would give him plenty of cover. And from here he could survey the house.

The electronic gates across the entrance would open as Wycombe approached and pressed his remote control. His car would glide in and the gates slowly close behind him giving Marvik plenty of time to run from his cover into the driveway but not enough to run the length of the driveway and accost Wycombe as he climbed out of the car, and for all Marvik knew there could be dogs, although he hadn't seen or heard any. He needed to get to Wycombe before he entered the driveway. In fact before those gates swung open. He had to assume that his car would be centrally locked and that he wouldn't be able to jump inside. He toyed with the idea of announcing himself perhaps to Wycombe's wife or a housekeeper with a request to speak to Wycombe. He could make up a story to gain admittance but he wasn't sure he'd be granted it. There was only one thing he could do, and that was to step forward as Wycombe pulled up and, as the gates slowly swung open, stand in front of the vehicle and refuse to budge until Wycombe was forced to let down his window and demand a reason for his behaviour, no doubt with one hand stretched out for his phone to summon help.

Marvik would hear Wycombe's car approaching and see the vehicle's headlights. He wouldn't be able to swear it was Wycombe's car though because he had no idea what he drove, but there would be time enough from when Wycombe pulled up for Marvik to reach him before he could drive in.

He could wait. No matter how long it took. He crouched down on a tree trunk, using it as a makeshift seat, and pulled up the collar of his jacket. The trees and shrubs gave him some protection from the wind and the fitful rain. He didn't let his mind wander but concentrated on the job ahead, focusing only on that and the outcome he required. He couldn't afford to miss this chance and he wasn't going to.

He heard several cars but none of them came this far. Then a vehicle approached. He saw the headlights. He sprang up and broke cover as it stopped outside the house, but with surprise and annoyance Marvik saw Helen climb out of a taxi. He cursed. She swung round and as she did another car approached and even before it reached them Marvik knew it was Wycombe. She was going to spoil everything. She must have overheard Strathen on the phone, or perhaps she'd seen the list that Vera at Danavere had forwarded, and she knew where Wycombe lived because they'd come here in the taxi after interviewing Amelia Snow at Bognor Regis.

'You're not going to stop me,' she blazed, as the taxi drove off and Wycombe's car drew nearer. She raced to the electronic gates and stood solidly in front of Wycombe's car as it swung towards her, just as Marvik had intended to do. Marvik registered Wycombe's shock and saw him reach for the mobile phone lying on the passenger seat.

'Esther Shannon,' shouted Helen.

Wycombe's hand froze.

Marvik stepped towards the driver's side. 'Let down the window,' he commanded. Again Wycombe's fingers flexed for his phone. 'I wouldn't do that if I was you, not unless you want the police and the judiciary to know why you withheld vital information.'

The window slid down. 'Who are you? What do you want?' Wycombe tried to sound confident but Marvik detected a hint of fear in his cultured tones.

Before Marvik could continue though, Helen, who had marched

around to the window, her expression furious, shouted, 'I want to know why you killed my sister.'

Wycombe's eyes widened with shock, then alarm. They shifted nervously towards the house as Helen continued, 'And if you don't tell me then I am going to make sure all your precious lawyer friends know exactly what you did.'

Marvik could see Wycombe rapidly mentally weighing up his chances. Deny it, bluff it out or admit it? Marvik said, 'We have proof that you knew Esther and that you forgot to admit this when defending the man convicted of killing her. Helen and I can make enough noise so that no matter how many times you say it's not true people will begin to think it is. No smoke without fire,' he sneered.

Wycombe threw an anxious gaze at the house. 'Can't we talk this over later?'

Helen thrust her angry face forward. 'No, we bloody can't. I want to know why you killed her or shall I go inside and tell your wife that you're a murderer.' She made to move towards the house.

'No!' His nervous gaze shifted between them. Then he took a breath. More evenly he said, 'OK. Let me move the car.'

'Not without me inside,' Helen said, making to climb into the rear. But Wycombe had the central locking on.

'Get out, Wycombe,' ordered Marvik. 'We'll discuss this over there.' He jerked his head at the woods.

'My wife will wonder why I've left the car here.'

'Then let her bloody wonder,' Helen snapped.

'She might call the police.'

'Good, then we can tell them you strangled my sister seventeen years ago.'

'They won't believe you.'

'You're forgetting we have proof,' Marvik said.

'You can't have because I didn't kill her.'

'But you did know her.'

Impatiently Helen interjected, 'I'll call the police for you. It will force them to re-examine my sister's murder. Or perhaps I should just call the newspapers.'

'No.' The car door opened and Wycombe scrambled out.

Eyeing them warily he stepped across to the edge of the woods. Marvik scanned the area to see if anyone was taking any notice of them but it was as quiet as a wet winter Sunday at the seaside.

Marvik threw Helen a pointed look, willing her to let him handle this, but she was too irate for that.

'OK then, so why did you kill her? What the hell had Esther done to harm you?'

'I didn't kill her,' he repeated.

Marvik quickly broke in. 'No, you just slept with her.'

'Not on the day she was killed,' he hastily replied.

'But on the previous night, the Friday before she attended the Remembrance Service, she was with you in your London flat. How long had you been having an affair with her?'

Wycombe ran a hand through his hair. Clearly rattled he said, 'This mustn't come out. My wife mustn't know. It will ruin me.'

'Should have thought about that before you decided to seduce my sister.'

'She was a grown woman. I didn't seduce or force her. It happened. We were attracted to one another. It was just one of those things.'

Helen snorted.

'I was sorry when she was killed.'

'Sorry!' Helen spat with fury.

If she'd had a gun Marvik thought she might have shot him. But Wycombe seemed to find refuge in her anger. He was regaining his confidence and there was a superior expression now on his angular face. He was a clever man and Marvik could see he was calculating how he could squirm out of this. Helen was mentally unbalanced, she didn't know what she was saying, she'd persuaded her boyfriend to go along with her. Wycombe had friends in high places, no one would believe them. The fact his name was on some guest lists that Esther had compiled meant nothing. It was time to take a different approach.

Marvik balled his fist and struck Wycombe, not with all his force, just a tap as far as Marvik's fists were concerned, but it was enough to make the man reel back and stumble to the ground. He put a hand to his bloody mouth and stared up at Marvik, shocked and petrified. Helen's surprised expression gave way to a grim smile of satisfaction and the anger seemed to drain out of her.

Marvik towered over Wycombe. 'Let's start again. You and Esther met while she was organizing an event for Danavere, her employer.'

Wycombe nodded. 'The first time was April 1996.'

'And the affair started when?'

Wycombe coughed nervously and put his hand in his pocket. Marvik stepped menacingly forward. 'I need a handkerchief,' Wycombe said, clearly terrified. Marvik nodded. Wycombe withdrew a handkerchief and placed it to his cut mouth. 'After that I called her at work and said that if she was in London again soon, would she like to have dinner with me. We could discuss how my Chambers, and my friends at the Bar, could help raise funds for the charities that Danavere supported. We had dinner two weeks later and it developed from there.'

Helen said, 'Did she know you were married?'

'Yes.'

'I suppose you told her your wife didn't understand you,' she sneered. 'Or that you would leave her when the time was right, which would be never.'

'I know it was wrong, which was why it had to end. I told her the night before she was killed that it was over.'

'Oh great. And you expected her to walk away?' Helen scoffed.

'She was upset. But she'd get over it. She did, and pretty quickly,' he added spitefully.

Wycombe was referring to Esther having slept with Blackerman. Marvik saw that Helen had also registered this and it confused her into a silence that Marvik took advantage of. He said, 'The next day she was dead. Did she threaten to expose the affair, call your wife, tell your Head of Chambers? Or perhaps when you went to visit her at the Union Services Club on Saturday evening to plead with her not to tell anyone about the affair, you discovered her in bed with another man. That really hurt your male ego. You waited until Blackerman left and then you went inside and strangled her, knowing the police would think it was Blackerman. You then made a pretence of defending him and making such a balls-up of it that he got convicted and you had your revenge.'

Marvik could feel Helen's eyes on him. It fitted with what he knew of the case. 'Blackerman has protested his innocence for years but you, through your contacts, have made sure he stayed inside and any appeal quashed. You and your cronies in the old-boy network have stuck together. You wiped the room clean of your fingerprints. And made certain that whatever DNA was found in that room somehow got contaminated. Besides, you were well in with the police, you knew Detective Inspector Bryan Grainger, and had worked with him on several cases, where you'd not only defended but prosecuted.' That was a guess on Marvik's part but not such a wild one and he could see he was right by Wycombe's increasingly horrified expression. 'So between you, you made sure that Blackerman went down for it. Grainger got a result and you got let off the hook.'

'This is ridiculous. It's not true,' he blustered.

His protest sounded genuine but there was something not right about the force of it. Marvik smelled a different fear, one that went deeper than he'd sensed before. Perhaps because he was close to the truth, or perhaps because for the first time Wycombe realized he could be in the frame for a murder he hadn't committed.

Marvik pressed on. 'When Grainger retired he thought back over his cases; perhaps he threatened to blackmail you. Perhaps by then he'd developed a conscience and wanted the record to be put straight. He asked to meet you in Brighton. When you saw he was serious you couldn't let the truth come out, so you watched him walk away and then cold-bloodedly ran him down. What was one more murder, after all? And you'd get away with that too. So where is she, Wycombe? Where's Charlotte? Have you killed her too? Did you take her out on your boat and throw her body in the Solent?'

'I don't know what you're talking about. I don't know anyone called Charlotte.'

Marvik stepped closer to Wycombe and towered over him. Wycombe shrunk back fearfully. Marvik saw the terror in his grey eyes. 'Oh, but you do. You'll tell me where she is – or do I have to beat it out of you?'

'I swear I've never heard of Charlotte and I didn't kill Grainger. I knew he was dead—'

'How?'

'I read about it in the newspapers.'

'Bollocks.'

'Duncan Ross told me.'

'Why would he do that?'

Wycombe looked taken aback and then quickly tried to recover himself. 'I know him through my work. He mentioned it to me one day when I was sitting at Chichester court.'

It was a lie. 'When?'

'I can't remember.'

'Is he blackmailing you?'

'Of course not. Why should he?'

'Because he was on the Esther Shannon murder case.'

'He's not blackmailing me.'

Marvik saw the relief on Wycombe's face. He'd got that wrong. More confidently now Wycombe added, 'I was with my wife the night Esther was killed.'

'And no doubt with her when Grainger was killed,' sniped Marvik. 'But perhaps we should do as Helen says and let the police investigate. They can check your alibi and no doubt if they do your wife will swear she was with you. She'll want to protect that lovely way of life you've given her.' Marvik waved his arm in the direction of the house. 'And maybe you'll call up your influential friends, the barristers and judges you know, the politicians and police commissioners, and ask them to exert pressure to bury the investigation. Perhaps you'll ask whoever you're in league with to silence me and Helen as you've silenced Esther, Grainger and Charlotte. You may also have silenced Ashley Palmer.' Marvik watched carefully for a reaction to the name and was pleased when he got one. It was fleeting, just a moment's surprise before it was gone. 'But even if you do, as Helen says, before they kill us there'll be enough time for us to stir up plenty of trouble and to make several people curious enough to start asking questions. And once they do, there'll be a stain on you that will spread like blood on that handkerchief.'

Wycombe stared at it as though he'd never seen it before. Marvik took hold of Helen's arm.

'What are you doing?' she cried as he pulled her away. 'You're not going to leave it like that?' She struggled to push him off but his grip was too strong.

'We're going to the police. No, on second thoughts we're not.'

'But—'

Marvik turned back and addressed the man on the ground. 'We'll let Mr Wycombe phone them and report how I assaulted him. I'll look forward to explaining why.'

He pulled Helen away, very much against her will.

'What the hell do you think you're doing?' she raged, as reluctantly she had no choice but to go with him. 'He's as guilty as hell.'

Marvik said nothing.

'Let me go,' she cried.

He spun round on her but didn't stop walking. 'Just do what I say.'

'Why the—'

'Do it.'

She glared at him. Marvik heard a car start up and turning he saw Wycombe's Mercedes glide in through the gates of his house. It was a mile to where he had parked Strathen's Volvo, and after about half a mile he let her go.

'So that's it? You're doing nothing,' she raged, rubbing her arm.

'If he's innocent he'll call the police and report the assault, and the police will interview me. But we both know he won't because the last thing Wycombe wants is the police involved and by not reporting it we know he's involved in Esther's death.'

'We knew that anyway,' she spat scornfully.

'We didn't. We only knew that his name was on the lists of three events that Esther organized.'

'But he admitted the affair.'

'To us he did. But how can we prove that? He could say he made that up to get rid of us, because I was threatening him. There is no proof, Helen. It's our word against his and I'm a former commando with a mental health problem, and you're the sister of a murdered woman who is also mentally disturbed by it. You want revenge on someone and you just happened to focus that revenge on him. And if he does report it and the police come to charge me with assault, how are they going to find me?'

'Eh?'

'He doesn't know who I am. He didn't ask my name. I didn't give it and you didn't utter it. Maybe he didn't ask because he already knows who I am, and if he does then he knows far more than he told us.'

She frowned as she thought this through. 'OK, so what's he going to do next?'

'That's why we're walking away. It's what I need to know.'

'I still don't understand.'

'Maybe you will soon. You shouldn't have come. How did you get away from Shaun?'

'He wasn't keeping me prisoner,' she snapped.

'He was trying to keep you safe.'

'Well he didn't do a very good job of it.'

And was that what Shaun would think? Marvik recalled their earlier conversation. Helen bolting for it wasn't going to boost Shaun's self-confidence.

'A neighbour knocked on his door and asked him if he'd fix a light for her. I ducked out as soon as he was gone.'

'When?'

'About three fifteen.'

'Did he see you leave?'

'If he did he didn't shout after me or chase me if that's what you mean.'

'He could hardly do that with his leg,' Marvik snarled.

'No,' she answered sulkily.

Marvik hoped she felt guilty. They'd reached the car. He zapped it open and swiftly appraised the area. There was no one in sight. Climbing in and stretching the seat belt across him he asked her how she had got there.

'The hard way, because my car is still outside my house, or I assume it is,' she grumbled. 'I walked to Hamble railway station and caught a train to Fareham and then another to Chichester where I got a taxi here. It cost me a fortune.'

Marvik pulled away and switched on the windscreen wipers. 'So what time was the train from Hamble?'

'Four minutes past four. It was six minutes late though.'

And Marvik hadn't received a message from Strathen to say that Helen had gone because he'd turned off both phones before he'd entered the court and hadn't turned them back on yet. Maybe Strathen had left him a message. He'd check later.

Marvik pointed the car in the direction of the main road, his eyes flicking to his mirrors and scouring the many turn offs and side streets on the way. There was very little traffic about. He said nothing but his head was buzzing. Soon he'd know if he was correct.

Within five minutes he was turning left on to the B2179 and another two miles took him to the junction of the A286 and the main road north to Chichester. Several cars sped past him heading south but there was very little going in his direction and nothing behind him but as he passed the road leading to the marina a car pulled out behind them. It kept a safe distance back. It was too soon anyway he thought for someone to be following them.

The countryside opened up on both sides, punctuated by a few scattered properties, their lights flickering in the heavy rain. The vehicle behind drew closer. The headlights were high, a Range Rover thought Marvik. He was drawing level with the turning to Dell Quay and a short cut that led up to Fishbourne avoiding the large and traffic clogged roundabout at Chichester. He indicated left. The Range Rover followed. But then the driver was probably doing the same: it was a popular rat run. After a hundred yards Marvik indicated right, on to a narrow lane. The Range Rover stuck behind him. Marvik again glanced in his mirrors.

'What is it?' asked Helen, twisting round in her seat. 'Jesus!' she exclaimed as Marvik rammed his foot on the accelerator. The Range Rover loomed large behind them. Suddenly it was level on the tiny narrow road. Nothing was ahead, except a sharp left-hand bend. It happened in a second. There was a sickening thud as the Range Rover rammed into the side of them. Helen cried out. Marvik tried desperately to keep the car on the road but the second and violent impact from the Range Rover pushed it over the edge into the undergrowth. He heard Helen's screams as the Volvo ripped and tore into the shrubs. Ahead was a dense wooded area. He had to avoid it at all costs. The impact could be fatal. With his heart racing, the blood pounding in his ears, he pulled hard right on the steering wheel. The car lurched and veered. He slammed his foot on the brake. He had seconds between life and death. Then nothing. Only silence.

EIGHTEEN

Marvik moved his head. A shooting pain almost fried his brain. He cried out. He forced himself to concentrate, to shut out the agony. Time to feel pain later. The urgent voice inside him told him he had to get away, the more he delayed the greater the danger. From what though? He tried to think, to clear his mind. After a few seconds – it could have been longer – he opened his eyes. The pain was still there but not so sharp now, instead it had turned to a deep throbbing ache, which he was much more accustomed to and which he could handle. Slowly his mind resurfaced and the vague notion of danger sharpened into the reality that he'd been forced off the road into the undergrowth and that whoever had done it could return at any moment to make sure he was dead. And not just him but the woman beside him.

He twisted round to find Helen slumped in her seat. Fear gripped his heart. He pressed his fingers to her neck. Thank God, there was a strong pulse. He retrieved a slim pencil torch from his jacket pocket and played its meagre light over her. There was no physical damage to her face, no cuts, and as far as he could tell no bones protruding from her slender body, but he'd seen dead men and women without a mark on them. She was alive, yes, but could she move? Would the driver of the Range Rover return to finish what he'd started? Or would he hope that the accident on a wet night and slippery road on a narrow twisting country lane had claimed two victims? Marvik wasn't going to hang around to find out. They'd already been here too long.

He shook her gently and called her name. There was no response. He tried again, this time shaking her with more pressure and gently tapping her face. If necessary he'd have to carry her, but his efforts were rewarded with a groan. He continued to urge her to wake up.

'Helen,' he repeated. They had to get moving.

'Huh?' she groaned, slowly surfacing into consciousness. But he didn't have time for 'slowly'.

'Can you move?' he urged.

'I . . .'

'I'll help you.' Swiftly he climbed out of the car and hurried to the passenger door, his eyes taking in his surroundings. They were on the edge of the wood. He'd managed to stop the car before hurtling too deep into it and miraculously without striking the trees. He strained his ears for the sound of human movement but all he could hear was the wind in the trees and the rain bouncing off the car roof. He wrenched open the car door, relieved that it hadn't been jammed by the collision. Swiftly, he ran his torch over Helen, again checking for broken bones and cuts, but she was unscathed. But his torch picked out the scars on her right forearm where the sleeve of the jacket had ridden up. They hadn't been done recently.

'Come on.' He took hold of her left arm.

Slowly she slid out of the seat, wincing and giving a small cry of pain, falling against him.

'I'll carry you.'

'No. I'll be fine. I'm OK,' she insisted, clearly making an effort to pull herself together.

Marvik swiftly surveyed the area. They were still alone. He had no idea of the extent of the wood or what was on the other side of it. Going deeper would give them cover but the killer, if he returned

– and Marvik felt sure he would – on seeing they had left the car would assume that was where they had headed. The natural instinct was to go deeper into cover so that meant they wouldn't. They couldn't go back either, because the road was in that direction. And heading east meant crossing the road he'd just been forced off. There was only one direction and it led towards the harbour.

Taking Helen's hand he half pulled and half dragged her westwards. He estimated the harbour was about a mile away. It was pitch dark, wet and the terrain was uneven and dangerous. Trees seemed to loom out of nowhere causing Helen to start. He was used to working in such conditions but Helen frequently stumbled against him and supporting her he led her as swiftly as he could through the undergrowth until they came out on a small clearing and a hedgerow. He guided her through a break in the hedge and into a field beyond. She slipped and he pulled her up. The ground was sodden, their shoes and boots were caked in mud. They were both soaked to the skin but Marvik was certain no one was behind them.

'Not far now,' he encouraged.

He didn't see her expression but he probably thought it dubious.

'Where are we going?'

'Where it's safe.'

Ahead in the gloom he caught sight of a building. It was a small church. It would be locked. They couldn't stay there. He urged her onwards. She groaned but he could tell she was beginning to recover from her dazed and confused state when she said, 'You sure know how to show a girl a good time.'

He smiled. 'Not far now.'

They had to be close to the shore by now. They were following the edge of a field, then another hedgerow and finally they came out on the shoreline of the Fishbourne Channel. It was a long trek north to civilization but not so far to the south where there was a sailing club, a handful of very expensive houses and a pub bordering the channel at the small waterside hamlet of the one-time Roman port of Dell Quay. There he could call for help. He just hoped the Range Rover driver hadn't come to the same conclusion. But if he had there would be too many people around for him to try anything and too many who would be able to remember him if necessary at a later date. If the tide had been in Marvik thought he might have stolen a boat and taken it across the channel, but there was nothing except mud ahead of them in the dark night. He couldn't even see the slither of water.

There was no Range Rover in the pub car park. Marvik didn't think they'd get much of a welcome given their bedraggled and mud-spattered state, but when he asked to speak to the manager and explained they'd had a car accident they were ushered towards the roaring fire, offered drinks and help. Helen was shivering violently. It was the shock of the accident as well as being half dragged through the sodden countryside. Marvik removed his jacket and placed it around her shoulders. She took it willingly.

They drew some curious looks from a handful of customers enjoying an early evening meal but thankfully the pub wasn't crowded. Marvik ordered a small brandy for Helen and the same for himself and then excused himself, stepping towards the door and far enough away from flapping ears but close enough to keep an eye on Helen. Her dark make-up had smudged and run down her pale, drawn face making her look like a vampire with her purple hair, and he silently applauded the manager for taking them both at face value and not turning up her nose at them, especially when he saw his reflection in the glass of the door. With his scarred and mud-smeared face he thought the manager would have had every right to summon the police and have them thrown out for looking like refugees from a horror movie.

He found three messages on his mobile phones: two on the pay-as-you-go mobile Crowder had given him and the other on his own mobile. They were all from Strathen and Marvik reckoned they were to tell him that Helen had done a bunk. He didn't play them but entered a number on his pay-as-you-go phone and pressed it to his ear. It was answered almost immediately.

'Where the hell are you?' Strathen demanded.

Marvik told him.

'I'll be there in five minutes, maybe three.'

'That soon!'

'Yes.' He rang off leaving Marvik puzzled but grateful. He returned to Helen, who was sipping her drink. She was still shivering but some colour was beginning to return to her cheeks.

'The cavalry's on its way. Won't be long. Stay here.'

'I have no intention of moving.'

He swallowed his drink and felt the welcoming warmth of the liquor slide down his throat. He told the manager that a friend was on his way to pick them up. Marvik stepped outside. The night was quiet. The weather was keeping most people at home, thank goodness.

As he waited for Strathen, several questions he'd postponed on their trek through the countryside resurfaced. Had the Range Rover driver returned to the Volvo and discovered they'd gone? If he hadn't returned then why not? That would have been sloppy but perhaps his intention was to scare rather than to kill. That didn't fit with the profile of Esther Shannon's killer though. Many more questions buzzed around his throbbing head but he put them aside as he caught the sound of a car approaching. He stepped back into the shadows until he saw the vehicle swing into the car park and a man climb slightly awkwardly from it. Marvik stepped forward.

'What the hell happened?' Strathen asked anxiously.

'Someone didn't like me being on the same road as him. I'm afraid there's a bit of damage to your car.'

'Sod that,' Strathen readily dismissed. 'Is Helen OK?'

'Apart from being cold, wet and in shock, yes. She's inside the pub. We need to get her somewhere safe.'

'Leave it to me.' Strathen reached for his phone as Marvik returned to the pub. He fetched Helen and they climbed into the rear of the taxi as Strathen climbed in the front and gave directions to the driver to head for Arundel, ten miles east of Chichester. Helen said nothing. Perhaps she was too wet and too dazed to enquire where they were going. Marvik had no idea who Strathen was taking them to.

Before they reached the market town with its eleventh-century castle, the family home of the Dukes of Norfolk, perched high on its hill, Strathen gave directions to the driver to turn off and soon they were winding their way through a small estate of bungalows. The driver pulled up outside a large one on a corner plot and the door opened immediately to reveal a couple in their mid-thirties.

Strathen paid off the driver and swiftly introduced Colin and Amy Chester. Colin Chester, like Strathen, was an amputee. Strathen didn't need to explain where they'd met, but he did. It was at the military rehabilitation centre at Headley Court in Surrey. Colin Chester was ex-army.

The bungalow had been extended and Amy Chester led Marvik and Helen to the bedrooms on the right of the property. 'The bathroom's next door,' she said, indicating beyond the guest bedroom.

'The main bedroom beyond the bathroom has an en-suite. The twins are in the bedroom opposite. They're five. They won't disturb you.'

Marvik could hear them talking through the slightly open door. He told Helen to take the main bedroom and en suite and he'd shower in the family bathroom adjoining the spare room.

Amy Chester said, 'I'll let you have some of Colin's clothes and Helen you can borrow some of mine. I'll bring them in. Let me have your dirty things and I'll run them through the washing machine.'

'This is very good of you.'

But she waved aside Marvik's gratitude. 'There are fresh towels in both bathrooms but if you need anything just ask.'

Marvik quickly showered and found Colin's clothes laid out on the king-sized bed in the tastefully decorated and modern guest bedroom when he emerged. They were a goodish fit. Chester, like Strathen, kept himself fit and both had good upper body strength. He bundled up his own sodden and soiled clothes and took them into the kitchen at the rear of the house which had been cleverly extended into the garden. He couldn't see how big the latter was but there were no lights of houses beyond it so either it backed on to bungalows or the countryside.

Strathen and Chester were seated at the table in the kitchen. Strathen spoke. 'Helen and I can stay here for a couple of days.'

Colin, a fair-haired man with a keen expression, said, 'For as long as you need to.'

'Thanks.'

'You're welcome to stay too, Art, but Shaun says you might have other arrangements. I'll contact the garage in the morning and get the Volvo towed here.'

Marvik felt bad about the Volvo being out of action because it would restrict Strathen's mobility. He began to apologize but Strathen made light of it.

'Taxis will do for now.'

'I can take you anywhere you need to go,' Chester volunteered.

Marvik wondered how much Shaun had told Colin Chester of their mission. Probably enough but not too much. Looking at him, Marvik saw a man intelligent enough to have joined up some of the dots but he wouldn't be able to complete the picture because not even he and Shaun could do that yet. Perhaps they might never be able to and that thought horrified him and made him even more determined to find out what the hell was going on.

To Strathen, Marvik said, 'Can you continue working from here?'

'Yes.' He was prevented from saying more by the arrival of Amy Chester with Helen. She was dressed in black trousers and a white jumper that fitted quite well. She was only about three years younger than Amy but without her make-up Marvik saw in her raw and exposed face all the pain and insecurity of her youth and the years of anxiety and anger following her sister's death. Amy Chester had her problems too; there was anxiety and concern in her eyes and in the lines of her fair face and yet it was softened by love, an emotion that was missing from Helen's and possibly his own, he thought with a pang of regret which he hastily pushed aside.

He would have liked a doctor to check Helen over but that would have meant revealing her location and he and Strathen had agreed they couldn't risk that. He didn't think Helen would agree to a medical examination anyway.

Colin Chester rose. 'You'd like to talk. I'll show you to the lounge. We'll call you when dinner's ready.'

Strathen smiled his thanks and after Colin Chester had left them in the comfortably furnished and modern lounge, Marvik asked one of the many questions that had been bugging him. 'How come you reached us so quickly, Shaun?' Marvik caught the sounds of the meal being prepared in the kitchen and the laughter and chatter of the twins in their parents' bedroom.

'As soon as I got back from Mrs Handley's flat I realized you'd given me the slip, Helen.'

'I'm not sorry,' she said defiantly. 'And neither am I sorry about showing up at that slime ball Wycombe's house.'

Strathen continued. 'It was just after four and I rang for a taxi, which took ages to arrive. By the time I reached the station the train had left. I tried ringing you, Art, to warn you where Helen was heading. I thought the taxi would reach you before Helen did but there was an accident on the A27 between Emsworth and Chichester. Both carriageways were blocked, the road closed and we sat there for two hours doing sod all. If I could have walked or run it I'd have done so. By the time we got through and I was at Itchenor outside Wycombe's house there was no sign of either of you. Then I got your call. Any idea who ran you off the road?'

'All I could see was a dark hooded figure in a black Range Rover.

The car came out of the turn off from the marina. How could Wycombe have summoned that kind of assistance so quickly? And why wait in the turn off to the marina?' More questions that had been gnawing at him.

'The driver knew you were coming from Wycombe's place and there is no other road you'd take to reach Chichester.'

'But we might have swung east and taken the road to Bognor.'

'He gambled you'd return to Chichester and take the main road back to Portsmouth and Southampton. And there are several ways he could have known you were at Wycombe's place.' Strathen addressed Helen. 'Someone could have followed you, which means whoever it is knew you were staying with me.'

'I didn't see anyone suspicious,' she declared, clearly thinking of her fellow train passengers.

'Perhaps you were too engrossed in thinking about what you'd say to Wycombe to notice,' Strathen answered, then quickly continued. 'But I don't think anyone followed you because it's far more likely there's a tracking device on my car.'

Marvik hadn't searched for one. Maybe he should have done.

Strathen continued. 'It's likely to have been planted when my car was at the marina where you left it, Art, before I collected it and I didn't check it over. I should have done. It's probably a live GPS vehicle-powered tracker, rather than a battery-operated one that would need recharging. It would have been sending a signal to report the exact location of the vehicle in real time, which means that whoever was tracking it at the other end knows you went to Weymouth and Bordon, then to Portsmouth and on to Itchenor and it wouldn't have taken much to assume that your visits to Portsmouth and then Itchenor were linked with Vince Wycombe. The driver of the Range Rover only needed to wait for you to drive away from Itchenor to know where and how to intercept you. The device could be under the radiator, behind the back bumper, in the wheel wells or in the wheel axle underneath the car. Instead of phoning the garage to collect the car it might be better if I went with Colin tomorrow and swept it before moving it in case the device is still transmitting.'

Marvik agreed. If his Land Rover had also been located then that too could contain a tracking device. Maybe it did anyway: there had been ample time to place one while he'd been away from the cottage. It had probably been fitted while he'd been taking Charlotte to Southampton last Thursday.

Strathen went on. 'There is also the possibility that my apartment is bugged and someone's been listening into my conversations, so they'd know you were heading for Wycombe's place. I did a sweep of it this morning and it was clean but that doesn't mean to say it is now or it was when I left. The apartment was empty between the time you left, Helen, and I returned from Mrs Handley's. I phoned you, Art, and left a message to say where I thought Helen was heading. It was careless of me.

'The other possibility is that Vera Pedlowe could have told whoever is behind this that I asked for the lists of those who attended the fund-raising events, and I also asked who attended the Remembrance Service in 1997. She told me that it was Roger Witley. He could be giving the orders from Germany.'

'If he's really in Germany.'

'Yes. Or perhaps he's relaying the information to someone here who is making sure the trail stays closed.'

'Whoever it is didn't tell Wycombe because he was surprised to see us. If Wycombe knows who Esther's killer is, or knows something about her murder, then surely someone would have got to him before us to make sure he said nothing.'

'Perhaps they judged he'd keep his mouth shut because he has a lot to lose.'

'Or he has nothing to do with her death. He had an affair with her, yes, and he failed to declare an interest at her trial but perhaps he really did believe Blackerman killed her.'

Helen looked highly sceptical. 'Unless he killed her and he's the bloke who's organizing the planting of all these bugs and nearly killing us. He had this maniac in that road waiting for us. Maybe he's just good at acting surprised.'

But Marvik could swear his reaction had been genuine.

Helen continued. 'Perhaps Esther found out something about him and threatened to tell the police, especially after he ditched her.'

Marvik said, 'If she did then she couldn't have named Wycombe to Blackerman otherwise he'd not have chosen him to defend him.'

Strathen said, 'But Wycombe could still be involved in her murder. Perhaps Esther overheard him discussing something with someone who couldn't take the risk that she wouldn't repeat it. And it could be a financial scam, as we previously discussed, prior to DRTI being set up.'

Marvik frowned as he recalled what Louise Tournbury had told him. 'Ashley Palmer's former girlfriend says he's scrupulously honest. According to her he'd have certainly exposed a fraud if he'd discovered it. Perhaps he confided his fears to the wrong person. And the same could have applied to Esther, except that DRTI didn't exist then.'

'But Danavere could still have been attracting finance from government sources. When Wycombe ditched her she also told the wrong person, and I don't mean Blackerman but her killer. Witley served in the same regiment as Jim Shannon. She'd certainly have admitted him to her room at the club. Esther believed she could trust him because he had known her father. Blackerman became the fall guy for Esther's murder and a perfect one because he'd slept with her. Palmer's been set up as having sold valuable information to a competitor before vanishing. Whoever it is has leaked this information to make everyone believe Palmer's dishonest and if his body shows up then they'll believe he's been killed by unscrupulous rivals.'

Marvik agreed it was a possibility.

Strathen continued. 'But the reason for Esther's death and Palmer's disappearance might not be fraud. I've been working on another theory, and one that was sparked by you, Art, when you suggested that Charlotte and Ashley might have met at a medical seminar. I haven't been able to check that out yet but I will.'

Marvik sat forward eagerly. 'Go on.'

'Perhaps what both Esther and Ashley discovered was a medical cover-up. Not drugs, because Danavere aren't involved in testing or manufacturing drugs, but it could be connected with the design and manufacture of a faulty medical device, and Wycombe could have been called in to give Danavere legal advice on it seventeen years ago.'

Helen said, 'But is that enough of a reason to kill someone?'

Marvik answered, 'Anything can be a reason to kill if someone thinks their livelihood, reputation, or way of life is threatened. Or if they believe they've been insulted or compromised. They might also be a psychopath or suffering from some kind of maniacal personality disorder.' He addressed Strathen. 'How would this work?'

'The MHRA, Medicines and Healthcare Products Regulatory Agency, is responsible for regulating all medicines and medical devices in the UK by ensuring they do what they're supposed to do and are safe. It's an executive agency of the Department of Health. It's responsible for the regulation of medicines, medical devices and equipment used in healthcare and for the investigation of harmful incidents. It also looks after blood and blood products, to improve blood quality and safety. So let's say that one of the medical devices designed by Chiron and manufactured by Danavere is being used or trialled in 1997 or just before then. It could be equipment used for the diagnosis or treatment of a disease, or for monitoring patients, or assisting them, like my prosthetic leg for example. But this equipment or device caused unwanted side effects on a patient or on someone using the device in order to help a patient. He or she could have been permanently injured, or possibly died as a result of the failure of the device – a faulty reading, maybe, or a misdiagnosis that led to the wrong treatment. The fault could have been caused by faulty design, hence involving Dr Shelley and his sister, or perhaps Danavere cut corners when they manufactured it. They made modifications to save money or time. They had to hush it up or they'd find they had a huge law suit on their hands which would effectively push them out of business.'

Marvik had it in a second. 'Ashley Palmer, in the course of his research, discovered old files on this.'

'Yes.'

'And there might have been more than one person who suffered as a result of the faulty equipment or device; they could have been using it or trialling it on service personnel or veterans.'

Hence the involvement of the intelligence services and possibly naval intelligence, thought Marvik.

Strathen added, 'The devices were hastily recalled under some pretext and destroyed, but not until after Esther had been killed to prevent her from telling what she knew or suspected.'

'If it's true then how the hell do we prove any of this?' Helen cried in exasperation.

'We can't, not yet,' Marvik answered. 'But we need to force the pace. I'm going to talk to Duncan Ross tomorrow and put pressure on him. I'll come clean about what I'm doing and ask him to tell me what Blackerman told him about his conversation with Esther in that lift.'

'And will he tell you?' Helen said dubiously.

'Probably not, but we'll soon know if he's involved.' He glanced at Strathen and saw he understood his meaning.

Helen said, 'But what are we going to do about Wycombe?'

'Nothing. We need proof. It's his word against ours and the police won't investigate, or if they do then whoever is behind this is powerful enough to see any investigation stalls.'

'I could go back to him.'

'No. You're staying here with Shaun.'

'I . . .'

'No, Helen. The risk is too great. I need you helping Shaun. Please.'

She made to protest but Marvik could see she was exhausted both physically and mentally. She capitulated. There was no further chance for debate anyway because Colin Chester came to tell them their meal was ready.

All further discussion was postponed until Marvik and Strathen were alone. Helen had retired to bed. Marvik said, 'I need to return to the Hamble and fetch my boat.'

'And I want to check out the flat and pick up my laptop. We'd better not use Colin's car because it could be traced back here; the same goes for calling a cab from here but if Colin drops us off at Chichester railway station we could get a taxi from there.'

Marvik swallowed two more strong painkillers to dull his throbbing head before setting out. Colin dropped them as arranged at Chichester station where they transferred to a taxi for the thirty-mile journey to Hamble.

There was no sign of anyone watching them when they reached Strathen's apartment but as he inserted the key in the door of his flat he said, 'Feels sticky.' Marvik knew he wasn't referring to glue or grubby hands but that the lock hadn't opened as smoothly as it should have done, a sure sign that it had been manipulated.

Strathen disabled the security alarm. They said nothing. In the office, Strathen flicked on the light. Everything looked to be in the same position, but only Strathen would know whether it actually was. He leaned over one of the desks and switched on a PC. Marvik stood directly behind him as though waiting to get into the seat and blocking the view to Strathen, who said, 'While that fires up I'll make some coffee. We'll need to download what I've got and take it with us.'

'Right.' Marvik stepped aside to let Strathen go ahead of him then followed him into the hall and into the kitchen. Strathen was carrying a holdall. 'I'll stuff some clean clothes in this. It'll be enough for a few days. Coffee first though.'

In the kitchen he turned on the kettle and opened the wall cabinet as though to retrieve two mugs. Leaving it open he also opened the tall fridge opposite so that it formed a barrier between them and the far wall and the door.

'Fresh ground coffee is called for after what you've been through.'

He tipped some beans into a sophisticated looking coffee machine, and as soon as it was grinding nosily along with the kettle boiling he jerked his head towards the window. It slid open noiselessly and smoothly.

Marvik climbed out and assisted Strathen – it was more difficult for him given his leg, and he couldn't crouch down low, but he managed well enough. Strathen indicated for Marvik to follow him, which he did across the wet lawn in the dark. They were heading towards the sea. In the cover of a small copse, Strathen paused and pulled out a slim torch. He opened the holdall. Inside was a laptop computer. He swiftly and expertly examined it and then the holdall and nodded the OK. They continued for another couple of hundred yards until they came to a hedgerow and a gate. Strathen unlocked it. Just beyond it to the right was a slip way and beside it were several kayaks.

'This is mine,' Strathen said. 'Help yourself to one of the others.' Together they pushed the specially adapted kayak down to the water where Strathen sat on the edge before easing his body and his prosthetic limb inside it. Marvik climbed into another kayak close by and put the holdall between his feet. Taking the paddles they struck out on to the water heading for the marina. It would have been an arduous journey for most but not for them. Marvik felt the months since he'd left the Marines slip away and he was back on a mission. He didn't know what Strathen was thinking or experiencing but he'd bet it was the same sense of exhilaration.

Soon they were drawing alongside Marvik's boat. The pontoons were deserted. They climbed on board, leaving the kayaks tied up on the pontoon. Marvik indicated the tracking device placed at the helm. Strathen nodded and together they went below. Strathen placed the laptop on the cabin table and switched it on while again Marvik indicated the listening device under the table. Marvik climbed back into the cockpit, started the engine and cast off. Some minutes later, as they headed east into the Solent, Strathen joined Marvik at the helm.

'Only the two you know about but there could be another tracking device on the hull above the water line.'

'Can we talk freely up here?'

'Yes.'

'I'm not bothered about being tracked, in fact it might tempt the killer out, but this time I'll deal with him on my own. I take it you discovered something in the flat.'

'The smoke alarm opposite the security alarm had been tampered with. It was slightly askew which means someone unscrewed it and placed something inside it. A listening device most probably along with a tiny security camera. I set the security alarm before chasing after Helen. Bloody stupid place to put the smoke alarm opposite, but then the builders didn't have any reason to think anyone was going to be bugged.'

'Was Mrs Handley and her lamp problem genuine?'

'As far as she was concerned, yes. And it was broken, but the timing was immaculate. Either someone struck very lucky or it was staged. I think if I were to question her more closely I'd find that she let someone in who, while she was making them a cup of tea, sabotaged the lamp and mentioned me, so that when it went kaput, on a remote control timing device – she didn't even have to switch it on – startling her, she immediately thought of me. Just as she did for any other odd jobs around the place. She'd been known to tell anyone who would listen, and even those who didn't, that she liked to give that poor man who only had one leg something to make him feel he was still capable. They must have been watching me, as well as you, for some time.'

'Because of Ashley Palmer.'

Strathen nodded. 'Remember we discussed the impression of that Isle of Wight coastguard cottage address on the Post-it note in Ashley's office and how convenient it was that I found it, and that Ashley might not have been fool enough to jot it down.'

Marvik nodded.

'Well my mistake was not checking to find out if the Post-it note holder had always been on his desk. I'm betting it hadn't, and that either Ashley, or someone else in the company or someone posing as a visiting rep or a cleaner, planted it there.'

Marvik was with him. 'It contained a listening device.'

'Yes. And by the time DI Feeny and DS Howe showed up, that listening device had vanished into thin air. Ashley could have been duped into taking it into the company himself. He might have been told to put it on his desk in an attempt to record any conversations to provide whoever he had confided in the proof that the faulty medical devices from seventeen years ago could be laid at the Shelleys' door. Part of the plan was for him to write down the address he was given, pressing hard enough for it to be read. Whether he ever went to that cottage is another matter but he probably believed that someone would and the scandal would be exposed.'

'He was met at Cowes and taken somewhere. Just as Charlotte was met at the Town Quay and taken away.' Marvik stared out at the pitch-black heavy sea, his thoughts a swirling mass of anger. He had to get this killer and make him pay. And if there was no evidence against him then he'd dish up the sentence himself. He'd kill the bastard. But he wasn't certain he or Shaun would ever be allowed to get that close. 'What else did you find in your flat?'

'There was a device under the wireless keyboard. It monitors keyboard strokes so that it can read passwords and logins. Everything is backed up off site and the passwords and login would have given our man access to all of it, which he could then have conveniently wiped off. But I didn't log in, as you noted, and haven't done so since that device was fitted so he won't have access to it. I changed the password and username, a moment ago, on the laptop. He may still find a way in but I doubt it. Where are you putting in to?'

'Chichester Marina. I'll call Ross in the morning and go on to Littlehampton from there unless he agrees to come to me.'

'They could be waiting for you at Chichester Marina.'

'But they won't do anything. It's too public even at this time of the year. Someone in the lock control room or the yacht club might see something. No, they'll wait until there are fewer around to witness an accident.'

'I'd better not call a taxi from there to the Chesters in case anyone is watching the marina – and of course Crowder, or whoever has placed the tracking device, will know when you put in there. Put me off at Sparkes Marina.'

That was at the southernmost tip of Hayling Island and at the entrance to Chichester harbour.

'I'll make sure it's clear before calling for a taxi to take me to Arundel. Crowder will see you've put in there and gone on to Chichester, so he might assume you needed to fuel up or changed your mind.'

'Unless he's responsible for putting that video camera in your apartment and knows we're together.'

'I'll be gone from Hayling Island before he can get someone over to me and if he does I'll certainly not lead them to the Chesters. I'll work tonight. I might have something for you by tomorrow that can help with your interview with Duncan Ross.'

Marvik hoped so because tomorrow it would be a week since Charlotte had vanished and a week was far too long.

NINETEEN

Thursday

It was just before one o'clock when Marvik moored up at Littlehampton. He'd phoned Duncan Ross earlier that morning from Chichester Marina. He'd wondered if Ross would take the call but he was put through without question. He recalled their conversation.

'It's Art Marvik. We met at Littlehampton Marina on Saturday.' Marvik thought it seemed a lifetime ago instead of only five days.

'Oh yes, the man who was thinking of joining the Metropolitan Police.'

It was evident by his tone that he didn't believe that, and that Ross had either got his name from the marina office and run a check on him, or he'd been given the information by someone else. Crowder or the killer? Or were they one and the same?

'I'd like to talk to you about Bryan Grainger's death.'

'Why?'

'I've spoken to his sister. I think there's something you should know. It might have a bearing on the case we were discussing.'

There was only a fraction's pause before Ross answered. 'I'll meet you in the same place, one p.m.'

If Ross was involved in a cover-up over Esther's death he was hardly likely to admit it and, just as Marvik's meeting with Wycombe had prompted an attempt on his life, so could this encounter. But this time, as he'd said to Strathen, he'd be prepared. And they needed to force this killer out into the open.

There was no sign of Ross when Marvik reached his boat. The hatch was open though and Marvik called out. Only silence greeted him. Marvik surveyed the area. The pontoons were deserted. The chilly March wind was blasting down the river. Perhaps Ross had brought the dog with him and had slipped away for a few moments to take it for a walk. But surely Ross, a copper, wouldn't leave his boat open and exposed to potential thieves. Marvik's spine tingled. There was something wrong. He could feel it and smell it. He climbed on board, his backbone prickling, his senses alert. He peered down the hatch into the cabin. His eyes met Duncan Ross's but there was no returning gaze and no smile of welcome, only the grimace of death.

Marvik swore softly and descended into the cabin. He eased his way carefully around the crumpled body. There was no need to test for a pulse but he did anyway. Ross's flesh was cold but not icy which meant he hadn't been dead for very long.

His eyes travelled over the suited body. Ross wore no outdoor jacket and the white shirt and maroon tie were still in place. There was no blood, no sign of a stabbing and no bullet wounds but around Ross's throat were the tell-tale signs of strangulation. And by the way he was lying, on his back, whoever had killed him had done so from behind. Either the killer had been waiting inside the lounge or in the cabin beyond it – but if he had then he must have gained access to the boat either forcibly or with a key – or Ross had told his killer he had a meeting. The killer had met Ross here at the boat and they'd boarded together. Ross had let his visitor go down into the cabin first then, when Ross's back was turned, the killer had struck. Judging by the thin, dark-blue mark around Ross's throat it looked to Marvik as though he'd been throttled with a fine cord.

So where was the killer now? Waiting for him? Possibly, but not on board this boat. Perhaps Ross had been told that Marvik was to be the victim. Instead it had been the killer's intention to frame him for Ross's murder just as he'd framed Blackerman for Esther's.

Marvik caught the sound of sirens in the distance. There was no time to lose. He leapt off the boat and sprinted to his own, knowing that somewhere in the car park or on the bank to his right the killer was watching him. He pressed the ignition at the helm. Nothing. He tried again. Shit! The sirens were growing louder. He didn't have time to stay and be questioned by the police. Even if he did and explained the purpose of his visit and the fact he was investigating Esther Shannon's murder and hoping to get some idea where

Charlotte was being held and by whom, he could see his story being dismissed as ludicrous. The man who had murdered Esther Shannon was in prison. And Charlotte's disappearance was much more likely to be laid at his door. After all he had been with her on Wednesday night. He had slept with her. Perhaps he hadn't dropped her off at Town Quay but had dumped her body in the Solent. And he had been at that derelict coastguard cottage on Wednesday night when Ashley Palmer had gone missing. The police would claim that Charlotte and Ashley had been lovers and he had been jealous and had murdered them both. He was a trained killer. And what would they say of his motive for Ross's death? His mind whirled as again and again he tried to start the engine. Someone would come up with a plausible motive, and his DNA and fingerprints were on Ross's boat. And that had been the only evidence that had secured a conviction against Terence Blackerman.

The engine spluttered and died. The sirens were so loud now the police must be on the approach road to the marina. Should he abandon the boat and make for the shore, and return when the police had left? But no, they'd block the road and interview everyone who was around.

He tried again as the flashing blue lights came into view. At last! The engine sprang into life. He breathed a sigh of relief, cast off the only line at the rear holding him to the pontoon and, jumping on board, pushed up the throttle and swung out of the marina and into the river. He risked a glance back. There were no police on the pontoons but he could see activity at the marina.

Keeping strictly to the speed limit, not wanting to draw attention to himself, he motored slowly down the river towards the sea. Only once did he look back and see uniformed officers on the pontoon. It wasn't until he was out to sea that he considered fully what had happened. Someone had given the police an anonymous tip-off. The killer most probably, and had the killer mentioned he'd seen a tall, muscular man with a scarred face climb on board the boat? You bet. Of course Crowder could back up his story but Marvik didn't know if Crowder was straight. And Crowder knew he was here because Marvik had kept the tracking device on board the boat. Again Marvik considered if Crowder was the killer, playing a sick game to suck him in and frame him, just as he'd done with Blackerman seventeen years ago. Had that lift accidentally broken down or had it been deliberate? Marvik wondered. But the killer wouldn't have known that Blackerman would sleep with Esther. No, that had been a bonus. And why had Esther got in that lift when according to Helen she'd been terrified of them? Had Blackerman told her something that had made her forgo her fears? Or perhaps she'd been feeling unwell and unable to face climbing the stairs. But that didn't fit with her having sex with Blackerman.

He turned his mind back to Ross's death. Who had Ross called after receiving his telephone request to meet? There had been a three-hour interval between that and their meeting. Ross had suggested the time, perhaps to allow long enough for the killer to arrive.

The boat bucked and rolled as Marvik ploughed through the rising waves being whipped up by the wind into whirls of grey and white foam. He thought back to Esther's murder. She'd been strangled with a tie, Ross had been strangled with a cord. The methodology suggested the same man. Last night's attempt to kill him and Helen by forcing them off the road didn't fit that pattern but then the killer might simply have seized the opportunity. And now Ross was dead and Wycombe too could be in danger. Perhaps the killer had already dealt with him.

Marvik headed as quickly as he could for Chichester harbour but this time he stopped before he reached the marina and moored up at Itchenor. From there he ran to Wycombe's house. He might be at home now that the trial in Portsmouth was over. Or perhaps he'd gone into his Chambers in London. Marvik needed to know.

There was no sign of the Mercedes on the driveway but it could be garaged. He pressed his finger on the intercom and waited anxiously. There was a CCTV camera mounted on the right-hand post giving a good view of anyone at the gate. Perhaps Wycombe was watching from behind his computer screen inside the house and was at that very moment summoning up the maniac who had tried to kill him and Helen last night, only this time requesting that he finish the job, just as he'd finished Duncan Ross.

Marvik pressed his finger again on the buzzer and kept it there for several seconds. He expected nothing so was surprised and pleased when a woman's voice said, rather loftily, 'Can I help you?'

'I'd like to see Mr Wycombe.'

'He's not here.'

She sounded apprehensive, understandably so. She was probably wary of visitors she didn't recognize.

'Is he at Chambers?'

'No. Who are you?'

Her nervousness increased. Time for a lie, thought Marvik. 'I'm a colleague of Mr Wycombe's. He engaged my company to discover certain information regarding a case he's been briefed to represent.' Marvik had no idea the language barristers or private investigators used but he hoped it sounded authentic enough to convince the woman on the other end of the intercom. He continued. 'I hoped to speak to him before he went to London. I heard that his case in Portsmouth had finished because of a change of plea to guilty.'

The buzzer sounded and the gates swung open. Marvik walked briskly up the driveway with heightened excitement. Just as he'd experienced on the pontoon at Littlehampton Marina he sensed something was also wrong here. And he'd heard it in the woman's voice.

The door opened before he reached it to reveal a slender woman in her late-fifties, elegantly dressed in trousers and a tight-fitting jumper. She looked troubled and wary.

'I'm sorry to disturb you, Mrs Wycombe—'

'My husband isn't here,' she cut him short, nervously playing with the necklace at her throat. Now he was closer he saw the strain around her mouth and fatigue under her blue eyes. Clearly she was very distressed.

'Do you know where I can find him?'

'I . . . I'm not sure. He left very early.'

'Mrs Wycombe, is everything OK?' He knew it wasn't and that it was connected to what had happened last night, possibly even this morning. Did Wycombe know about Duncan Ross's death? Had he killed him? Somehow Marvik couldn't see the aloof barrister doing that but then the stakes were high. High enough perhaps for him to kill to prevent his secret from being disclosed and ruining his life.

'Can I help?' he asked with concern.

She pushed her hand through her short, highlighted blonde hair. 'You say you're working on something my husband's involved in.'

He could see that she desperately wanted to confide in someone. His timing couldn't have been better. He took an educated guess and answered, 'Yes. The Esther Shannon case.' She looked at him blankly. Clearly that meant nothing to her. He tried again. 'It involves a man called Terence Blackerman.' Bingo! Her eyes widened and then a shadow of fear crossed them. His heart skipped a beat as he saw her hesitate over whether or not to confide in him but he could see she had to tell someone what was troubling her.

'Do you want to come in?' she asked, stepping back.

He did. Very much. He entered the wide, spacious, immaculate hall and she led him into an elegant and expensively furnished lounge that gave on to landscaped gardens. Beyond it he could see the sun glinting on the water of Chichester harbour. He glimpsed the pontoon at the end of the garden but there was no boat on it.

She waved him into a seat behind a low oak chest scattered with magazines on interior design and yachting and took the seat opposite him, wringing her hands entwined in her lap.

'When Vince arrived home from court yesterday he was very distracted, and his clothes were filthy and wet. His lip had also been bleeding and he looked dreadfully pale. I thought he'd had an accident but he told me he was fine. I could see that he wasn't. He was very curt with me, which is totally unlike him. If I didn't know him better I'd say he'd got into a fight. He went into his study, without even bothering to change. I left him alone but when I called him for dinner he said he didn't want any. I asked him if he was ill, perhaps he'd had a fall which had shaken him up, it would explain his dishevelled state. But again he snapped at me and told me not to fuss. He said he had a lot of work to do.'

She took a breath and again fiddled with her necklace.

'Go on,' Marvik encouraged.

'I went in to tell him I was going to bed. He'd been drinking heavily, which is completely out of character. It took me a long time to get to sleep because I was listening for him to come up to bed but eventually I dropped off. When I awoke this morning Vince wasn't in his room. He hadn't been to bed at all. I've tried his mobile number but there's no answer. I rang his Chambers but they haven't seen or heard from him and the boat has gone. I don't know what to do. I was on the verge of calling the police when you arrived.'

Marvik quickly calculated that Wycombe must have left in the early hours of the morning on the high tide or a couple of hours after it, because the pontoon wasn't accessible at all states of the tide.

'Did he take anything with him? Any clothes or personal belongings?'

Her skin paled. 'I don't know.'

'Shall we take a look?' He rose to indicate there could only be one answer to that question. He was anxious to get into Wycombe's study and suggested they try that first.

The study faced the rear of the house and looked out over the garden. It was contemporarily furnished and very tidy. One wall was lined with books while the others boasted modern paintings. The large desk contained only a telephone, a couple of books, some pens and pencils and very little else. Marvik sat and opened the drawers. None were locked and there wasn't much inside them except the usual stationery.

She said, 'I can't see his laptop computer or his briefcase.'

Marvik crossed to the filing cabinet. Again it was unlocked and held only files connected with the household bills and similar items. If Wycombe had been foolish enough to have notes or evidence here of his affair with Esther then he'd taken it with him. He raised the topic of Terence Blackerman and asked how she had heard the name.

'I followed Vince in here a couple of minutes after he came in. I was very concerned about him. He was on the phone. I heard him say, "They'll find out what happened to Blackerman." Then he spun round and saw me and clamped his hand over the receiver and said not to bother him.' Her face flushed and Marvik guessed her husband had expressed his wishes more forcibly than that.

Marvik mentally replayed the scenario. Wycombe, startled and scared by Marvik's revelations and theorizing, had immediately telephoned Esther's killer. But instead of being reassured that everything would be dealt with and he need have no fears, Wycombe had taken to his heels in the early hours of the morning. He'd known that what had happened in 1997 could no longer be contained and that he would become the next victim. Marvik didn't think that Wycombe had taken his boat to Littlehampton and killed Ross although that was still a possibility. A remote one though. Mrs Wycombe confirmed that the boat they owned was a large and powerful motor boat, which Marvik knew could travel a long distance very quickly.

His thoughts had taken him to Wycombe's bedroom where his wife discovered he'd taken some clothes.

'Is his passport still here?' asked Marvik.

'I don't know. It's in the safe and I don't know how to open it.'

He suspected she'd find it gone when it was eventually opened. They returned to the hall.

'What's happened?' she asked nervously.

It wasn't his place or his job to tell her. 'Have you ever heard your husband speak about a DI Duncan Ross?'

'No. I don't think so. Do you think that Vince has had some kind of breakdown? He's been working too hard and perhaps he just needs some time to get away, only I wish he'd answer his phone or send me a message.'

'Perhaps I could have the name of his boat and his mobile number. I'll see if I can get hold of him.'

She gave it to him without querying why he didn't already have it if he was working for her husband as he'd said. He gave her the pay-as-you-go mobile number with instructions that if her husband contacted her, or if anyone asked about his visit, she contact him.

'Shall I call the police?'

'That's up to you. Have you tried his friends? Could he have gone to a relative?' Or perhaps, Marvik thought, Wycombe had a lover. He'd had one seventeen years ago; what was there to say he didn't have another now. 'Perhaps he'll send you a message. Or it might be best to talk to his deputy at Chambers and see if they know where your husband could be.'

'Yes. I'll do all that. Thank you. I wouldn't want to bother the police unnecessarily.'

And that would give him a few more hours, possibly another day or two before the police made the connection with him. The same could not be said for Ross's murder. Time it seemed was running out fast. And not just for him. Maybe it had already run out for Vince Wycombe, because Marvik thought that if he wasn't already dead, it was only a matter of time before he would be.

TWENTY

In the pub at Itchenor, Marvik rang Strathen on the Chesters' landline from the pay phone. Keeping his voice low he said, 'Ross is dead. Strangled.'

'Shit!'

'And Wycombe's missing. His boat's gone, *Perfect Alibi*. See if you can trace it.' Marvik relayed the gist of what Mrs Wycombe had told him, adding, 'I think Wycombe's terrified and has done a bunk.'

'Because you can expose him about his affair with Esther or because he knows why she was killed? Or both,' Strathen said, answering his own question.

'From what Mrs Wycombe said it seems clear to me that the killer told Wycombe on the phone last night that if he doesn't keep his mouth shut then he'll get the same treatment as Bryan Grainger. It was a bit stupid of Wycombe to call the killer; the police will be able to trace the call, if they need to, and they will when Mrs Wycombe reports him missing.'

'To an address yes but not necessarily to the killer, the line could be used by others, unless Wycombe rang a mobile registered to the killer. But if it is someone from intelligence who's behind this then they'll make damn sure it's not traceable, or if it is, it's covered up.'

'I'd tell Crowder only I can't trust him. Whichever way we look at it Wycombe's in deep shit. He's a risk to the killer. I saw Ross's body, Shaun, it's a professional killing. And if it's not someone from intelligence then it ties in with the killer being a serviceman or veteran who had access to the Union Services Club and knows how to kill.'

'There's no confirmation that Witley is in Germany. Vera told me where he was supposed to be and I called the company. I asked to speak to him but they said he cancelled his meeting yesterday and he checked out of his hotel yesterday morning. He's not answering his mobile phone. Vera gave me the number because I told her that I needed to speak to him urgently in connection with Chiron and Ashley Palmer. I haven't gone back to her yet to say I can't get hold of him but I will in case she's got any news. She'll have to inform the other directors and one of them might have heard from him. We're trying to find out if and when he came back into the UK, Helen's using her ace telephone skills on the airlines. He doesn't drive a Range Rover, but his wife does.'

'So a cover up over a dangerous and deadly medical device is looking more than a possibility with Witley running scared.' Marvik didn't even know what Witley looked like. Strathen said he'd email a photograph to Marvik's phone.

'I've been thinking about Grainger's death,' Strathen continued.

'He was an ex-copper; he'd have made notes. If he put them on his computer he'd have backed them up either on a CD or a USB, which could have been found and taken by whoever broke into his flat. But it's also possible he used an online backup service. Helen says Amelia Snow cleared out her brother's flat but found no notebooks, only her mother's diaries. Maybe he wrote his password and user name in those and details of where he backed up his information. I know it's foolish to write these things down, I wouldn't and neither would you, but then most people haven't had our training. But even a copper or a retired copper's memory can be fallible.'

'Good idea. We need to get hold of the diaries.'

'We'll call her and ask if we can collect them or look at them. I've also been on to my contacts at the Queen Elizabeth Hospital Birmingham, Royal Centre for Defence Medicine, Critical Care Unit. No one I spoke to remembers Charlotte mentioning a guy called Ashley Palmer and no one remembers him visiting anyone there. Emma Longton checked the visiting log for me, he's never been there, and Vera says that Ashley never attended any medical seminars or conferences.'

But Louise Tournbury's words came back to Marvik. She'd said that Ashley was working on developing better movement for amputees and those suffering from neurological illnesses and that he'd been in touch with some charities. She couldn't remember which ones but if Marvik put that with what Stisford had said about Blackerman visiting the armed forces nursing homes then maybe there was something there. Stisford had mentioned two places: St Vincent's on the Isle of Wight and the Queen Alexandra Hospital Home at Worthing. He relayed this to Strathen.

'I know them both. The one at Worthing is for physically disabled ex-service men and women, and provides rehabilitation. The other is a nursing home for injured and disabled service personnel.'

Marvik quickly continued as the thoughts began to coalesce. 'If we can discover that Ashley Palmer visited the same nursing homes as Blackerman did in 1997 then Palmer might have been following the same trail. It could confirm that he'd discovered something in Chiron's records that points to this being linked to a medical device that was given to or trialled on service personnel back in 1997.'

'I've got a list of all the service rest homes up on the computer. They won't have information on Blackerman visiting them, it's too far back, but they will if Ashley Palmer's been there. Helen and I will get cracking on ringing round them now. What are you going to do about Ross?'

'My prints and DNA are on his boat. I'm not on the fingerprint or DNA database so the police won't be able to make an immediate link to me but there's probably a recording of me phoning Ross this morning and arranging the meeting, and the marina office will have my name from when I moored up on Saturday. Once the Sussex police get that they'll contact the Hampshire police and Feeney and Howe will come looking for me. I can explain Ross was already dead but that will take time and I can't afford losing any. So I need to keep moving as long as I can. Palmer went missing from the Isle of Wight; if he visited the St Vincent's Nursing Home then perhaps he was lured to the island by someone using that connection. Perhaps he'd become friendly with someone there. I'll head there by boat but call me if you get anything from the other rest homes or on Wycombe.'

Strathen said he would. Marvik headed for his boat and cast off. He toyed with the idea of returning to his cottage. Would anyone still be watching it? Perhaps the police had already made the connection between him and Ross and would be waiting for him. Why hadn't Crowder been on the phone to him? Because he already knew what was happening? Because he was engineering all this? But again Marvik couldn't think why he'd go to the effort of enlisting his help if he was the killer. He could simply have abducted and killed Charlotte and left it to the police to follow up any leads. But he obviously knew a hell of a lot more about this and because of his reticence and the way he had decided to manage this affair a man was dead, thought Marvik angrily. Marvik wondered how Crowder would feel about the news that a fellow officer was down. If indeed Ross had been a fellow officer. Crowder might not be police.

He set a course for East Cowes Marina but Strathen rang him before he was out of the harbour.

'We've struck it lucky. Thinking about where Grainger died I decided to try the Brighton armed forces rest homes first. Ashley Palmer regularly visited St Jude's on Marine Parade.' Marvik felt a frisson of excitement as Strathen continued. 'I've told them you're a relative and that you're on your way to speak to them because Ashley's gone missing and you're wondering if any of the residents he spoke to might be able to help you. I didn't ask them about

Danavere, Blackerman or Bryan Grainger because it would have
raised their suspicions. I'll leave that for you to broach. But it looks
as though Grainger might have been returning from there with
information that was damaging to the killer.'

'And Amelia Snow?'

'Not answering her phone. She could be out shopping or painting.
Helen's going to try again in half an hour.'

Marvik hurriedly made for Brighton. Ninety minutes later he'd
moored up at the extensive marina and was heading for Marine
Parade. He stopped for a few minutes at the junction with St James's
Street where Bryan Grainger had met his death. Grainger had been
coming from the opposite direction; he wouldn't have reached the
nursing home. He was heading there. But that might not have been
for the first time. Perhaps he was returning to double check his facts.
Perhaps he'd told DI Duncan Ross what he'd discovered and that he
was going back to collect the evidence, only he never got there.

Marvik hurried on. He found the substantial Edwardian house
set slightly back off the road and overlooking the sea. A blonde
woman in her late-thirties wearing a royal blue overall over navy
trousers answered the door to him with a friendly smile. Marvik
quickly introduced himself. She stepped back to let him in, her
smile turning to a frown of concern.

'Mr Strathen said you were on your way. I'm sorry to hear that
Ashley's missing. He's nice and the residents love him.' She intro-
duced herself as Angela Deacon. 'I told Mr Strathen the last time
Ashley came here was the Sunday before last.'

That was the Sunday before he went missing on the Wednesday.
'Has anyone else been enquiring about him?'

'No.' She threw him a puzzled look before her expression cleared.
'Oh, you mean the police. No, they haven't contacted us and as far
as I'm aware no one else has.'

'Can you check with your colleagues?'

'I already have, Mr Strathen asked me to.'

'Has anyone come recently who you haven't seen before, or you
don't know, to visit a resident for the first time?'

'No.'

'Would you know if a man called Bryan Grainger visited here
in 2004?'

'Sorry, no. We don't keep records and no one will remember
from so far back.'

Marvik had thought as much. He stopped outside the lounge. He could hear the sound of a television but it wasn't overly loud. 'When did Ashley begin visiting here?' he asked.

'About nine months ago. He used to visit Ken Jamiestone.'

'Were they related?'

'No.'

'Do you know why he came to see Mr Jamiestone?'

'No, sorry.'

'Can I talk to him?'

'I'm afraid not. Sadly he died on Wednesday.'

Marvik tensed. 'What was the cause of death?'

'Heart failure.'

'He had a heart condition?'

'Not that we were aware of but he did suffer from a number of conditions including high blood pressure.'

'So there was a post-mortem.'

'No. The doctor who attended him here didn't see any need for one. His funeral was this morning.'

How bloody convenient. 'Did he leave any notes, letters, diaries or say anything about his conversations with Ashley?'

'He didn't leave any correspondence. He had arthritis in his hands so he didn't write. But he might have told Les Meade what he and Ashley talked about. Les and Ken were very close. He's in the lounge. Would you like a word with him?'

'Please.'

There were a number of residents watching television and a couple snoozing in front of it, but in the far corner gazing out of a large bay window that overlooked the sea, and sitting alone and in a wheelchair, was an elderly man wearing a black suit and black tie, looking reflective rather than sad.

Angela introduced Marvik and explained why he was there. Les Meade studied Marvik keenly and with curiosity and waved him into the seat next to him. Angela took her leave. They were far enough away from the other residents not to be overheard. Marvik began by apologizing for disturbing him and offered his condolences.

'I'd like to ask you if Mr Jamiestone said anything to you about his conversations with Ashley,' Marvik began.

'Have you been in the services?'

'Yes, Marines. Commandos.'

'Thought so, can always tell. But you're out now. Got those scars in action?'

'Yes.'

'Don't want to talk about it, quite understand. Those of us who saw real action never do. It's only those who haven't and think they have that bang on endlessly about it. Anyone would think listening to them they'd fought off whole tribes of villains and insurgents.'

'Was Mr Jamiestone like that?'

'No. Ken was all right. I never thought he'd go that quickly. It was a bit of a shock.'

'I'm sorry.'

Les Meade took a breath before continuing. 'Ken was an ammunitions officer in the army, joined in 1963 and served twenty years. Ended up a Warrant Officer, saw service in the 1960s like me in the Indonesian-Malayan conflict and did several tours in Northern Ireland during the Troubles in the 1970s. We both served in the Falklands War, and fortunately we both came out unscathed. Not like others we knew. He was seventy-five in January but his health was bad. Not only high blood pressure and arthritis but he had Parkinson's which was why young Palmer came to talk to him.'

Angela Deacon hadn't said that although she had mentioned Jamiestone had other pre-existing medical conditions. He remembered what Strathen had said about Ashley Palmer's research, that he'd been developing an intelligence software programme that could help those suffering from Parkinson's disease, something to do with using electrodes to record signals from the brain to the muscles and it was that software that had been registered by a German company. Perhaps Jamiestone had simply been part of Palmer's research and nothing to do with any deviant medical device from 1997.

'Or that was what Ashley said or rather Ken told me,' Meade continued as though reading Marvik's mind. Marvik studied the thin body hunched in the wheelchair and the lined and tired face and looked through the frailty of age and saw intelligence and alertness in the pale grey eyes.

'Go on?' He leaned forward.

'Ken told me they spent most of the time talking about Ken's career in the army.'

Marvik's interested deepened.

'Ashley was a very keen diver. Ken had been a diver in the army working on diffusing underwater explosive devices. Then in civvy street he worked as a commercial diver, first for the oil rigs and then for a dive operator, taking divers around the world on marine expeditions. Ken really enjoyed talking to Ashley. Said it was nice to have a young person who wasn't condescending or thought you were gaga because you were old. They got on really well.'

'Did you see Ashley write any of this down?'

'He had a phone and a small computer that he used to make notes on.'

Which had vanished along with him.

Meade said, 'Has this anything to do with him disappearing?'

Marvik thought it was time to be partially honest with the elderly man because Meade would know if he was bullshitting and then he'd clam up. 'It could but I'm not sure how. How did Ashley find Ken? What made him come here and approach him specifically, aside from his research on Parkinson's disease, which incidentally happens to be true?'

'Ken was also an amputee. Didn't Angela tell you? Obviously not judging by your expression. He lost his left leg in a diving accident. It was on a wreck somewhere off the Channel Islands. He got trapped on this wreck, something sliced through his leg and his oxygen was running low. They managed to bring him up but couldn't save his leg. He told me that Ashley had been in touch with ALPS, the charity, and found him that way because he was working for a company that worked closely with the manufacturer of prosthetic limbs and his work could help those fitted with them, is that also true?'

'Yes.'

'He's a clever lad.'

'Very.'

So Ashley had wanted someone with a neurological illness and an amputee. Palmer had also needed a former serviceman and Ken Jamiestone fitted the bill. But was the diving connection significant? Maybe. He recalled what Louise Tournbury had said: *one application can have implications for other things, there is always crossover, or so Ash said. His head is always buzzing with ideas, he's a natural inventor.* And Marvik also recalled Strathen's words about how an application could be used in surveillance, defence and security. Had Ashley Palmer tracked down Jamiestone because he'd been involved in the trials of a faulty medical device or perhaps knew someone who had, or was it something completely different? He asked Meade the same question he'd put to Angela Deacon, hoping to elicit more information.

'When did Ashley first visit Ken?'

Meade gave this some thought before answering. 'The time goes so quickly and you lose track of it here, but it must have been April or May.'

And Palmer had been working for Chiron for at least a couple of months by then. 'How often did he come?' Marvik asked.

'To begin with quite regularly, once a fortnight, then there was a gap, in the summer. Then he came back quite a few more times in late autumn and before Christmas. I did wonder why Ashley didn't show up at Ken's funeral but then I thought nobody probably knew where he lived. I asked the staff and they said there was nothing in Ken's room to give Ashley's address and they didn't have a phone number for him and I thought the poor lad probably doesn't even know that Ken's passed away and it'll be a shock when he turns up. But now you say he's missing.'

'Angela told me that Ken died last Wednesday, and that Ashley was here on the Sunday before his death.'

'He was.'

'Do you know what they talked about?'

'The usual I guess. Ken's job in the army, working on ammunitions and diffusing unexploded devices, his diving career.'

'And did Ken have any other recent visitors?'

'No.'

'How did he seem when Ashley left?'

Meade's face clouded over. 'He was down, which wasn't like him, especially after one of Ashley's visits. Usually he was very upbeat and talkative but he stayed in his room. I guess he'd started to feel ill.'

That was possible but Marvik thought it far more likely that Ashley had told him something that had depressed him. But what?

'When was Ken's diving accident?'

'In 1997.'

A shiver ran down Marvik's spine. That was no coincidence. Ashley *had* been on Esther's trail. 'Did Ken say anything to you after Ashley's last visit, anything at all? It might help me find him.'

Meade screwed up his face in thought. Marvik didn't prompt him but stared out at the sea in the declining afternoon sunlight feeling that at last he was getting somewhere.

'I don't know if it means anything but he said, "You think you know someone but it shows just how wrong you can be."'

'Was he talking about Ashley Palmer?'

But Meade shook his head. 'No, because I asked him if he and Ashley had fallen out. He said they hadn't but he couldn't help wishing he'd never come here.'

So Palmer had told Ken something about someone and by revealing that knowledge he had upset Jamiestone. With his heart knocking against his ribs, Marvik sat forward and said, 'Did he mention a man called Terence Blackerman?'

Meade looked shocked, then confused. 'How do you know Blackerman?' he asked a little sharply.

'How do you?' Marvik rejoined, because clearly Meade did.

'I knew him when I was in the navy and he was a navy chaplain. But he also used to visit here before Ken and I came here.'

Bingo! Another connection. Marvik hardly dared to hope that he was at last on the right trail.

'And Ken couldn't have been referring to him because we all knew what Blackerman did. I take it you also know?'

Marvik nodded.

'Is he still in prison?'

'Yes.'

'Seems such a waste.'

'Why do you say that?'

'Because the Blackerman I remember from my navy days was a genuinely kind and caring man. But he did sleep with the woman he killed. I forget her name.'

'Esther Shannon.'

Meade nodded; clearly it meant nothing to him.

'Do you think he killed her?' Marvik was interested in getting the view of someone who had known Blackerman.

Meade shrugged. 'We're all capable of killing and we've all done it.'

'But not navy chaplains, they don't carry arms.'

'No, but he'd have seen a lot of death, perhaps it affected him.'

Marvik knew that wasn't the truth. Once he might have agreed, and he had more or less thought the same last Wednesday when Charlotte had told him about it. But that had been before she had been abducted and before the events of the last few days.

There was something niggling in the back of his mind. Quickly and mentally he reassembled their conversation, searching for what was nagging at him. It was something Meade had said, or rather he hadn't said. Then he had it.

'You said that Terence Blackerman used to visit before you and Ken came to live here. How did you know that?'

'I came to see a couple of my navy colleagues and Ken used to visit an army comrade of his, Patrick Rydall, a former ammunitions technician like Ken. They worked together. Blackerman also saw him.'

Marvik's pulse quickened. 'But Blackerman was navy, not army.'

'Makes no difference: a chaplain is a chaplain and Blackerman wouldn't pick and choose who to speak to and who not to because of their service background. Rydall had multiple sclerosis.'

'Did Ken tell you what Blackerman and Patrick Rydall discussed?'

'No.' Meade looked thoughtful. 'It's strange though, what Ken said before he died, how you think you know someone only you never do. Because I thought of that when the chaplain today at Ken's funeral mentioned things about Ken that I didn't know and which he'd never spoken about. But then that's the chaplain's job, isn't it, not only to hear your dying confession but to look into your background and tell the mourners about you.'

'And what did you learn about him?'

'How he was abandoned as a child, left in a shoe box outside the local hospital. How he survived the bombing when all the other kids in the shelter were killed. How he overcame childhood illnesses and God knows what to achieve what he did. He was a fighter was Ken. I'll miss him.'

Marvik stretched out his hand. Meade took it firmly and smiled sadly. Marvik left him to his sorrow with a feeling of excitement and several thoughts racing around his head. He still didn't have all the pieces and he certainly didn't have enough to make sense of all that had happened but he was getting very close, and Meade had given him a big chunk of the puzzle, or at least he thought it was. Perhaps it was fraud on a huge scale that Palmer had uncovered, and Esther before him. Or perhaps it was a faulty medical device that had resulted in fatalities. Perhaps Grainger had been killed because he'd also unearthed this and Ross had been party to it. But as Marvik turned left out of Marine Parade and into Broad Street, past the place where Grainger had lost his life and then into St James's Street, he knew that whatever it was diving had something to do with it and an accident that had occurred in 1997. He needed to know when in 1997 and who Jamiestone had been diving with. And he needed to know everything there was to know about Rydall and why Ken, the day before he had died, had been distressed about finding out the truth about his former buddy.

TWENTY-ONE

The library didn't close until seven p.m. which meant Marvik had at least two hours to obtain the information he wanted. He'd called into a local shop and asked the way and had been given a free street map showing its location. As he hurried through the streets he began to wonder if Grainger had been coming from the library on the day he'd been killed.

Seated at a computer terminal Marvik called up the British Sub-Aqua Club website. It listed all the recreational diving related fatalities that had occurred in UK waters since 1964. Jamiestone's diving accident might not have been recreational. He'd soon know.

He clicked on the Diving Incident Report for 1997 and was soon viewing on screen the incidents that had occurred that year. The report listed the fatalities, decompression incidents, boating and surface incidents, ascents, techniques, equipment and miscellaneous incidents, but Marvik quickly scrolled to the section on injury and illness. No names were given and neither was the location mentioned but there couldn't be many incidents which had resulted in a man subsequently losing part of his leg. There was, however, nothing listed under that section. Undaunted he scrolled back to fatalities and found it.

It had occurred in September 1997 north-west of the Channel Islands at Hurd Deep. Marvik's mind raced. It was an area he knew well, not because he'd dived there but because of its history. It was a deep underwater valley in the English Channel supposedly named after Captain Thomas Hurd RN by Admiral Martin White, born on Hayling Island in 1779. It harboured the wreck of HMS *Affray* which sank in 1951 but it held a darker purpose and one that connected with Ken Jamiestone and Patrick Rydall's army careers.

Rapidly he read on. Three divers had been exploring the wreck of HMS *Affray*. Two were taking photographs. It was planned that the third diver would continue to fifty-seven metres, on his own. One of the divers taking the photographs began to experience problems. The other went to assist while the third diver continued his descent unaware of what was happening. The distressed diver's regulator fell from his mouth. The other diver tried to replace it but it was rejected. He tried the distressed diver's second regulator, this was also rejected. The distressed diver had become unconscious but the diver got him to the surface and the dive boat operator called the coastguard. Then, aware that the other diver hadn't resurfaced, the diver went down again and found his buddy partially trapped by an obstruction. He managed to free him and escort him to the surface. Both divers were air lifted to Princess Elizabeth Hospital Guernsey, where the first diver who had been assisted to the surface died and the other diver suffered serious injury resulting in the amputation of the left lower limb.

With his brain racing Marvik consulted a few more websites, his photographic memory registering the most critical information. He then turned to the website on multiple sclerosis, not because Helen's mother had died from it but because Patrick Rydall had contracted it. He read how MS affected the nerves in the brain and spinal cord, causing problems with muscle movement, balance and vision. The causes could be genetic but it was also linked to a lack of vitamin D and possibly a virus that attacked the auto-immune system.

Finally, just as the library was closing, he called up a website on Parkinson's disease and read that it was caused by a loss of nerve cells in the part of the brain called the substantia nigra, responsible for producing a chemical called dopamine. Dopamine acted as a messenger between the brain and the nervous system, and helped to control and coordinate body movements. If these nerve cells became damaged or died, the amount of dopamine in the brain reduced, meaning that the part of the brain controlling movement couldn't work so well. Movements became slow and abnormal. He scrolled to see what caused the loss of nerve cells associated with Parkinson's disease and discovered that it could be genetic but could also be environmental caused by exposure to toxins such as pesticides and herbicides used in farming, those used in industrial plants and air pollution related to road traffic. There was no mention of exposure to toxins released in the sea, but as Marvik logged off he thought about Ashley's passion for the marine environment,

Jamiestone and Rydall being divers and responsible for ammunition, the location in which he'd been diving, his own service training and what he knew about Hurd Deep.

Heading towards the seafront he called Strathen. Before he could relay what he'd discovered though, Strathen said, 'Wycombe's boat's been found in the English Channel. There's no sign of him. The coastguard boarded it after it was reported drifting into the main shipping channel.'

'So was he pushed or did he jump?' It was a rhetorical question. They might not know until his body was found, *if* it was found.

'Helen's spoken to Amelia Snow. She says there were no notes in her mother's diaries but she has kept a few books and CDs that were her brother's. She says we're welcome to look at them. Colin's going to drive Helen over to collect them. It's OK, I'm going with her.'

Swiftly Marvik relayed what he had learned. He asked Strathen if Palmer could have been working on an application that could be used in diving. The answer was yes. He'd been working on 3D object detection. Louise Tournbury had said the same.

'I'm going back to the rest home to see if I can get anything more from Les Meade. See what you can get on Patrick Rydall and Ken Jamiestone.'

It was getting late. He was asked to wait while one of the carers went to enquire if Les Meade was willing to see him. He was and Marvik found himself being shown into Meade's room on the first floor. It was spacious with an adjoining bathroom and Meade was sitting in his wheelchair at the wide bay window overlooking the sea. There was a television set but it was off and Meade asked him to turn off the lamp which the carer had switched on as she'd entered the room. The black suit jacket had been replaced by a beige cardigan but Meade was still wearing his white shirt and black tie.

'I guess this must be urgent for you to visit me twice in one day,' he said as Marvik drew up the chair and placed it next to the elderly man. Marvik apologized for the intrusion but Meade dismissed that with an impatient gesture of his left hand. 'I'm glad you've returned. I've been thinking a lot about Ken and young Ashley since you left.'

'I'm hoping you can give me more information about Ken and Patrick Rydall.'

'What do you want to know?'

So much, thought Marvik, but he needed to get his thoughts in order. 'Which regiment did they serve in?'

'The Royal Army Ordnance Corps as it was then. It didn't become the Royal Logistics Corps until it joined up with the Army Catering Corps, the Royal Pioneer Corps and some of the Royal Engineers in 1993. That's how they became buddies. I told you they were both in the Falklands War like me.'

'Ken's accident was when he was diving in 1997, while Patrick Rydall was a resident here. Do you know who Ken dived with?'

'Another buddy in the army, Tom Hilton.'

'Was he the man who died?'

'Not then, but shortly after on a dive somewhere off the Isle of Wight. The man who died wasn't army. Sidney Rathbury. He was a chemist or something like that.'

Marvik took a mental deep breath. Louise Tournbury's words again reverberated around his head. *The sea is a huge dumping ground . . . people think it doesn't affect them but it does.* It matched with what he knew and what he had just read on the Internet.

'Ken was diving at Hurd Deep, wasn't he? North-west of the Channel Islands.' And Marvik knew why.

'Yes.' Meade eyed him curiously and a little warily.

'The dumping ground for both chemical and conventional munitions after the First and Second World Wars.' It was no secret.

Meade nodded.

'Did Ken talk to Ashley about this?'

Meade hesitated.

'Please, Mr Meade, it's very important.'

He nodded.

'And Ashley's interest wasn't just Parkinson's disease and the diving accident in 1997, was it? His interest went back to when the munitions were dumped there but not as far back as the Second World War. More recently than that.'

'How did you know?' Meade said warily.

'I'm a former marine. I know about ammunition. Ammunition sea dumps can contain TNT, picric acid, hexogen, and octogen – highly explosive substances which will eventually leak and contaminate sea life and the food chain. Some experts say that it will take about five hundred years but who really knows. Shells and ignition systems contain metals that slowly dissolve in sea water and that means they also have an effect on the marine environments. Huge amounts were dumped but the cost of bringing them up and destroying them is so vast as to make it impossible. Were Patrick Rydall, Tom Hilton and Ken involved in dumping the ammunition there?'

'Yes. But it was legal and authorized by the Ministry of Defence,' Meade said in defence of his late friend.

Marvik knew that. 'The dumping of munitions was banned globally under the London Convention of 1972, or rather the dumping of highly toxic radioactive waste was; the disposal at sea of intermediate and low-level waste still continued. It didn't get completely banned until 1993 although most of it stopped in the mid-1980s. But there was also an emergency dumping at Hurd Deep in 1974, authorized by the Ministry of Defence,' he said, recalling what he knew and had read in the library. 'Were the three men on that dumping?'

'Yes. Ken said that he, Paddy and Tom were responsible for making sure the sealed containers were safely ditched. It was munitions and low radioactive material.'

Or that was what they were told. Suppressing his excitement Marvik continued. 'Why did Ken and Tom go back in 1997?'

'I don't know. He didn't say.'

But Marvik knew why. He studied the old man's face closely and could see that it was the truth. Had Ken Jamiestone returned to make sure the cargo was safe? Or had he wanted to check that whatever had been dumped was what they'd been told rather than dangerous and highly toxic substances? Was that what he'd told Ashley Palmer?

Anxiously, Meade said, 'What was it that was bothering Ken?'

Did Marvik tell him? Did he fob him off? Meade deserved more than that.

'I'm not an idiot,' Meade added, seeing Marvik hesitate.

'It might be dangerous to know.'

'You think I worry about that now when I have nothing to lose and when I've never worried about it before when I had everything to lose? Danger was my job, just as it was yours. Still is by the looks of it.'

He was right. But it wouldn't be for much longer when he took Drayle's consultancy job. If he was still alive to take it. 'It could be dangerous for others.'

'Then I'll keep it to myself.'

Marvik could see by the steely glint in the elderly man's eyes that he would. He began to relay what he knew, what he'd read online and what he'd pieced together.

'In 1997 a report was commissioned by the National Radiological Protection Board to carry out an independent assessment of the waste dumped and whether it posed a danger. I believe that Ken, Tom Hilton or Patrick Rydall got wind of the report or read about it in the media. Or perhaps Sidney Rathbury approached one of them, concerned about what was down there. Not trusting the government backed report to reveal the truth, Rathbury persuaded Tom Hilton and Ken to go with him to check. It wasn't an official dive because the diving accident is logged by the British Sub-Aqua Club, which only lists recreational dives, and it claims that they were diving to explore the wreck of HMS *Affray*. The dive went wrong. Sidney Rathbury got into distress, Hilton got him to the surface and then went to help Ken who was trapped, possibly while trying to explore what was inside one of those canisters or containers that were dumped. Anyway the report was published in November 1997; its findings were announced to Parliament. It concluded that the dumping was well within the International Commission on Radiological Protection's recommended dose limit for members of the public and that the dumping was of no radiological significance. The report also concluded that the majority of the wastes disposed would not present a hazard even if accidentally returned to shore.'

'A whitewash?'

'Possibly.' And Marvik wondered if Wycombe had been officially consulted as a legal expert to ensure that, whatever language was used in the report, it would bear scrutiny and wouldn't expose the government or the Ministry of Defence to damaging claims if anyone subsequently discovered otherwise. A conversation between Wycombe and a government official discussing it might have been what Esther overheard and threatened to tell when Wycombe ditched her but Marvik didn't think it was.

Meade said, 'So Ashley Palmer was on to this?'

'Yes. He was a keen marine environmentalist. Maybe he stumbled on it through his work with Chiron and Danavere, which brought him into contact with Ken for the purposes of his research. Ken telling him about his diving accident and background got Palmer curious. Or perhaps Palmer, working on his diving application, was keen to test it out and had researched and read about munitions dumping. He'd have certainly known about it and would have had a keen interest in it from his involvement with MPCU – it's a marine environmental charity,' Marvik explained.

'I believe that in the summer, when Ashley was absent from visiting Ken, he returned to the dive location with the same aim as Ken in 1997, to see what was really there. Ashley's application could not only detect the containers but what was inside them and analyse their contents. After that dive he did some further research and maybe dived again. He came here that Sunday before he disappeared when he had all the evidence and told Ken what he'd found, therefore depressing him. It's possible that what was ditched wasn't simply ammunition and radioactive waste but chemical weapons, the leakage of which could have triggered Ken's Parkinson's and even possibly Patrick Rydall's MS.'

And Ashley Palmer would have decided to expose it.

Meade said, 'This toxic cargo could be leaking.'

'Yes and if this is what Palmer unearthed and was about to reveal, someone would make sure he disappeared before being able to do so.'

'Because it proves we were developing chemical warfare?'

'Most people know we were but developing chemicals and dumping something that is extremely harmful is another matter. I think there was someone else with Ken, Patrick and Tom in 1974 on that dumping, who also returned with Ken, Tom and Sidney Rathbury in 1997 and who is responsible for covering up what was really dumped there.' And perhaps he'd been responsible for sabotaging Sidney Rathbury's diving regulator and wrecking the dive, and for Tom Hilton's subsequent diving accident off the Isle of Wight. Hilton might have witnessed something on the dive boat, the pilot tampering with the regulator, that made him suspicious. He had to be eliminated. Ken had been safe though because he was below. Was that person Witley? Whoever it was, Patrick Rydall on his deathbed had told Blackerman. Esther hadn't been killed because she knew too much; she had been killed to keep Blackerman silent. Because Rydall had told him something about that dive in 1974 that was too dangerous to know. The dying don't lie.

Meade said, 'What will you do now?'

'Tell the right person.' Except Marvik didn't know who that was. Blackerman had told someone and that had cost him his freedom.

Palmer had also confided what he'd discovered and was now most probably dead. He couldn't afford to make the same mistake.

Marvik took his farewells, promising to return to tell Meade what happened if he was still around to do so. He hoped it was a promise he could keep.

As he hurried back to his boat he rang Strathen and brought him up to speed.

'Witley wasn't in the same regiment as Rydall or Jamiestone and he wasn't an ammunitions technician so it can't be him,' Strathen said. 'But he could still be involved if he's in on a fraud and has been threatened with exposure if he doesn't do as he's told. Perhaps Palmer confided in him, and Witley ran to whoever is pulling the strings on this. And that could be the intelligence services, acting under orders from a higher authority and we both know of one organization which wouldn't want this coming out. The Ministry of Defence.'

'A government minister now or back then?'

'Ministers come and go. I was thinking of someone more permanent. A civil servant.'

Marvik was with him. 'Sir Edgar Rebury.'

'Yes. He was Permanent Secretary for Defence in 1997 and . . . hang on, I'm just looking him up. He was a junior civil servant in 1974 at the Ministry of Defence. He was not only the first Chairman of DRTI in 2000 and stayed there until 2010, but he's also a patron of ALPS.'

'That's it!' Marvik exclaimed. 'That's who both Blackerman and Palmer confided in. Palmer wouldn't normally have had access to such a powerful man but as a patron of the charity he'd have been able to approach him believing he could trust him.'

'Yeah, and Rebury told MI5.'

'But is this so vital that they'd need to clean it up?'

'Possibly, and Crowder could be making sure it is cleaned up with no loose ends left lying around.'

'But why kill DI Duncan Ross? OK, so he could have threatened to admit that he'd withheld or doctored evidence in connection with Esther's murder but I can't see the intelligence services waiting this long to dispose of him. And there must have been another man on that dive boat at Hurd Deep, someone who was also involved in dumping that stuff in 1974. Perhaps Sir Edgar Rebury will tell me if I'm persuasive enough.' Marvik realized he didn't even know what Rebury looked like. 'Is there a photograph of him?'

'Yes. I'll send it over along with the one of Witley.'

'Where can I find Rebury?'

'Southampton.'

'That close!' Marvik said, surprised, as he turned into the marina.

'According to the ALPS website he's attending a fund-raising bash at the De Vere Hotel, along with a number of other luminaries.'

'I'm on my way.'

'Art, be careful.'

But the time for caution had passed.

TWENTY-TWO

How to persuade Rebury to talk, however, was another matter. Marvik pondered this as he cast off and made his way out of the marina. If it came to it he would have to use force. Charlotte's life could still depend on it. How long would it take him to get to Southampton by boat? Too long. Perhaps he should have hired a taxi. Would Rebury have protection? If so Marvik would deal with it. Who was working with Rebury on this? Could it be Witley?

Perhaps Helen and Shaun would find something in Grainger's meagre belongings that would tell them. Perhaps the police, searching Ross's house, would discover something that would make them reopen the case and set Blackerman free. But no one wanted that murder in 1997 reopened. Rebury would use his influence to make sure it never was. Marvik had to make sure of the opposite.

His mobile phone pinged and he retrieved it from his jacket pocket to see that Strathen had sent him over two photographs. One of Sir Edgar Rebury, stout with dark hair framing a jowly face in his mid-sixties, and the other photograph, Strathen said, was Roger Witley. In the dim light from the helm Marvik's heart skipped a beat as he stared down at the rounded face and stocky build of a man in his mid-fifties. It was the same man he'd seen with Nick Drayle on Thursday, the day he'd dropped Charlotte off at the Town

Quay. With his mind racing he rang Strathen but there was no answer. He rang the Chesters.

'He's not here,' Amy Chester informed him. 'He left about ten minutes ago.'

'To go with Helen to Bognor Regis?' That didn't explain why he wasn't taking calls on his mobile though. Perhaps he couldn't get a signal.

'No, Colin's taken Helen.'

Marvik felt a coldness in his stomach at what her words might imply. 'Did he say where he was going?'

'No, but he said that if you called, you'll know where.'

He did. Southampton.

Marvik glanced anxiously at the clock at the helm. It would take Strathen about an hour to reach Southampton by car. It would take him two hours, or rather another ninety minutes if the weather held, because he'd already been travelling for half an hour. He increased his speed. He could make good time out at sea, but motoring into Southampton he'd have to slow down and abide by the speed limits. Whichever way he looked at it Strathen would get to Rebury before him. Would that matter? Strathen would get the name of Rebury's accomplice from him and he'd call it through. Or would he? Not if Strathen thought he had a point to prove to himself. That he was still up to the job. He'd go after the killer himself and alone.

The boat rocked and bucked in the waves. Marvik opened up the throttle and sped along the Solent. There was little time to lose. He skirted around a giant container ship and eventually he was heading into Thorn Channel and Calshot Reach towards Southampton but here he had to slow down and keep to the speed restrictions. It felt as though he was travelling backwards.

He consulted his watch as he eased into Ocean Village Marina, anxious and impatient to get to the hotel. Strathen hadn't called in so perhaps he hadn't located Rebury. Perhaps Rebury hadn't shown up at the charity bash: with a chill of dread Marvik wondered if Rebury had already been dealt with. He could tell all. He was a risk. Perhaps that's what Strathen had realized and had hastened there to protect him. But why not tell him? Marvik wondered with trepidation.

He switched off the engine and reached under the helm. Then, after locking the boat, within minutes he was running through the modern complex and along the main road past the buildings that had once been the offices of the major shipping companies, and the entrance to the port, not daring to think that Strathen had also been dealt with. It was just after eleven. The charity dinner and dance would be in full swing.

At last he reached the hotel, pushed back the glass doors and stepped into the chrome and tiled lobby. He drew a few apprehensive looks. Not that he cared about those. Quickly, consulting the function room boards, he found the location of the charity dinner dance and made for it. The room was crowded, hot and noisy. About a hundred people in evening dress were seated at tables or were on the dance floor. At the top of the room was a long table for the VIPs, he assumed, and there were two spaces on it, one of which had to be Rebury's. He made towards it when an elegantly dressed woman in her late-forties intersected him.

'Can I help you?' she asked pleasantly but warily.

'I'm looking for Sir Edgar Rebury, it's important I talk to him.'

'He had to take an urgent call.'

'When was this?'

'About fifteen minutes ago.'

Could Strathen have called him? Perhaps from the lobby of the hotel. But there had been no sign of Rebury or Strathen in the hotel lobby.

He thanked her and hurried out. He was too late. They had already left. But hastily he checked the restaurant and bar, not expecting to find them and he didn't. He crossed to the reception desk and asked for Rebury's room number, confident that when he visited it Rebury wouldn't be there. But Rebury wasn't booked in. Marvik left anxious and puzzled. He stood in the rain, contemplating his next move, eyeing the expensive motors in the car park. Then his gaze alighted on a vehicle in the far right-hand corner, a Bentley Mulsanne with a personalized registration number, and his heart quickened. If he wasn't mistaken it belonged to Edgar Rebury.

He raced towards it noting the two men inside. He could tell by their build that neither of them was Shaun. Perhaps he was wrong. Perhaps Rebury had sod all to do with this, or perhaps it wasn't his car. There was a smaller, stouter man in the passenger seat, whose build matched what he'd seen in the photograph of Rebury and beside him a taller, leaner man in the driver's seat. His chauffeur or bodyguard. Or perhaps someone from the intelligence services who had already silenced Shaun. Whoever it was Marvik would have to deal with him first. As he drew level the door swung open and Marvik halted, his mind rapidly trying to assimilate what and who he was seeing. He stared at the man in his early-sixties wearing a dinner jacket and felt a mixture of wrath and disappointment as several facts slipped into place.

'Glad you could make it, Art. We didn't think you were ever going to come.'

'Where's Shaun?' Marvik demanded of Nick Drayle, quickly stifling his shock.

'You'll find out soon enough. I suggest you get in.'

He could suggest all he liked; Marvik could get the better of Drayle. He was thirty years younger and far fitter even though the older man kept himself in shape.

'And if I refuse,' Marvik said, tensing, in readiness for action.

'Then I'll just have to persuade you.'

'With what?' But Marvik already knew. This ruthless bastard would use Charlotte's life as a bargaining tool, if she wasn't already dead. How could he believe him if he said she wasn't? But Drayle withdrew a firearm from his jacket pocket, one of many he kept secured on his business premises: guns and ammunition had been his business in the army and were still his business. God, what a fool he'd been. Drayle had the muscle and means to mount a surveillance operation. But Marvik hadn't known enough about Drayle's past to put it with Esther Shannon's murder. Why should he have suspected him? But something Strathen had told him about DRTI resounded in his mind along with some of the other things that had occurred but there wasn't time to consider that now.

'Bit public for a shooting,' Marvik said lightly, calculating how he could get out of this and find Strathen. Where was he?

But Drayle said quietly and evenly, 'At night? In this weather? In a remote corner of the car park? Hardly. I could shoot you and leave you here and no one will find you until they staggered out of that dance. And Edgar and I would have enough witnesses to say we were inside.'

'But you both left – and how are you going to explain being wet?'

'We heard a disturbance while we were discussing an important matter after Edgar received a phone call from Strathen. By the time we got here, you were dead and Strathen had disappeared. I can come up with a number of plausible stories as you should know by now and they'd be believed.'

But would they be believed by Crowder? By then though it would be too late for him and Strathen.

'Where is he?' Marvik snapped. Strathen couldn't be far; there hadn't been the time for Drayle and Rebury to take him anywhere. 'I need to know he's alive.'

'He is.'

But for how much longer? He and Shaun would be silenced just as this man had ensured Blackerman stayed silent by killing Esther Shannon. He'd also killed Bryan Grainger and Duncan Ross and probably Ashley Palmer or had Witley killed Palmer?

Drayle called to Rebury, who hauled his squat body out of the car and walked hesitantly around the front of the car to stand beside Drayle.

'Go back inside and if anyone asks where I am say I've got called away on business.'

'But I can't—'

'Do it,' Drayle commanded.

Rebury licked his lips nervously and brushed his wet hair off his sweating forehead before scurrying off. Good, it was just him and Drayle. But Marvik was wrong. As Rebury hastened off another figure loomed out of the darkness behind Drayle. A man closer to Marvik's age and one he also knew. His stomach churned in anger, his fists balled.

'Your boat keys, Art,' Lee Addington said, holding out his hand.

Marvik had no option but to hand them over.

'Get in,' Drayle ordered.

Marvik made to climb into the Bentley knowing what was coming next. He steeled himself and tried to dodge the blow but there was nowhere to go and the butt of the gun came down forcibly across the back of his head, wielded by a man who had strength and skill and knew exactly where to hit and how to stun. A lightning flash of pain shot up into his skull obliterating all thoughts before the next blow. Another stab of pain. He could hear voices. He couldn't make out what they were saying. He was being manhandled into the Bentley and his pockets were being searched. His vision faded. Desperately he tried to focus but the images were blurred. If he could just move. If he could reach out. If he could concentrate, focus, stay conscious, but already he was slipping into darkness. He needed to preserve his strength for the ordeal that was to come. The struggle between life and death. And he needed the energy and presence of mind to be able to take his chance, the best one he had, when he had it, knowing even through the haze of impending unconsciousness and the pain radiating through his head that Drayle was planning a manner of death for him and Strathen that would leave him in the clear. But despite all his resolve and efforts the black abyss opened up and Marvik sank into it.

TWENTY-THREE

G radually a soft drone pierced his subconscious. He couldn't place it. He forced himself to concentrate even though his head hurt like hell. His body was rocking gently then it swayed more violently. He smelled leather. Then the soft drone became a purr, then the sound of a car engine. And slowly he began to resurface.

The car stopped. His head was thumping like a giant piston engine. A strong hand on his arm. He was hauled out. He fell to the ground. The gravel grazed his scarred face. Good. The sharp pain jolted him more fully awake but he feigned a dazed state in the hope that he'd fool Drayle into making a mistake. As far as he could tell there were only the two of them and the gun. And that made a difference. He wasn't planning on ending up like Esther, Palmer, Grainger and Ross. And Wycombe. He'd forgotten Vince Wycombe. He must surely be dead. God knows how many more people this man had killed. He prayed that didn't include Charlotte but why would he stop at killing her when one more life meant nothing to him? He'd wrecked so many lives, including Helen's and Blackerman's. *Helen.* Was she safe? She must be because Drayle had made no mention of her and Drayle could easily have threatened him with her life. Neither had he mentioned Charlotte so perhaps there was the possibility she was still alive. But where was Shaun?

His head was clearing and his mind sharpening. He picked out the shape of a petrol tanker and a bus used for anti-terrorist training purposes and knew they were on Drayle's estate in the New Forest, which bordered the Solent. He made to stand up.

'Slowly,' Drayle warned. 'Don't try any heroics, Art, because I won't hesitate to shoot you.'

Marvik knew it was no idle threat. He felt sick inside that he had trusted this man. How had he not seen his evil and deceit? Because he hadn't wanted to or because this man was an expert at camouflage?

'Where's Charlotte Churley?' he asked.

'I was going to ask you that.'

Had he got that wrong? 'If you haven't got her then someone else knows that Terence Blackerman didn't kill Esther Shannon, and they'll know that you did.'

'I doubt that very much. There is nothing or no one to link me to Esther Shannon's death except you and Shaun Strathen and you'll both be dealt with.'

'And her sister?'

'An unbalanced bitter woman with a history of self-harming and mental health problems. No one will believe her. Besides, we can deal with her later without her two knights in shining armour to protect her. A suicide perhaps while the balance of mind . . .'

'There are too many deaths, Nick. Don't you think someone will start asking questions and keep on asking them until they get to the truth?'

'You mean Detective Superintendent Crowder. I've handled coppers before, he'll be no different. He'll have something in his background that he won't want revealed.'

'Just as Duncan Ross and Bryan Grainger had?'

'Grainger was clean but ambitious. Ross was dirty. It didn't take much for him to play ball especially when his cooperation was requested at a high level.'

'From Rebury?'

'Let's say Edgar put pressure in the right quarters. The police got a quick result and it stuck.'

'Because of Wycombe's pathetic attempt at defending Blackerman, and Wycombe was easily persuaded because of his affair with Esther and the fact he didn't admit it. Did you kill him?'

'He might not be dead.'

In the lights of the Bentley, Marvik saw the mocking expression on Drayle's face and balled his fists. He caught the sound of a boat in the distance. Was it his being piloted by Lee Addington? There were questions about Addington and that ill-fated maritime operation that had cost Harry Salcombe his life that Marvik wanted to put to Drayle but he might never get the chance.

'Where's Shaun?' he again asked.

Drayle waved the gun at Marvik to move around to the rear of the car and indicated that he wanted the boot opened. As he did dim lights flooded the yard. Drayle had them on a remote switch and there was no one within miles to see them. Even if there had been no one would have questioned it, as Drayle often ran night-training sessions.

Marvik prayed that Shaun wasn't already dead and his body bundled inside the boot. If he was he knew that Drayle expected him to carry it down to the shore and on to his boat which Addington was bringing round, and was planning an accident for them. Drayle wouldn't want them killed on his land. They'd be taken out into the Solent where an explosion – something Drayle and Addington were expert at – would rip through the boat leaving nothing but its charred remains and theirs too, *if* they were ever found.

Holding his breath Marvik opened the boot of the car. Strathen was alive. Thank God. Relief flooded through him. He helped him out. He was in some discomfort even though his grim expression didn't betray it.

'Is this the bastard that killed Esther?'

Marvik nodded.

'Is Helen OK?' Strathen added, worried.

Marvik didn't know.

'Walk,' Drayle ordered, indicating the way to the shore.

It was difficult for Strathen. Or was it? In a flash of intuition borne from undertaking many missions together Marvik knew that Strathen was exaggerating his disability to delay their progress and to give them time to get out of this. He also knew that Drayle would underestimate Strathen. Good, that suited them.

The rain had turned to a thin cold drizzle. The hard standing gave way to grass and the landscaped gardens in front of the offices. Marvik recalled what he knew of the place. There was ten yards of grass before more hard standing, about twenty paces before the pontoon, another twenty and then the boat would moor up at the end. Once on the boat, when it arrived, they'd be finished. They would have to make their move by then. He didn't look at Strathen beside him but knew he was thinking the same.

Marvik said, 'What was the chemical that you dumped in Hurd Deep in 1974?'

'There was no chemical. Only low radioactive waste.'

Marvik turned to glance at Drayle but it was Strathen who answered. 'That's what Palmer found. And only that.'

Of course! And that was what he had told Ken Jamiestone and why Ken's words to his friend Les Meade were *you think you know someone but you don't*. Ken had been referring to Drayle and to what he had done, because Drayle had been with Ken, Rydall and Hilton on that ammunitions dump in 1974. But not all the munitions had been dumped.

'You sold the munitions,' Marvik said. And Ken had found that so hard to take; the fact that not only had Drayle duped them but he'd actively helped those terrorists who had maimed and killed their comrades. Because Marvik knew who Drayle had sold them to. It had been the 1970s and the height of the Troubles, as Les Meade had mentioned. Without disguising his contempt, Marvik said, 'You built your business on the back of selling munitions to the IRA in Northern Ireland to kill servicemen, police officers and innocent men, women and children. You framed Terence Blackerman after killing Esther Shannon because he'd heard a dying confession from Patrick Rydall which made him wonder not only if the chemicals that had been dumped were dangerous, but if what was supposed to have been dumped actually was there. Blackerman's suspicions grew when he was told that out of that diving party one man had died and another had lost his leg. Did he make some enquiries and discover that the dive operator and pilot of that boat in 1997 was you? Blackerman confided his concerns to the wrong man: Sir Edgar Rebury.'

Drayle said nothing. He didn't have to. Marvik knew he was right. The pontoon was ahead. There were lights along either side of it and on the end. As they stepped on to it Drayle ordered them both to turn to face him. There was no sign of Marvik's boat and Marvik caught a glimpse of irritation on Drayle's face. Addington should have been here by now. Drayle's hand was steady, his expression resolute.

'If you're thinking of trying something, Art, let me remind you that I have the gun and Shaun will certainly die before you can strike out. But perhaps you'll take that risk.' Strathen made to step forward. 'Or perhaps it's best if I kill you, Art, because maybe Shaun doesn't care any more if he lives or dies. Must be bloody awkward living with a false leg.' Drayle levelled the gun at Marvik's head. His hand was firm, his eye contact even and hard. Strathen eased back.

Marvik continued calmly though his mind was racing furiously. 'As a junior civil servant in the Ministry of Defence, Rebury somehow made sure that you were to oversee the dumping of munitions in 1974 and probably some consignments before and after then. He altered the cargo lists omitting the containers carrying the ammunition and created new paperwork authorizing you to collect it from the depot where it was being stored. You did and handed it over to the IRA. You and Rebury agreed to split the proceeds of the sale of ammunition. Once he was implicated he was yours for as long as you wanted, able to dish out lucrative contracts and make sure you secured funding from the government and the European Commission whenever you had a programme that fitted. By the time he stepped down from DRTI you no longer needed him. You had and have powerful contacts of your own. And it probably wasn't only the IRA but any terrorist who could pay the asking price for munitions. Terrorists aren't fussy about where their weapons come from or what kind of state they are in, and if they blow themselves up or wound themselves adapting them to make them live again then it's the risk they take.'

Marvik caught the deep throb of a boat engine in the distance as he studied the man in front of him, wondering if war had made him less human. Had it brutalized him? Was that why he had killed and destroyed so many lives? This man had seen five years of bloody conflict in Northern Ireland and yet he had still sold munitions to the IRA. No, it wasn't war because inside Drayle was a Machiavellian personality. Over the years Drayle had done whatever he had to do to get what he wanted. He'd used deception, manipulation, theft, physical coercion and murder. He was a selfish, cruel man who cared nothing for others in the pursuit of his personal goals.

The boat was drawing nearer. There was still time and Marvik wanted to know it all.

'You entered the Union Services Club on the eighth of November 1997 and watched from a distance, probably from the entrance to the rear corridor, until you saw Blackerman leave the bar but there was a woman with him. Esther Shannon. They got in the lift together. That didn't worry you. You knew Blackerman's room number because Rebury had contacted him earlier saying he was investigating his allegations and asked where and how he could get hold of him.' That was speculation on Marvik's part but he could see he was correct.

'But when you reached Blackerman's floor nothing happened. The lift didn't arrive. You saw that it had got stuck. You waited. When eventually it started moving it stopped at floor thirteen and stayed there before descending. Had Blackerman returned to the bar? You tore down the stairs but stopped at floor thirteen, where you saw John Stisford but you didn't know him and he didn't see you. What did you do then? Go down to the bar?'

'He wasn't there, or in the restaurant and he hadn't left the building.'

'Was Rebury waiting outside?'

Drayle said nothing but his gaze flitted out to sea for a second. Strathen shifted forward an inch, as though to rest his prosthetic leg before Drayle's gaze was firmly back on them.

The boat was drawing closer. Marvik continued. 'You worked out that Blackerman had gone into Esther Shannon's room so you returned to the thirteenth floor and waited. You began to wonder if Blackerman was telling Esther what Rydall had said. You knew her through Danavere who were heavily committed to the service charities and so too were you, the acceptable face of your dirty business.'

'A legitimate and clean business.'

'Built on dirty money. And you knew Wycombe because you'd met him at charity bashes like the one we've just seen back there in Southampton. Perhaps you didn't know then that he and Esther were having an affair but you soon discovered it. Then in the early hours of the morning you saw Blackerman come out of Esther's room and that gave you an idea. You could make certain that Esther would never reveal anything she might have been told and you could frame Blackerman for her murder.'

The boat's engine grew louder.

Marvik continued. 'Esther admitted you to her room because she recognized and knew you from the fund-raising events. You must have spun her some yarn, possibly about donating something to those who had fallen in the Falklands. She was moved and emotional after the Remembrance Service, thinking about her parents, upset because Vince Wycombe had ditched her and perhaps even feeling a little guilty over letting Blackerman make love to her. You strangled her, cleaned up and left Blackerman to take the blame.'

Strathen stepped forward but stumbled. He fell heavily at Drayle's feet. Drayle smiled.

'You bastard,' Strathen cursed, his face contorted with fury and frustration as he struggled to get up. Marvik made to help him but Drayle stepped forward.

'Leave him,' he ordered, levelling the gun at Marvik. 'He can't do any harm down there, and Lee's just coming in.'

The throb of the engine was now much louder.

Marvik steeled himself. Keeping his eyes on Drayle he said tautly, 'You threatened Blackerman that if he breathed a word of what had happened in 1974 and in 1997 his wife and son would be killed, just as Esther had been killed. Blackerman, probably full of guilt at having taken advantage of Esther while she was vulnerable, even though she had probably been willing, and, knowing that Rebury, a man in high office had betrayed him, thought he had little chance of convincing anyone of his innocence. He didn't know that Wycombe was also being blackmailed by you. Maybe he expected to get off, the evidence wasn't conclusive, but Wycombe helped to have him convicted because of your threats to expose his affair and maybe even to implicate him in Esther's murder. Blackerman's wife died but his son was still very much alive. Everything was going well until Paul Williamson, Blackerman's son, died of injuries sustained in Afghanistan.'

The boat engine faded. It was going past. It wasn't Addington. Drayle scowled and peered into the black night before quickly putting his eyes back on Marvik. Strathen gave a cry of pain and shifted.

'Let me help him, Nick.'

'No, he stays there. Where the hell is Lee? He should have been here by now.'

It was Drayle's first sign of agitation and therefore weakness and Marvik seized on it. 'Perhaps he's run out on you, Nick,' he sneered. 'Perhaps he's going to double cross you with whatever you and he got from Harry Salcombe because I take it that was staged and that Addington made sure Salcombe was shot and that I was injured, before he took whatever Salcombe was carrying on that trip.'

'Then I'd better shoot you now.' The gun came up.

'No. Kill me instead,' Strathen quickly interjected. 'You'd be doing me a favour.' The gun came down a fraction. Drayle smiled. It broadened as the sound of another boat drew closer. This time it was fast and heading for them.

'At last,' Drayle breathed.

Marvik hastily continued. 'Blackerman has been protecting his family all these years by saying nothing of what he knew. The price he paid was prison for a crime he didn't commit, and Paul went to his grave believing his father to be a killer.' Marvik felt the anger knot his stomach. 'After Charlotte's visit, Blackerman thought he no longer had anyone to protect, that he could speak out, so he asked to see the prison governor, only by the time he'd been granted an interview the word had got to him that if he so much as breathed a syllable about you Helen Shannon would meet the same fate as her sister. Only this time you didn't personally have to get your hands dirty. You had Lee Addington to do it for you.'

Drayle looked on calmly, his face immobile, his head still.

'Grainger was suspicious about Esther's death but said and did nothing because he was due for promotion and a quick result meant he'd get it. When he retired though, and no longer had a position to protect, he went to Ross and began to hint that he knew there had been something funny about the Blackerman case. He dug deeper into Blackerman's background and made the connection between his visit to Patrick Rydall in the Brighton nursing home and Rebury. He came to the same conclusion as we did, that Rebury was involved. He told Ross what he suspected. Ross told you. Grainger might start making a noise to get the case reopened and you couldn't have that. Within a week Grainger was killed in a hit and run.'

The boat had slowed on the approach to the pontoon. Marvik couldn't see it. He had his back to the water but it would be here soon. There was little time left.

'Ross knew it must be you but he was already right in it up to his scrawny neck. He wasn't going to jeopardize his pension and he didn't have the balls to blackmail you. The price for his cooperation was for him to see his days out and take his pension. And perhaps there's a nice villa in Spain or Italy waiting for him when he sails his boat into the sunset. Only now he won't because you killed him, in the same manner as you killed Esther, strangulation. Ross could prove nothing against you and he was basically lazy, as well as corrupt. When I came sniffing around, he again ran to you. You killed him at a time when you knew I was meeting him and you thought you could frame me for his death.

'You could have just killed Blackerman but that was too simple for you. You wanted a hold over people, so you could use them if possible again. Esther was expendable, just someone to kill for the greater good, your reputation and greed. All Blackerman could do was to keep protesting his innocence. But no one was listening. Charlotte knew nothing but you couldn't take that risk. In prison Blackerman could have told Charlotte the truth and you weren't sure if she had told me. Where is she, Nick?'

'I've no idea.'

But Marvik couldn't believe him. He couldn't see the boat but he heard it draw up and halt at the pontoon.

'Move,' Drayle ordered. Strathen was still on the ground but he rose to a kneeling position on his good leg. Marvik went to assist him. Their eyes connected for a split second. Drayle barked, 'Leave him. Get moving.'

Marvik did but not towards the boat. He jumped to the side as Strathen lunged forward, arms outstretched, grabbing Drayle tightly by the legs with both his hands, his prosthetic leg stretched out to the side and slightly behind him, his other knee bent and, using his powerful shoulders, in one swift movement he swept Drayle off the ground and pressed his powerful upper body into Drayle's chest, pinning him to the pontoon. Marvik rammed his foot on Drayle's hand. He gave a cry of pain and Marvik bent down and retrieved the weapon just as four uniformed police officers leapt off Marvik's boat and ran towards them.

Strathen said, 'I always knew those martial arts techniques and all that upper body building would come in handy in civilian life one day.'

Marvik reached out a hand. Strathen took it and pulled himself up as an officer put the cuffs on Drayle.

Eyeing Drayle with contempt, Strathen said, 'Never underestimate a cripple. Not everyone with a false leg walks with a lopsided gait.'

Strathen had just exaggerated it, as Marvik had noticed. And Drayle would never have expected someone with a disability to get the better of him. Marvik looked up to see Crowder alighting from the boat. He could hear other boats approaching fast and see the lights on them. 'Did you get Addington?'

'Yes. And we also interrupted Sir Edgar Rebury's dancing, although he didn't appear to be enjoying himself very much.'

'Will you have enough to charge and convict them?'

'Yes.'

Drayle said, 'Don't be so sure.'

'Oh, but I am. Addington seemed very keen to tell us when we picked him up boarding Marvik's boat. And Sir Edgar Rebury seemed almost relieved to get out of your clutches. There'll be others too, including Terence Blackerman, who can now speak out.' Crowder nodded at the uniformed officers to take him away, as a police launch drew up and behind it a RIB. Drayle still looked confident but Marvik didn't think he would wriggle out of this one, not even with the best lawyers.

'Is Helen safe?' he asked.

'Yes. We intercepted her and Colin Chester as they left Amelia Snow's. She didn't seem very happy about it but she did pick up a box of CDs from Mrs Snow and one of them is not a jazz CD as it purports to be.'

Strathen excitedly interjected. 'It's Grainger's back-up.'

'Yes.'

Marvik said, 'And Charlotte? Will he tell us where she is?' He looked over to Drayle climbing on to the police launch. Four uniformed officers jumped off the RIB.

'He doesn't need to. She's safe and well.'

Marvik was momentarily stunned before it dawned on him what had happened. 'You abducted her?'

'Abduction is too strong a word. I persuaded her, with her commanding officer's full approval and knowledge, to come with us. She boarded our boat at Town Quay after you had dropped her there. I told her we needed her help in relation to Terence Blackerman. She was concerned about you, Marvik, and what she'd told you, but I said that you were working for us to help get to the truth about Esther Shannon's murder. She's in a safe house in Bembridge on the Isle of Wight and will be able to return to her unit shortly.' He broke off to give instructions to the police officers to seal off the premises. Turning back to Marvik and Strathen he said, 'We'll have a team in here tomorrow taking the place to pieces.'

They made towards Marvik's boat. Crowder continued. 'Addington told us where Drayle was taking you but we already knew you were here because of the tracking device. Where is the one that was at the helm?'

'Inside my shoe.'

Crowder nodded and gave a brief smile.

Strathen said, 'How long have you suspected Drayle?'

'Of fraud for three months. The National Intelligence Fraud Bureau alerted us.'

'Who is "us"?' enquired Marvik, climbing on board. They descended into the cabin. Marvik nodded Crowder into a seat and he took up position opposite with Strathen beside him.

Crowder continued. 'The National Intelligence Marine Squad. It's a new unit. It's my job to use whatever resources I see fit to help tackle marine-related crime across the UK and the Channel Islands, both recent and cold cases.'

'But this isn't . . .'

'Marine related? Isn't it?'

'You knew about the munitions being dumped.'

'Or rather not being dumped. No. The connection came through an investigation into DRTI.'

Strathen interjected, 'Because DRTI is responsible for maritime safety and security.'

'Yes. Six months ago the National Fraud Intelligence Bureau first began to uncover irregularities in the funding process at DRTI and it pointed to Rebury going back years. Funding from the UK Government, the European Commission and other private sources had been going to DRTI but not all of it was ending up where it should have done. It was a complex paper trail but Drayle's maritime security business, established in 1976, seemed to grow very quickly and even quicker after 2000 when DRTI came into being and its chairman was Rebury.

'The National Intelligence Fraud Bureau found that although other companies tendered for marine security contracts, Drayle won them. They suspected that Rebury was making sure that Drayle got the contracts from UK and overseas governments and private companies in exchange for a commission and between them they'd created a complex system of false accounting. The NIFB alerted us at the National Intelligence Marine Squad or NIMS for short. We began digging into Rebury's past and current activities, which included looking at Drayle and others Rebury seemed to be closely connected with – Chiron, Danavere and the service charity ALPS. At that stage the investigation had no connection with Terence Blackerman or the Esther Shannon murder.' Crowder addressed Strathen. 'We knew you were a former special forces communicator with an exemplary record and that you'd decided to go it alone after your injury. You were working for Chiron. We weren't sure if the Shelleys were involved, they're probably not, but we'll look a little closer at them.'

Marvik said, 'And when you began to look more in depth at Danavere you found that Esther Shannon had worked for them and Blackerman had been convicted of her murder.'

'Yes, and that subsequently Bryan Grainger had been killed in a hit and run in Brighton. We learned that Blackerman had always strenuously denied killing Esther but wouldn't say who he believed had killed her. Perhaps he didn't know. Perhaps he was just spinning a line. Then Blackerman's son was injured and sadly died. Prison intelligence alerted us that Charlotte Churley had made an application to find Blackerman. When she requested to see him, and he accepted, it was the chance we had been waiting for. If Blackerman was innocent and had been threatened then Charlotte visiting him could force our killer out into the open.'

'You sent that text message to Charlotte telling her where I lived, hoping that she'd come and see me.'

'Yes. We knew that you and she had been close and that you were living on the Isle of Wight, and that you also worked for Drayle. We also knew about the Salcombe incident.'

'Which was staged.'

'Yes. Although we didn't know that then and we don't know what Harry Salcombe was carrying but we're hoping Addington will tell us. You were the perfect choice to help us.'

'It would have been nice to have been briefed.'

'But that would have influenced your actions and we didn't know how far the deception went or who had killed Esther Shannon.'

'It might have saved Duncan Ross's life.'

Crowder nodded. A small silence fell between them. Marvik broke it. 'And there was no email sent from me to Charlotte?'

'No. I just thought that might increase the pressure to find the truth.'

'It bloody worked,' muttered Marvik. 'Was it your officers following Charlotte and who broke into my house or was that Addington?'

'We had no need to follow her; we knew where she was. We were tracking her on her mobile phone, remember.'

So it had been Addington who had broken in. And after having done so and planting a tracking device on Marvik's car, he had arrived here on Drayle's boat while Marvik had also been here to discuss his future with Drayle.

'How did Drayle know about Charlotte visiting the prison?'

'He'd been keeping tabs on Paul Williamson's movements over the years. It was in his interest to do so, otherwise the threat wouldn't hold. When Paul died, Drayle knew Blackerman was free to speak out, and that was the last thing he wanted. Perhaps he planned for Blackerman to have an accident in prison, or to be found dead, having taken his own life after hearing the news of his son's death. Drayle has his own form of prison intelligence, and word got to him that Charlotte was to visit.'

'And Addington was sent over to follow her,' Marvik continued. 'He must have come by boat, moored up at Newport, and followed her from the prison to my cottage. He kept watch on us all night, then after we'd left he broke in, saw that I'd been looking into the Esther Shannon murder and relayed this information to Drayle.'

Crowder nodded.

Marvik said, 'The CCTV images from Town Quay that you showed me were doctored.'

'Yes.'

'Who was watching Helen's house?'

'We were but we didn't break in either the first time or the second, when you returned alone. That was Addington. But he didn't know we were there.'

Strathen said, 'So Drayle bugged my apartment, probably sending Addington in there to plant it, and then Addington was sent to run Art and Helen off the road.'

'Yes.'

Strathen continued, 'And Ashley Palmer confided what he'd discovered at Hurd Deep – or rather what he hadn't discovered – to Rebury, who promptly told Drayle. Drayle approached Palmer who was unaware that Drayle was the man on that dive in 1997 and involved in what happened there in 1974. Drayle told Ashley to keep quiet about it until they could present it to the right authorities.'

'Is Witley clean?' asked Marvik.

Crowder answered. 'As far as medical applications go he probably is. I don't think he was selling that type of information to Danavere's competitors.'

Strathen again interjected. 'But Ashley liaised closely with Witley on the progress of his work and when Witley discovered that Ashley's research could also have applications in surveillance, he went to Drayle with the information.'

'Yes. It's likely that Witley's in league with Drayle, creaming off software applications connected with defence and security and has been selling them on to terrorists on behalf of Drayle and taking a percentage. When Ashley went missing and his medical research applications showed up in Germany, along with the fact that Vera Pedlowe told Witley you were sniffing around asking about Esther Shannon's murder, Witley got scared. Perhaps he didn't know the full extent of Drayle's involvement in Esther's murder, but Witley was connected with Drayle. The French police have picked him up. He claims to have had a breakdown, stress, too much work. But he'll talk.'

Marvik shook his head sadly, his mind churning over all that had happened.

Strathen said, 'Ashley was told by Drayle to write down that Isle of Wight coastguard cottage address and press hard on the Post-it note so as to draw suspicion away from where he was really heading. Drayle told him that others were suspected of leaking information, me probably, and that it was a trap to catch me.'

Crowder answered. 'It was probably Addington who picked him up by boat at Cowes and took him out into the Solent. Perhaps he or Drayle will tell us where his body is.'

'Poor sod,' Marvik said. And to think he had worked and had been about to resume working for a bastard like Drayle. He felt sorry for his staff and his family. But perhaps his staff wouldn't be that shocked to learn the truth or sorry to hear of his fate. He'd never met Drayle's wife. Had she ever seen signs of her husband's Machiavellian personality? Maybe it had exhibited itself at some stage. But he'd never seen it. Maybe the signs had been there but he'd chosen to ignore them. Drayle had seen his weakness, his uncertainty and unease at leaving the Marines. He'd smelled his fear and he'd used him for his own corrupt ends. Crowder on the other hand had sensed something else about him and used that to catch the bastard. That felt good.

Crowder said, 'I mentioned that I can use whatever resources I need on the National Intelligence Marine Squad. I need people who are unafraid of asking questions, who know about surveillance and covert work, who know the marine environment and who can take risks. I'm not promising that the assignments won't be dangerous because they will and I won't be able to acknowledge your role publicly. But I'd like you both on board.' He rose. 'Call me. You have my number.'

Crowder stretched out his hand. Marvik took the firm grip in his. Strathen did the same. They watched him leave. Neither of them spoke as the engine on the RIB fired up and they heard it speed out into the Solent.

Finally Strathen said, 'Crowder's given me another chance. I'm going to take it. Are you?'

Was he? Did he want the kind of job Crowder had offered? He could handle it. He knew that now. Crowder had given him back his confidence and he was grateful for that. But accepting it meant resuming the nomadic life he'd lived for so long.

He studied the man across the table, eyeing him keenly. They both deserved another chance and they'd given Helen one. Maybe now she'd be able to stop running and face up to the truth of her sister's death. And Blackerman's torment was also over; he'd be free to resume his life, albeit one that had been broken and destroyed by Drayle. And Marvik recalled the exhilaration he'd felt and the adrenalin surge during the investigation, the feeling that he was once again alive and accomplishing something of value.

There was only one answer. 'Looks as though we've got a call to make.'